"A psycl ... ıd intrigue. It
felt like ... op on the first
page and plenty of twists and turns thereafter."

Rev. David Nofziger, M.Div., LSW
Director, Hope Alive Counseling Services

"Not only did this captivating story of young love keep me up half
the night reading, the historical context gave me new insight into
a period of strife between the Protestant and Catholic worlds.

"Young lovers being pursued by rogue bounty hunters, family strife
and forgiveness, the purity of Christian love, all amid a historical
background so real you think you are actually there—what more
can a reader ask? Great book!"

Jeanne A. Calvert, Assistant Professor, University of Saint Francis
Author, *Oakwood, Ohio: Past and Present* and *A Paulding Journal*

"This is not my normal choice of reading material, so for me to
have read this book in seven hours non-stop, it had to be awesome.
The storyline is exciting and the characters come to life on the
pages as I was reading. I can't wait for a sequel. Well done!"

Lisa Cox, connoisseur of thrillers

"The characters make thoughtful and prayerful decisions. The
research added an additional layer of intellectual interest to a
marvelous plot and fascinating story."

Ann Gustafson Frake
Author, *Emerald Elephant, Golden Bee*, and *Crystal Dragon*

"Purity is a lost character quality, and unity is important for
believers as we push closer to the Day. It is encouraging to read a
novel reviving their importance."

Reverend Sharon Fox
Director, HARC Ministries (Healing Addictions
through a Relationship with Christ)
Author, *HARC Life Skills* and *Creating Authentic Relationships*

Honorable Deception

Honorable Deception

...where twisted paths lead

KAREN BOWDEN-COX

TATE PUBLISHING & *Enterprises*

Published by Tate Publishing & Enterprises, LLC
127 E. Trade Center Terrace | Mustang, Oklahoma 73064 USA
1.888.361.9473 | www.tatepublishing.com

Tate Publishing is committed to excellence in the publishing industry. The company reflects the philosophy established by the founders, based on Psalm 68:11,
"The Lord gave the word and great was the company of those who published it."

Book design copyright © 2008 by Tate Publishing, LLC. All rights reserved.
Cover design by Kandi Evans & Beth Cox
Interior design by Jonathan Lindsey

Published in the United States of America

ISBN:978-1-60604-543-5
1. Fiction: Religious: Romance/Historical   2. Fiction: General: Historical
08.08.21

Dedicated to the "High and Lofty One,
who inhabits eternity, whose Name is Holy" (Isaiah 57:15),
who "knows the thoughts He thinks for you ...
thoughts of peace,
and not of evil,
to give you an expected end" (Jeremiah 29:11).

Acknowledgements

So many people have affected my life and the writing of *Honorable Deception*.

First, I wish to thank my elder son, Steve Cox, for presenting me with the *Christian Writers Market Guide* 2007 as a 2006 Christmas gift.

Next, I wish to thank my younger son, Chad Cox, the expert engineer; my granddaughter Beth Cox, a technician par excellence; and Julie Mitchell, librarian extraordinaire of Paulding County Carnegie Library, for helping me navigate the technological seas of this twenty-first century.

Other librarians aided in processing books and leading me to needed information. Thank you, Sue Thomas and Pamela Kretz of Cooper Community Library in Oakwood and Rhonda Gerken of Defiance Public Library.

My busy daughter-in-law, Lisa Moore Cox, combed through the final draft of this manuscript. Thank you, dear.

Many gifted students crossed my path during my teaching career. One who stands out for her remarkable talent as a writer is Barbara Maxwell of Centerville whose life was cut short before the world could fully appreciate her innate abilities. Students who kept my pen active included Roberta Cohen, Janet Wolery Carder, and the late Holli Hotz Dickerhoff of Delphos. Elizabeth "Buffy" Heller, Allison McKenzie, Rich Littell, David Himes, Karen McCormick,

Claudia Rosell, Dean Wolfe, Sharon Speidel, Kim Howland, and Mary Dale Walters of Centerville also challenged me to hone my craft. It is true that students teach teachers.

Relatives led me to family archives. Thank you, Emil "Skip" Chiles, Kathleen Ford Biery, Mary Stambaugh Bowden, Pastor Virgil Caskey, and Roger Cobb for sharing our rich family heritage. A posthumous thank you to my Aunt Mildred Bowden Cobb, Roger's mother, and my Aunt Elizabeth Bowden Chiles, Skip's mother. Second cousin Anne Gasper Erny helped enormously by locating the Hempleman lineage online for all of our grateful hearts.

Friends Sue McMillen, Anne Sheehan, Patty Weber, Reverend Sharon Fox, and Michelle Retcher pushed me toward the finish line.

Never to be forgotten is my lifelong forever friend, Donna Davis Wermer, who ministered to me in sorrow and rejoiced with me when good tidings arrived. Linda Merris Shopoff and Carole Girod Johns Jose are also such friends.

Native German Christina Schmiedl Hayes, Chad's mother-in-law, broadened my perspective and understanding of Germany, as have native German Emil Schoch and his wife Barbara. Henry zum Felde, founder of German Lutheran Heritage of Northwest Ohio, also aided in my research.

Thanks also go out to the Reverend David Nofziger, whose love of godly reading stretches through the cosmos. Also, I humbly thank Pastors Tim and Jill Tracy and Pastor Tim and Lisa Hacker for their sound doctrinal teaching and solid Christian lifestyle.

A hearty thank-you to Blane and Lori Olinghouse whose daughter Cassie and her fiancé, Matt (son of Donny and Linda Verhoff), became chaste models for the main characters of *Honorable Deception*. Matt and Cassie are now married.

My deceased brother, William Lee Bowden, deserves a nod of acknowledgement for paving a literary pathway for me. Our mother, the late Nellie Fae Bowden, stockpiled classics for us to read; our father, William Wesley Bowden, read voraciously.

Who came onto the scenes unannounced except Robert Edwin Cox, Jr., my departed and beloved husband? His memory lives on. Thank you, all.

Chapter 1

The young man lay on the marble flooring as a single strand of coarse rope bound his wrists and ankles behind his contorted body. Slowly Lord Sturzhelm wound the narrow necklace around his victim's neck. Charlotte, the eldest daughter of Lord Harry Sturzhelm, held a four-year-old document in a tight grip as she towered above her betrothed.

The young man's father surveyed his son's agony, turned his back, and walked into the shadowy corridor, wanting to see no more. The victim's mother collapsed in tears on the cold floor in front of him, begging him to submit.

Lord Sturzhelm, his feet securely anchored, pulled the cord to tighten the rope around the neck of his prospective son-in-law. The lord's thunderous laugh echoed throughout the young man's home. Lord Sturzhelm's wife, looked from the tortured young man to her daughter, Charlotte.

The sound of the malicious laughter faded, only to be replaced by the tapping of Charlotte's foot close to the young man's writhing form.

He struggled for breath as the rope cut deeply into his neck. With each movement that loosened his bands the minutest, Lord Sturzhelm yanked the yoke more securely. The raw filament dug into flesh. Blood began to creep into the fiber of the hemp.

Yet the young man preferred disfigurement, even death, over his option.

Darkness crept into his consciousness. His military training failed as he sought for an advantage. Soon lucid thoughts gave way to a gathering whirlpool of gray confusion and spinning black oblivion.

SATURDAY, SEPTEMBER 13, 1751—EARLY EVENING—HESSEN-CASSEL

Lord Hempleman stomped out of his bedroom suite, shouting for Raymond. The Hempleman chamberlain raced from the servants' quarters, clambered up the oak staircase, and intercepted his lord, who was halfway down the steps.

"You called, sire."

"Yes! Yes! I have a thief in my household. Let us go to the study. I am sure we can remedy the situation quickly." Trailing the rapid pace of Lord Hempleman, Raymond wondered who the victim would be this time.

Catching the knob of the study door with his long arm, Raymond opened the hand-carved wooden barrier and stood stiffly beside the opening with both heels snapped together. Lord Hempleman raced through the aperture toward his desk.

"Come in! Come in!" Lord Hempleman ordered. Raymond obeyed, quietly shutting the door behind him.

Pacing back and forth in front of his massive desk, the aging lord's substantial physique struck terror in Raymond's racing mind. *Who will be the accused?*

Running his wide hand through his straight hair, Lord Hempleman announced his verdict.

"It is that young thing from Giessen. I was doing her father, the professor, a favor by hiring her. See what a kind heart earns you these days? Get Margarette in here right now! But do not tell her why she is being summoned!"

Bowing slightly, Raymond left the room.

Mid-evening chores would find Margarette placing night clothing upon the beds of the ladies and tidying up their chambers for the night. She would be easy to locate. Raymond hurried up the staircase and onto the second floor. He heard humming coming from Mistress Hayley's room. Giving his usual three taps on the door, Raymond heard a soft, "Who's there?"

"Raymond, *Fraulein.*"

The door opened. Margarette, a loose curl falling loosely from her braided hair, stood with dust cloth in hand. Raymond and his wife had grown to love Margarette, a sweet girl who was so full of laughter, good stories, and a helping hand. Now his order was to escort the strawberry-blonde beauty to her unraveling without a hint of what lay ahead.

"Good evening, Mr. Yarger. Am I needed elsewhere?"

"You are wanted in the lord's study, Margarette." He turned on his heel. Margarette trailed behind the brisk-walking head steward, her mind racing as she wondered what this might possibly concern.

The two walked down the hallway to the staircase, clipped off the steps one by one, and emerged into the home's grand entranceway where a shadowy figure moved off to their right. Raymond saw nothing. It was Margarette who caught a glimpse of the apparition.

A brisk knock. An equally brisk, "Yes, come in," told Margarette more than she wanted to know.

Lord Hempleman sat at his desk shuffling maps, ledgers, and official papers. "Raymond, you are to stay."

Raymond anchored himself stiffly beside the white marble fireplace.

Margarette glanced with her lovely blue eyes from one man to the other. She attempted to keep her knees from shaking and her hands from fidgeting. No one of her status was called into the lord's study except for serious discussion.

Without looking up, Lord Hempleman broke the silence. "Margarette, I shall get right to the heart of this matter."

Margarette drew her eyebrows into a deep furrow.

"As you know, the family is expecting my eldest son back from Togo shortly," Lord Hempleman's eyes now passed from the trifles on his desk and riveted on Margarette.

Margarette nodded her knowledge of this event; her cheeks gathered color and her heart began that uncontrollable patter as she thought of Master George. Lord Hempleman slowly narrowed his eyes, fastening them in a death grip on the tender maiden.

"The family is planning a welcome-home party for my eldest son." The lord paused and raised his left eyebrow before returning his gaze to the papers on his desk. "All preparations were going well until this evening. I asked my wife to wear her emerald necklace on the night of the homecoming. Of course, she consented, but when she looked for the heirloom amongst her jewelry, the necklace was not there. Both of us had been admiring it two days ago, thinking it would be fitting for Master George's party. But now it is gone. Vanished!"

So this was Lord Hempleman's plan. How easy for him! Margarette tried to shield gathering tears, but the crystal droplets fell onto the dust cloth she held in her small, trembling hands.

"There! You see, Raymond! She has admitted her guilt—" Lord Hempleman sniffed in mockery while placing his hands on his desk and leaning toward the accused before spewing out his conclusion. "—by her tears. How convenient! Now that is as good as a verbal confession!"

Raymond remained stoically immobile, hating both himself and his lord with equal intensity. To defend Margarette would jeopardize his and his wife's positions. Not to defend Margarette branded the girl as a thief.

Margarette knew better than to speak. She would receive the consequences of someone else's actions. Her only consolation was a verse she had read recently. *Vengeance is Mine, I will repay, saith the Lord.* But the words were only a temporary consolation. The possibility of the God of heaven and earth extracting justice, let alone vengeance, on behalf of a lowly servant demanded more faith than Margarette possessed.

Not one to miss an advantage, Lord Hempleman stood squarely on his feet and towered over his domestic. "I'll not make this public, Miss Duffy. All I require is that you leave our premises *immediately*. I will have Raymond attend to the necessary details for your departure. You have one-half hour to pack your belongings. Raymond will inspect your valise when you are finished. You will wait at Cassel Inn until the next coach to Giessen leaves." Lord Hempleman pivoted to face the huge window overlooking the main street that wound around Cassel and the moat beyond. "Leave now, Miss Duffy. Pack. Then wait outside at the back entrance for Mr. Yarger." The lord then turned his head toward his chamberlain. "Raymond, stay here for your orders."

Quiet tears flowed down Margarette's oval face as she exited the study. *I would have left upon the lord's request. He did not have to accuse me of theft. I know my station in life. I told George that his attentions toward me could be ruinous. But for his father to falsely accuse me! Oh, poor Papa. Poor Mama. They will be ruined! I am ruined!*

Inside his study, the *Landesvater* of the Hempleman manor in southern Hessen, the former military commander turned constable, lifted his weight on his toes, then set down his heels before abruptly executing an about face. He walked to his desk, inserted a key, opened the side top drawer, and took out an envelope, which he handed to Raymond. "This will be adequate for the trip to her home. See to it."

"Yes, sire," Raymond bowed, thereby catching a glimpse of green and gold in the desk drawer before Lord Hempleman slowly pushed it shut and locked it again. Looking straight toward Raymond with his piercing dark eyes and sardonic smile, Lord Hempleman challenged his servant to speak one word of protest or correction.

Raymond stood immobile, stunned. "That will be all. See to it," Lord Hempleman roughly dismissed his hireling.

When Raymond's footsteps echoed on the marble flooring, then faded into mere clicks on the smooth stone toward the rear of the mansion, Lord Hempleman sank into his desk chair. He had never done such a lowly deed before. As a constable, he certainly leaned the scale of justice on the side of the nobility often enough, yet this was more difficult than he had imagined. He had thought of Margarette Duffy as a good household servant. Yet his son was drawn to this rare beauty, and that would never do. *A commoner! A foreigner! A Roman Catholic! Never!* Lord Hempleman's eldest son would marry above himself, honor his betrothed of four years, sail to Togo after his honeymoon, and enlarge the fortune of two families.

As for Raymond catching sight of the "stolen" necklace, that would work in Lord Hempleman's strategy too. It was good for the servants to know that their lord could orchestrate "justice" as it served his own purposes. *Perhaps I should have planted the necklace in Miss Duffy's room*, he mused, *but getting in and out of the servants' quarters requires great care. What is done is done! This will do quite adequately—and completely.*

Lord Hempleman reached for his vial of wine, smiled to himself, and poured a small quantity of the red liquid into his monogrammed silver goblet.

Concealed behind the massive tapestry in the grand entranceway, Lady Hempleman emerged from her hiding place and hurried up the staircase on cushioned slippers, wondering, indeed, if her coveted emerald necklace no longer rested in its jewelry case. Nearly racing through the master bedroom and then into her separate bedchamber, she sank to her knees in front of the chest at the base of her bed. *Oh, I need my household keys.* She glanced around the candle-lit room to locate her decorative pillow. It lay on a chair by her table. She reached for it and began massaging the soft down with trembling hands. Yes, the keys were in their customary spot inside the pillow where, years ago, she had inserted a pocket to secure them.

Lady Hempleman selected the correct key and opened the chest. Mounds of bedding and fabric lay on top of her rather large jewelry case resting near the bottom. The narrow, tapered fingers of the aging lady felt for the familiar ivory-carved box with its brass latch, hook, and lock. *Ah, the jewelry case is here.* She pulled it from its depths and clutched it tightly. Breathing a gentle sigh, she placed the container on the carpet and inserted a second key into the lock. Soon she was sifting gold, gems, chains, and rings through her delicate fingers. She could not locate her coveted jeweled necklace.

Her search was interrupted when she heard her husband's footsteps in the entranceway below. Next his steps echoed on the staircase. Lady Hempleman shoved the jewelry box under her feathered mattress, closed the trunk lid, and walked to the small table in front of the window, seating herself nonchalantly in her favored chair. As Johann's footsteps reached the master bedroom, Anna poured herself a goblet of wine and took only a small sip. There would be little wine for her tonight. However, she needed to convince her husband that she was soundly intoxicated and desirous of sleep before he retired for the night.

Johann eased his head through the doorway. "Oh, I see you are still awake, Anna."

Anna nearly sang the invitation. "Would you have a drink of wine with me, dear?"

Johann entered agreeably. "Don't mind if I do."

"What was all that horrible shouting about, dear? You know I hate shouting. My head aches with all the turmoil."

"Just a small incident. Everything has been taken care of." Johann's frame swallowed the miniature chair as he sat on the adjacent seat across from his wife and took a long draught from the full goblet his wife offered to him. "I have released that maid from Giessen, the daughter of the scholarly Scot that I trusted." Johann shook his head as if in disbelief. "I had a strong inkling that something was afoot just this morning. That grew into a strong suspicion as the day wore on, so I checked your jewelry box while you were in the nursery with Siegfried. Your emerald necklace was missing.

I knew at once that the little thief had stolen it. I did not want to bother you with my responsibilities, so I took care of the matter." The lord swirled the remainder of the wine in his goblet and cast a wary look toward his wife. "Do not worry, dear. I will do my best to get it back. I realize how much your mother's heirloom means to you." He paused a moment to watch his wife's reaction before saying, "I need to be more cautious about whom I hire."

His wife fought against her rising anger, remembering the wise advice of her mother. *Do not reveal your ability to reason, Liebe Anna. Learn what you can while keeping your emotions in check.* Anna smiled sweetly at her husband. "So Margarette confessed?"

"Yes," he lied. "I am still piecing the story together. She apparently has sold your heirloom to one of *her* relatives for whom I have issued a warrant. I *will* do my best to get it back for you, Anna."

"You are so thoughtful. Not every woman has the security of a constable in her life. So, who is the relative?"

Johann stood before setting down his empty vial. "Another nobody. He will swing from a rope soon." Then he kissed his wife on the top of her head. "I will be turning in for the night. I have a big day ahead of me tomorrow. Sleep well, my dear."

Anna glared at her husband's back as he swaggered into his chamber. *I will never get my necklace back if I leave it to you. It will be hanging on the neck of your most recent whore if I do not find it tonight. I know that Margarette has no idea where I hide my jewelry. Even though I sometimes have too much wine, I know that girl. She is innocent.*

Anna picked up her embroidery hoop and sat close to the candlelight. After Johann's breathing became an even, heavy snore—one that found its way through the walls and heavy door that separated them—she took her jewelry case from under her mattress. Her necklace was not there. Resuming her embroidery by the light of a candle, she listened to the clock mark the quarter, half, and full hour before rising to stare into the courtyard below her balcony. All the while, she plotted.

Chapter 2

SATURDAY, SEPTEMBER 13, 1751—EVENING— NORTH ATLANTIC OCEAN

George Hempleman awakened from his nightmare. The sound of Charlotte's tapping toes on the marble floor in the Hempleman household was nothing more than the dripping of rain outside his cabin. George sat upright and shook his head, grabbing for the side of his berth as the *Venture* swayed starboard and the ocean waves lapped against the hull of the ship. Despite the storm, George sighed in relief. He was glad to be in the safety of an ocean storm as he realized that the roaring of Lord Sturzhelm's laughter in his dream had been the howling of the Atlantic wind.

George's relief dissolved when his awakened thoughts became as tumultuous as the waves crashing against the ship. He remembered a series of afternoon conferences with Lord Sturzhelm, Lord Wolff, and Lord Hamler about their stakes in Togo, Africa. The wind had been increasing in velocity when he had returned to the cabin. *How long had he slept?*

He swung his feet onto the flooring while calling to his *friseur.* "I need my boots and cloak." His attentive servant quickly aided his master.

"Going on deck, Master George? It is mighty nasty there."

"I need the air, Hans. I will be back after dinner, that is, if dinner is being served in this kind of weather."

George walked out of the cabin onto the main deck where the pelting rain lashed his tall frame. Lightning stole from the heavens as the hesitant thunder roared in obedience to the flashing commands. Drenched sailors scurried past George in response to anxious commands that resounded above the fury of the wind. Men shouted as they wrestled with bundles of ropes and sails flapping wildly in a strange dervish.

Seizing what stability he could find on the bulwarks, George edged toward the companionway, laid hold of the railing, and mounted the steps to the bridge as the wind tore wildly at his cloak. He felt somewhat relieved when he heard the voices of his traveling companions within. George knocked soundly on the door. All speech halted. Heavy footsteps thudded. Then the door opened abruptly. The normally serene Lord Hamler pulled George quickly from the storm.

"Get in here, lad. What are you doing? Risking your life?"

George regained his footing and lost all semblance of protocol. Lord Hamler, Lord Wolff, Lord Sturzhelm, and two uniformed crewmen dwarfed before the square body of Captain Van Devoorde, who braced himself in a crouched stance while straining against the helm.

At that moment, a wave lashed against the *Venture* and swallowed the wooden structure in an avalanche of water, foam, and debris. George grabbed for Lord Hamler as both of the men fell, crashing into their other two companions. Seawater flowed into the bridge.

SATURDAY, SEPTEMBER 13, 1751—LATE EVENING—CASSEL

With valise in hand, Margarette walked the dark streets of Cassel trying to remember the directions Raymond Yarger had given her. All was quiet in the neighborhood where the Hempleman family occupied the home reserved for the city constable. However, as Margarette edged her way toward the city's central district, she heard laughter. It was not the laughter that had often filled her home in Giessen or the laughter that sometimes filled the Hempleman parlor when guests arrived. This laughter came from a cavernous depth into which Margarette did not want to fall. She vacillated between livid anger toward Lord Hempleman and stark fear as she surveyed Cassel Inn a short block away. Shadowy figures, multiple couples, isolated humanity entered and left the doors of the inn and the nearby stable in a macabre dance. Unidentified forms then froze in a tableau of horror.

When Margarette had arrived in Cassel over a year ago, she had gotten directions from a polite pedestrian and walked directly to the Hempleman home. The light of the sun on that bright afternoon had driven into darkness the scourge she now saw before her. *Lord Hempleman is a constable! He knew who would be out on these streets at night. How could he?*

Wondering where she could safely spend the night, Margarette slowly and observantly spun around. Then she looked up. In the shadows she could see a steeple towering off in the northeast. She clutched her valise tightly and altered her direction.

"Hey, sweet one. Why are you hurrying?" a raspy male voice called.

Margarette quickened her pace.

"I won't hurt you, darlin'. Let me help you," the man's voice echoed against the city's stone structures as the sound of leather on pavement quickened.

Margarette broke into a full run.

"Scared, are you? I may give you a reason for that." The man's voice was louder, closer.

Margarette was a full block away from the church and cloister. On her left was an open courtyard. She dashed toward a fountain, hunched down, and began to scream. When all the breath had left her lungs, she collapsed in a heap upon the cobblestone pavement, unable to believe that someone somewhere had not heard her plea for help.

Holding her head immobile, Margarette rolled her eyes as far to one side as they would move. Then she moved them in the opposite direction. She saw no activity and heard no noise except laughter in the distance. Then she smelled an odor of stale tobacco, liquor, urine, vomit, and unwashed flesh. Before she could rise to her feet, she felt a hairy arm clamp around her small frame and pin her arms while another burly hand muzzled her mouth.

"Now I have yah, sweet pea," the man said as his matted beard pushed against Margarette's tender cheek.

Chapter 3

SATURDAY, SEPTEMBER 13, 1751—MINUTES BEFORE MIDNIGHT—CASSEL

When she was sure her plan would work, Lady Hempleman dressed for bed and pretended to sleep. The mechanical bird in the downstairs' clock reported that it was midnight. Anna waited a few minutes, listening for Johann's snoring in the next room. It was smooth and consistent. With keys in hand, she tiptoed from her room through the room of her husband, shadows and imps following her to the staircase. Anna paused. The children were sleeping. She heard Maurice groan followed by a rustle of feathered comforters. Then all was still. Not even baby Siegfried whimpered in the nursery. Anna knew the staircase well—which steps creaked when she stepped on the right, left, or center. Being the wife of a constable had taught her many lessons.

At the bottom of the stairs, Anna made her way to her husband's study. The candles in the entranceway chandelier had been extinguished hours earlier, so the only light came from small candles in sconces on the wall. Anna let familiarity guide her to her destination. Unbeknownst to her husband, Lady Hempleman had duplicate keys to every lock she knew of in the house. It had taken several years to accomplish this feat and much "hush" money, but tonight it might work to her advantage. She did not want to lose her emerald necklace, even if she could never wear it publicly again.

Inserting and turning the key to the study made more noise than she desired, but in an instant, she was inside the room and inching her way toward her husband's work desk. Keeping a secure grip on what she thought was the correct key, she mused. *It is good that I refrained from much wine tonight. Otherwise, I would be trembling right now. Steady now, fingers.*

The candlelight from the foyer pulsated to the rapidity of Anna's own heartbeat as she inserted a key into the desktop lock. It cooperated. She gently eased the heavy desktop to its resting spot, ran her fingers through the slots above the base. *It is not here! Well, he has put it in one of the drawers then.*

Anna unlocked the second section of the security desk, then tugged at the bottom drawer. She wished more light were coming through the doorway. *Where is the full moon when it is needed?* The drawer screeched open. Anna froze, then consoled herself. *It just sounds loud to me.* Nothing but papers and a few small books lay in the bottom drawer. She tried the middle drawer, which creaked loudly. She had not planned on the noise factor. *What was that? Is Johann up?* Anna hesitated, then ran her right hand through the contents of the drawer. There was no necklace. Footsteps sounded from the master bedroom above her. Anna quietly shoved the drawer shut and pulled on the top one. It slid open more easily with only a slight squeak. She reached in and felt for the necklace. There it was! She gripped the recovered jewelry, slid the drawer shut, locked the drawers, and quickly lifted the desktop back in place before locking it as well. The footsteps were now on the staircase and approaching rapidly.

Anna looked to the right and left. *Where might I hide?*

As Margarette wrestled with her captor on the stone pavement, she nearly succumbed to his foul smell and superior strength. *I must keep my wits about me.* She remembered jostling with her two older brothers when they were youths. Being seven years younger than

Charles and four years younger than Hank, she had devised some combative techniques in the frequent scrimmages.

Pushing on her satchel with a rush of adrenaline, Margarette forced the grip of her adversary to loosen as she bit down on his fingers, which he had tightened on her open mouth. Turning abruptly in a twist, she crashed her luggage against the side of his head again and again. When his curses stopped, Margarette struggled to her feet. Tears streamed down her youthful cheeks. She had never before committed such a violent act. As she looked down upon the human dung lying at her feet, her first impulse was to seek aid for the filthy, ragged, fetid man.

However, sanity and self-preservation overrode her compassion. Slowly, she backed away, still amazed that no one had heard her screams or the scuffling.

But someone had heard. The clatter of approaching horse hooves resounded in the night air. Slipping off her shoes, Margarette darted through the shadows toward the church and cloister. She did not want to be caught in an interrogation where Lord Hempleman might be the one asking questions.

Carrying a single lit candle, Johann circled his desk more times than Anna wanted to count. On one of these circuits, Lord Hempleman unlocked his desk and rummaged through the top drawer. Not finding the necklace, he cursed, then quietly vowed, "Whoever has taken the necklace will pay with his life." He stood immobile, leaning over his desk momentarily while nervously tapping his fingers on the desktop. *Did Raymond take the necklace? I know he saw it in the drawer. Maybe he spoke about it with another servant who saw an opportunity. But that is unlikely. Could Anna be so bold as to distrust me and think me capable of taking her necklace? I think not. Regardless, she is upstairs sleeping off her drink.* Lord Hempleman walked to the window. As he parted the pair of draperies to check the security of the window, Anna held her breath. She stood a mere handbreadth away.

"The latch is secure," Johann said, reassuring himself.

Anna nearly burst into a quiet exhale when Johann pushed the drapery closed. He walked across the room and into the entrance-way. The main door of the home remained bolted. Returning to his study, his pacing began in earnest.

Several times he came so close to Anna's chilled toes that she feared the intensity of her heartbeats would expose her hiding place. When the clock indicated the half hour, Johann set the candlestick on his desk and repeatedly slammed his broad right fist into the open palm of his left.

Anna trembled with fear.

"I know someone is in here. You will answer for this, you felon. I will send you up for the rest of your life. Maybe I can persuade the judge to hang you."

Anna muffled a giggle at her husband's verbal outbursts, not in amusement but in restrained anxiety. Yet his temporary discomfort pleased her. In the drama of life, she never dared to upset her husband. He was not one to lose a single battle.

For nearly an hour, Johann roamed the room, slammed his fist on the desk, pulled books off the shelf, and threw them carelessly around the room. One came dangerously close to hitting his wife's trembling legs, which were all the while absorbing the cool air of the September night. Anna wished she had worn more than a robe over her nightwear. Additionally, her feet were now numb from the marble flooring. Anna wondered if a prayer would work. *Lord, please do not let him find me. Do not let him go upstairs to check my room. Also, Lord, please, please, please, do not let me sneeze or cough.*

Some time after the clock registered three, Johann sank into a comfortably padded chair of soft leather, stretched out his long legs, and declared. "I do not plan to leave, whoever you are. So make up your mind to turn yourself in. The quicker you do, the better it will go for you."

One hour later, Johann's snoring nearly drowned out the ticking of the clock. After another quarter-hour interval, Anna peeked out from behind the drapery, slid her slippered feet across the room, careful to avoid stumbling over any of the books her husband had slung about the room. Then she slipped out of the open door and tiptoed through the entranceway and up the staircase. From the second storey, Johann's snoring could barely be heard. Anna held her breath as she walked the width of the master bedroom, opened her bedroom door, and eased her trembling body on the other side of the wooden frame. Only then did she heave a sigh of relief as she leaned against the cold structure. Thoughts of wine seemed wonderfully tempting.

But first, where to hide the necklace? My pillow. Of course. Finding her sewing box in the darkened room that caught only minimal light from the outside balcony, she took her scissors and cut a small slice near the hem of the linen pillow casing. Then she paused. *I do not want my precious jewelry floating aimlessly amongst the feathers.* Her solution was simple. She chose a loose satin glove from her dresser drawer and tucked the necklace into the glove. Then she sewed several stitches through the glove's soft outer fabric. Easing the gloved jewelry into the pillow's down, Anna allowed the feathers to deeply envelop both glove and necklace. Then Anna's fingers pulled needle and thread through the linen to close the telltale gap in the pillow. *I hope I do not have feathers lying around. At the break of dawn, I will check the entire room. Now, for the most brilliant part of my plan!*

Anna removed the cushioned slippers from her small feet and rubbed the cold away before sliding her feet into small shoes with leather soles and heels. She took a deep breath, rubbed her arms to stimulate circulation, and splashed some wine on her mouth and face before walking rather noisily out of her room and toward her husband's bed. She ruffled his bedding. "Johann, where are you? Johann!"

She ran out of the room, down the steps, and into the entranceway. "Johann? Are you here? Johann!"

Soon Raymond approached in his robe with a single tall candle in his hand. "Lady Hempleman, are you all right? I heard you calling."

"Oh, Raymond, I cannot find Lord Hempleman. I awoke and did not hear him in his room, so I have come searching. I do hope he is all right."

"I am sure that he is fine, my lady. I will look around. You might be wise to go back to your room. It is quite chilly down here."

"Oh, I cannot leave until I know that Johann is safe. You must understand!"

Raymond was not one to argue.

Lord Hempleman heard the chatter. "What is going on out there?" he called from the study.

"Oh, it is Johann!" Lady Hempleman ran into the study. "Johann, are you all right? I woke up and could not find you in your bed. Raymond was about to begin a search. Are you okay, dear?"

"I am as fine as a person can be who has been subjected to criminal activity twice in a few short days. Raymond, get me my woolen robe. It is freezing down here."

Raymond scurried up the staircase.

Anna approached her husband and put a tender hand on his forearm. "Whatever do you mean by criminal activity, dear?"

"What I mean is that we had a thief, I mean, an intruder in our home tonight. He may still be here. Where is Raymond?"

From the top of the staircase, Raymond wheezed, "Right here, my lord."

When Raymond arrived with the robe, Lord Hempleman allowed his steward to help him don the warm garment before instructing, "Raymond, inform the staff to assemble in the study. Now! We will get to the bottom of this."

Lord Hempleman then turned to his wife. "You must go to your room. This is nasty business." To his chamberlain he said, "Raymond, escort my wife to the safety of her room before alerting the servants. I will wait for you in the study."

Lady Hempleman followed Raymond up the stairs and through her husband's bedchamber. At the door to her room Raymond inquired, "Shall I check your room for its safety, *die gnädige Frau?*"

Anna thought of the feathers that might be lying about. "No, no, no. I am sure if we do have an intruder, he would not venture up here. No. You may return to Lord Hempleman. I am fine."

So the faithful servant left to tend to his master's request.

Anna tittered as she listened to Raymond's fading footsteps. As she felt the safety of her room caress her, she moved toward the beckoning wine bottle on her table. Her delicate fingers stroked the neck, tenderly picking up the small yet commanding master and hugging it close. Removing its cork, she took a long, satisfying swill, then placed the liquid companion on her nightstand. As the Black Forest clock signaled five, Anna literally collapsed onto her bed, tugged the comforters closely around her chilled form, and rested her head on the soft, feathered pillow that had this night dramatically increased in value.

Chapter 4

MONDAY, SEPTEMBER 15, 1751—LATE MORNING— ATLANTIC OCEAN OFF THE COAST OF SPAIN

Two days and 300 knots after the storm, George surveyed the European coastline as he stood starboard on the ship. *Almost home.* Releasing his strong wide grip from the wooden rail of the square-rigged merchant ship, he turned to face the sunset.

He had always been obedient to his parents, compliant with their requests and demands, but what they had asked him this time was more than he could allow. He was determined to make his own choice in this matter. Hopefully, his parents would understand. If not, he would seek an alternative. George knew his decision would change the destiny of his family. As the eldest son of Lord Johann Hempleman, he was in line to receive his father's title. Beyond that, his father had orchestrated a plan to move the Hemplemans from lower nobility into a higher strata. Young George was crucial to the unfolding of the family fortunes.

That meant his moving to Togo for at least a decade to establish a 10,000-hectare cotton plantation, which would enhance his family's dwindling financial resources. This he would be willing to do. But marry Charlotte Sturzhelm? Never!

George's reverie returned to his real love. Just thinking of Margarette made his thoughts soar. He remembered the first time he had seen her nine years ago. George had been only ten years old, his brother Maurice only eight—the same age as Professor Duffy's daughter.

Ah, the Professor's daughter!

Professor Duffy had recently moved his family from Scotland, seeking employment as a tutor until he could gain a full position in a German university. George's father had been glad to gain Professor Duffy's expertise for a low premium while the new immigrant gained mastery of the German language. The industrious Scot with his two young sons joined other laborers to work the fields on the Hempleman manor. Yet Professor Duffy carved out time to teach mathematics, history, Latin, French, and English to young George and Maurice Hempleman.

George had caught far-away glimpses of Professor Duffy's family in the fields and near the cottage in which they lived on the Hempleman lands. But he had never seen Margarette up close until the day she had walked with her father in the market district of Cassel.

Young George watched the passing carts and pedestrians while standing beside his stately mother who was admiring lace displayed in a store window. It was then that Professor Duffy rounded the corner, holding the hand of an effervescent strawberry-blonde whose wind-swept locks crept out from under her bonnet and caught the sunshine in a radiance more dazzling than red gold. Suddenly George's dark brown eyes stopped roaming and riveted on the young lass.

"Good day, Master George," Professor Duffy said, tipping his head ever so slightly.

George harnessed his emotions in a gulp and returned the greeting as his mother turned to smile at the tutor before returning her attention to the store's merchandise. But George would not, could not, remove his gaze from the petite sprite who continued walking down the street with her papa. George could still see Margarette's calico dress swinging from side to side to the tempo of her dancing curls.

Even when George's mother took his hand and led him in the

opposite direction, George stole occasional glances, pivoting in an awkward gait until the Duffys merged into the noisy nebulous mass of shoppers.

That had been in 1742. For George it had been love at first sight. Of course, he had never let anyone know. His future was already in the preliminary planning stages. When his father had taken the office of constable in Cassel in 1745, it was only two years later that Lord Sturtzhelm corralled George's father into signing a betrothal for his daughter Charlotte to Lord Hempleman's eldest son, George.

MONDAY, SEPTEMBER 15, 1751—AFTERNOON— ROAD FROM CASSEL TO DARMSTADT-GIESSEN

The coach that wended its way to Giessen jostled Margarette's small frame. Opposite her sat a Roman Catholic priest.

Two nights ago Father Marc had taken the frightened girl under his care when he had first heard crying, then seen a disheveled, rank-smelling, nearly incoherent bundle of humanity in the church graveyard. His priestly paternal instincts wrapped around the wayfarer. Quickly he had sent a monk to contact Mother Julia in the adjacent convent.

Margarette was escorted by the kind lady to the convent, where she was given a warm, early breakfast. A sponge bath followed while novices washed her soiled clothing before any questions were asked.

Later Father Marc and Mother Julia heard her tale, and Father Marc dispatched three burly brothers to check on the welfare of the man left beside the fountain. His loud snoring made him easy to find, and the promise of a hot meal and medical care softened him into accepting temporary housing in the monastery travelers' house.

By midmorning, a messenger was sent to Cassel Inn to learn when the next coach would leave for Giessen. Two tickets were purchased so that Margarette could rest in the security of a Christian companion on her trip home. Father Marc also offered his services to talk with Margarette's father.

Mother Julia had introduced Margarette to several nuns who lavished her with kindness, told her stories of their own rescues, and served her *pickert* with freshly pressed apple cider. Unable to suppress a smile while remembering these kind moments, Margarette shut her blue eyes and attempted to think of the current jostling in the coach as a suspended cradle swung by loving Hands.

TUESDAY, SEPTEMBER 16, 1751—BAY OF BISCAY

Dusk replaced the sun's fading rays. The *Venture* sailed on dark seas. In two days, the vessel was expected to enter Amsterdam's busy harbor. George felt a sense of relief that he had only a brief time left listening to Lord Sturzhelm's loud snoring and incessant thrashing about on his bunk. George's proposed father-in-law was a torrent of crescendos asleep as well as awake. Even now his heavy footsteps on the ship's wooden deck shattered George's peace. Turmoil stalked as Lord Sturzhelm did the same. George knew that even with the darkness closing around him, he could not avoid the encounter.

"So, young man! Enjoying the sea breezes, I see. It has been a good trip, a fine adventure, despite that nasty little episode we had two nights ago. Yes, we have accomplished a lot on this trip."

George smiled dutifully before asking, "Where are our friends?"

"Lord Wolff and Lord Hamler have gone to their quarters for the evening. That gives us time for a bit of father and son chit-chat." George cringed as Lord Sturzhelm's loud laugh boomed above the din of the sailors' banter, the cry of the wind's surge, and the collision of the waves against the ship's bow. "Your home in Togo will be completed by the time of the wedding. A fine home it will be! Nothing too good for my daughter, I always say."

"Yes, sir," George conceded.

"Yes, indeed. It is a perfect plantation home. Charlotte is good at management, and she will have the home operating at top efficiency while you tend to the cotton. Yes, indeed, you will have a good life."

When George forced a smile, which turned into a smirk, he was grateful that the moon shone on Lord Sturzhelm's face while hiding his own.

From the inception of the Sturzhelm-Hempleman liaison, George had attempted to be congenial to his father's benefactor. But George considered Lord Sturzhelm a braggart. The successful entrepreneur mixed this deficiency with being socially too confident and financially too aggressive. Lord Sturzhelm, in George's opinion, was the superlative of poor breeding and opulence.

George's thoughts wandered to the submissive wife Lord Sturzhelm had chosen, one who had extended her husband's vast fortune.

The man stalks acquiescent people, George reasoned as his thoughts turned toward his own family. *Look what Lord Sturzhelm has done to my father. Lord Sturzhelm barks, and my father fetches. Then my father roars, and our whole household trembles in fear.*

It was true that George's father, reared in the military, had learned obeisance to authority, and it worked to his advantage. However, that attribute did not come easily to young George despite his six months in military training. He had more than a bit of his mother's high spirit plus his own penchant for manipulation.

As Lord Sturzhelm rambled, saying little of substance, George mentally removed the nobleman's mustache and bushy sideburns, substituting an elegant feminine hairstyle on the shorter man's balding pate. Before young George stood Charlotte, his betrothed. But massive dark locks could not turn Charlotte into a woman of beauty. Her short stature would have been an asset were it not for the protruding chest cavity that mimicked Lord Sturzhelm's. It was true she did not yet possess the rotund center section that dominated Lord Harry's physique, but it was sure to come. The prominent nose, protruding eyes, and enlarged ears set on a square face marked her as the daughter of Lord Sturzhelm. Suitors were non-existent, except for young George.

Of course, Lord Sturzhelm could cite the reason for that omission. The dominating lord had selected Master George Hempleman as a fitting mate for Charlotte while George was only fifteen. Then the powerful lord had corralled Lord Johann Hempleman into signing a binding betrothal for his handsome, promising eldest son. George shuddered despite the September heat. *What a shame Charlotte had not inherited her mother's fine looks and demure demeanor.*

But even that would not have turned George's heart away from Margarette Duffy.

Staccato steps announced Captain Van Devoorde's nightly rounds on the deck urging his passengers to their berths. The sea and darkness could pose problems for passengers who had not developed sailor legs. The good captain just felt better when everyone was battened down.

"Time to call it a day, Lord Sturzhelm," the stout officer called out.

"Yes, indeed, Captain."

"Will you be making your way back to Togo again?" Captain Van Devoorde queried.

Lord Sturzhelm laughed loudly, a trait Charlotte had been able to avoid. "No. This is my first and final voyage. But my future son-in-law here will be taking my daughter to Togo in a mere six months. He needs to be on the plantation before planting season." Lord Sturzhelm rumbled and shook in his delight, reminding George of the massive destruction Mount Vesuvius had brought on the unsuspecting residents of Pompeii.

Excusing himself, George made his way to his berth. His attendants, as well as Lord Sturzhelm's, had earlier readied the bed clothing of their lords' elevated, separate bunks. The four now huddled in round masses on their floor pallets.

From the time he turned fourteen and was isolated from female supervision, George coveted the servants' even breathing and occasional snores. The rhythmic vibrations soared around him like the soothing tunes and soft lullabies he no longer heard from his mother's lips. But those melodic sounds brought no solace tonight.

He had been gone from Cassel for nearly seven months. How had Margarette changed? How had he changed? The humid, warm Togo climate had stolen a few pounds, which made his broad shoulders more pronounced. The unrelenting sun had branded his skin a deep brown, which blended more easily with his coal black hair, a distinctive Hessian characteristic. Would Margarette be pleased with the new George? More importantly, would she still be waiting and willing to become his wife?

George quietly slipped on his nightshirt, adjusted his covers, rolled onto his side while clutching his pillow, and allowed the waves to lull him into festive dreams.

Chapter 5

TUESDAY, SEPTEMBER 16,
1751—DUSK—BEYOND ALSFELD

The road trip had been a treat for Father Marc. While the adult passengers had observed the privacy of the others, one loquacious lad had kept a running conversation with Father Marc. The lad's parents had tried to deter his inquisition, but the six-year-old had expressed the need to know why the priest dressed differently from others. Did his collar itch? Who understood the Latin he spoke during Mass? Why was he not married? Was God really able to listen to and watch everyone and everything on earth? And when would he actually meet God Himself?

The priest had chuckled with each new topic, trying his best to answer each question to the young boy's satisfaction. At their Alsfeld destination, the boy's father and mother thanked the white-haired cleric for his patience while young Marc, for that was his name, told the priest, "I want to be just like you when I grow up." Father Marc laughed but the young lad's parents clasped their son's hands tightly, leading him away from the charisma of the Roman Catholic cleric. As the family left, Father Marc shrugged his shoulders and forced a smile. He was accustomed to rebuffs in the Calvinist-dominated region.

Alsfeld, with its picturesque half-timbered structures, had also been the stop for the night. Since the rural town had a deep religious heritage, Father Marc had felt quite safe sleeping on the straw-strewn floor of the central market inn. It was not comfortable, but the authority of Father Marc's office and the magnitude of his presence had provided Margarette the security she needed to stretch out, gather enough straw to cradle her head, and catch a few winks before dawn.

After a light breakfast, and just before sunrise, the two remaining passengers entered the coach headed southwest to Giessen. Exchanging initial pleasantries with her traveling companion, the young lass then grew reticent. The priest granted her privacy while the wheels beneath them rumbled toward her home. As the day ebbed, Margarette pulled her cloak more tightly around her small frame, despite the warm temperatures. Her eyes, which periodically glistened with tears, locked in a blank stare on the shifting scenery.

In the privacy of the cab, Father Marc quietly studied the young lady opposite him as the fading sun filled the landscape with soft autumn hues. "Shall we formulate a strategy or just let events take their course?"

With tears gathering in her eyes, Margarette confessed, "I am just so ashamed to have to tell my parents that I have been dismissed from the Hempleman household under the stigma of a theft. But, Father Marc, I never stole anything from their home. Never!"

"I believe you, child. It is obvious that Lord Hempleman intends for his son to marry Lord Sturzhelm's daughter and wants no one to interrupt that marriage."

"But will my parents and family be disgraced because of my dismissal? Papa sacrificed so much when he came to Germany to begin life over again in a foreign country. He is established now with a good reputation, but everyone will begin asking him and Mama why I am home. You know, Father Marc, that the tongues will wag."

"It is unfortunate but true, Margarette. People want to protect themselves, but oftentimes that leads to gossip, then slander, and sometimes violence. God hates all three. It is often the well-meaning people who start the process. They hope to shield themselves from those they consider disruptive. Rather than seek the truth, people are often content to believe a lie. I deal with this all the time."

"So what do you suggest?" Margarette asked while drying her tears with her kerchief.

"I suggest that you trust the wisdom that your scholarly father will give to you. From what you have told me, he seems to love you dearly and has dealt well with the welfare of your brothers and sister."

"Oh, yes!" Margarette confirmed. "Charles Junior is married to the daughter of a glover and cobbler and has taken up the trade. Hank is a coxswain on the Rhine and loves the adventure. Suzanna married a miller's son, and young Will and Anthony are advancing well in their studies. Will is determined to be an officer in the Hessian army, and Anthony wants to be a professor like Papa. Charles and Suzanna even have children. I will be so happy to see them all again. If only it could be under different conditions. Oh, Father Marc, what am I to say?"

"What do you think, Margarette? Does the father of such a family as yours deserve to be trusted with the truth?" Father Marc smiled while raising his white eyebrows in near jest.

Margarette settled back in her seat, sighing. "I hope so. I certainly hope so."

WEDNESDAY, SEPTEMBER 17, 1751—EARLY MORNING—ENGLISH CHANNEL

A heavy wind with a lashing rain and mountainous waves tossed Captain Van Devoorde's ship dangerously close to shore. This was not a morning for sleeping. The able captain's orders transferred from his officers to all hands on deck. The well-practiced crew combined their individual expertise to cause the convoluted situation appear like everyday activity—despite gigantic ridges of water tossing the ship and lifting it airborne before slamming its keel onto the ocean surface again and again.

In his cabin, George planted both feet on the flooring. He steadied himself with one hand on the wooden bunk and another on the privacy rod above him when Lord Sturzhelm quite literally rolled onto the floor with a thud. All four male servants hustled to aid the squalling lord, who demanded to be placed firmly and upright on the edge of his berth.

"Get my boots and breeches, Franz! I am going to see what is going on out there! You, Louis, fetch my hat and cloak! I paid for a smooth-sail! One storm is enough for any trip. We will see about this!"

Lord Sturzhelm's groom scuttled to get his lord's legs into the fine-spun linen breeches before sliding the impatient man's feet into his leather boots. The *frieseur* stood by with the lord's cloak and hat. George wondered if Captain Van Devoorde or the Lord Himself would be in trouble for Lord Sturzhelm's discomfort.

Once clothed and shod, Lord Sturzhelm leaned on each of his servants as they walked him onto the deck of the ship.

What looked like utter confusion to the untrained eye masked the efficiency of trained sailors. Ropes in capable hands lowered sails and shifted others, catching the wind to guide the square-rig out of a shallow and rocky shoreline. Though the rain and winds did not abate, Captain Van Devoorde's ship sailed steadily toward the central channel of the Zuider Zee. The final nautical miles into Amsterdam would be thankfully uneventful.

At breakfast, Captain Van Devoorde was noticeably absent, having taken a quick repast with his men rather than subject himself to the never-ending clatter of Lord Sturzhelm's unsolicited observations.

George picked lightly at his breakfast, knowing that the cuisine on shore would be much more palatable. Also, if all worked well, perhaps Lord Sturzhelm would take a nap in one of Amsterdam's fine inns while George found more worthy company at a table. But for now, George needed to play his part, listening to the angry outrages of Lord Sturzhelm.

"No, indeed! If I were captain of this rig, I would never have continued in that storm toward the Zuider Zee. I would have detoured into Rotterdam's harbor until the storm lifted. It was not a good call."

When not one of the passengers in the dining area responded, Lord Sturzhelm continued. "I may decide to cancel all future dealings with Captain Van Devoorde. The man cannot be trusted. I will have a heavy investment to consider when the cotton starts coming in from Togo. I do not want it lying on the bottom of the sea. No use there. What do you think, Hamler?"

"The good captain did bring us safely out of the storm, sir," Lord Hamler commented.

"I cannot believe you!" Lord Sturzhelm jutted out his square jaw. "You agree with me, like any reasonable man would, do you not, Wolff?"

Lord Wolff added his assent with a ready, "Absolutely, Lord Sturzhelm." Then as soon as Lord Sturzhelm concealed his face in a mug of hot coffee, the merry man winked at George as if to say, *One storm a day is more than enough.*

Lord Sturzhelm set his massive cup on the table with a thud. "There you see, Hamler. Wolff agrees with me. Hamler, you should have more sense. Van Devoorde put all of our lives at great risk, not to mention the cargo he has aboard. No, I will locate another merchant ship and another captain who is more highly recommended. Enough of this foolishness! Why, if ..."

A knock on the cabin door preceded Captain Van Devoorde's entrance. Perhaps he had been listening all the while.

"Are you ready to put those feet on solid ground, men? We will be docking early tomorrow morning. I will get you passengers off and on your way before removing cargo. Alert your servants to be ready for debarking."

Lord Sturzhelm coughed indignantly. "My servants are ready,

Captain Van Devoorde! I was on top of that matter before bedding down last night!"

"Good. Good." The amiable captain chuckled. "I can count on your readiness every time, Lord Sturzhelm."

George stifled a laugh.

As quick as an adder, Lord Sturzhelm looked askance at young George who dodged the unspoken reprimand by picking up his coffee mug and taking a long draught.

Lord Sturzhelm was not accustomed to being mocked. *I am glad I will be sending this new son-in-law of mine to Togo. He could be a handful. Perhaps I can keep him down in Africa more than ten years. Say twenty or thirty, maybe his entire lifetime.*

THURSDAY, SEPTEMBER 18, 1751—MORNING—GIESSEN

Lydia Duffy scoured the last of the breakfast dishes, a skillet that had held *Reibekuchen*. It was a favorite of the Duffy family since they had moved to Germany. Anthony was studying his math and German in the parlor. With the guttural sounds Lydia overheard, Anthony had apparently finished with his math and was now trying to master the German *o*'s and *u*'s for which there is no Scottish equivalent.

"We need to speak more German in our household," Lydia reminded herself aloud. She set the skillet on the sideboard, wiped her clean hands on her apron, and was about to reach for the dishtowel when her quick eye caught the dazzling radiance of a young woman's tresses. Lydia leaned forward to peer out of the window, careful not to move the lace curtains shielding her own image.

"It's Margarette!" Lydia Duffy said to herself. "She is with a priest! Whatever does this mean?"

Smoothing her red hair, then repositioning hairpins to hold her massive locks in a tight bun at the base on her skull, Lydia ran from the kitchen to the parlor.

"Anthony, pick up your school books and go to your bedroom. Margarette is outside and a priest is with her."

"Ah, Mama, let me stay. I have not seen Margie forever."

"Off with you, son! Do as you are told. We will be having some *Weisse Nuremberger Lebkuchen* with tea later."

"Do not give it all away, Mama."

"Hush. Now, off with you."

A soft knock sounded at the door as Anthony swept up his school articles.

"Mama, it is your daughter. I have come home."

Mama swung the oak door wide, surveying Margarette who was obviously as trim as ever. *At least she is not in trouble that way.* But Margarette's eyes betrayed a solemnity Lydia did not want to face.

Pulling Margarette into a warm embrace, Lydia studied the aged priest who smiled approvingly. When Margarette relaxed in her mother's arms, Lydia whispered, "Now what is all this about?"

Margarette burst into tears. Never releasing her loving grip, Lydia ushered her daughter into the parlor.

"Perhaps I can explain a bit of what Margarette has been through, Mrs. Duffy," Father Marc offered.

"Forgive my bad breeding, Father. Please be seated. I will prepare us some tea. Have you had your breakfast?"

"We ate in Giessen Inn. We arrived late yesterday, too late to come barging in on your hospitality," the cleric explained. "But a cup of tea would be wonderful."

"I will just be a moment. You two must relax. Get settled. Then we can talk. Wipe your nose, Margarette."

Margarette recovered slowly from her initial outbreak. "I told you that Mama is a gem, Father Marc."

Lydia returned with a tray of tea and healthy slices of *Weisse Nuremberger Lebkuchen* for both the priest and Margarette. She seated herself beside her daughter before pouring steaming cups of tea. "Please help yourself when you are ready, Father." She beamed the invitation.

"How could a man resist?" Father Marc returned the smile and extended his hand toward Lydia. "Father Marc, here."

A slight touch of red rising to her fair complexion, Lydia extended her hand as well. "Of course, Father Marc. I am Mrs. Duffy, which you already realize. Forgive me for the late introduction."

"Forgiven and forgotten, ma'am," the good priest grinned while reaching for the plate holding the layered cake.

"Where is Papa?" Margarette looked around the room. "And Will and Anthony?"

"Anthony is in the boys' room. Will has gone with your father to the university," Mrs. Duffy answered before addressing Father Marc. "My husband has a full schedule. Will reads in the library while his father is busy with students. They will be back at noon. Now, tell me why you are here. We were not expecting Margarette until after the new year."

When the cleric paused and glanced at Mararette, tears again began to fill her blue eyes. "It is not good, Mama. In fact, it is awful." She took a deep breath, then expelled it. "Lord Hempleman dismissed me, Mama. He accused me of stealing and said he would not press criminal charges if I left quietly and immediately."

"Stealing? Stealing what, Margarette?"

"A necklace belonging to his wife."

The priest set his unfinished plate down, leaning toward Mrs. Duffy. "Lord Hempleman has been known to, shall we say, fabricate a story, ma'am. He has been seeking ways to rise on the social scale and is currently engaged in a venture with some higher-ranking nobleman. The scenario becomes more complicated. This higher-ranking nobleman has a daughter of marriageable age. Lord Hempleman has a son of equal age. However, it seems this young Master Hempleman has eyes for your daughter."

"Margarette!" her mother chastised.

"Mama, I have done nothing wrong, nothing inappropriate."

"Well, he must have had some encouragement somewhere. It would certainly be easy enough for him to compromise you!"

"Mama, I am not lying to you. George has been away in Africa for months."

"So it is *George*, is it? Margarette, you had better tell me the truth about yourself. You are accused of stealing. Now the nobleman's son has taken a liking to you. What is going on?"

"Mama, I am trying to tell you, but you keep interrupting me."

"Perhaps we had best start this conversation with prayer instead of tea and treats, ladies. What do you say?" Father Marc intervened.

"Absolutely!" Lydia agreed.

After the prayer, Lydia listened attentively to her daughter's plight. Soon she grew indignant towards Lord Hempleman as well as his son.

"So this young George appears to have designs on you, Margarette. You know that is impossible. Marriages do not cross social barriers. Even the Good Book says we are to be content in our station."

Father Marc intervened. "Yes, we are to be content with our lives, Mrs. Duffy. But only God knows what our lives hold. I am not going to judge this young man harshly just yet."

Encouraged, Margarette moved to the edge of the couch and took her mother's hands into her own. "Oh, Mama, if you could just meet George, you would realize what a gentleman he is."

"Has he ever kissed you, Margarette?"

Margarette lowered her eyes and presented the practiced explanation she had formulated. "Just once, Mama, but only on my hand. I was walking down the hallway as he walked out of his room. We nearly bumped into each other. I backed away, but he continued to stand there grinning at me with a sparkle in his eyes that danced like the eyes of an elf. Slowly he moved his arms from his side and slightly outward with his hands spread wide, beckoning me. I was so embarrassed that I turned to leave, but he said, 'Do not leave, Margarette. Someday I am going to marry you.' I was astounded. Then he took my right hand in both of his, raised it to his lips, and said, 'Remember, I am going to marry you. There will be no one but you for me.' He let loose of my hand, gave me a quick wink with those dark eyes of his, turned, and walked down the hall."

Lydia was lost in a moment from the past. "Just like your father, Margarette." She jerked her head to recover and turned to Father Marc. "So what are we to do with this situation?"

"I am here to help your husband with a solution."

"My husband will never allow Margarette to marry a nobleman. It is not done. It is impractical. It is asking for a life shut off from all social interaction. My daughter would be a pariah. She deserves better than this. Margarette, you are not seriously in love with this young man, are you?"

Margarette's silence gave her mother the answer.

"Impossible! Your father will think of something. He always has a solution." Mrs. Duffy picked up her cup of tea, which was now quite cold, put it nearly to her lips, and then quietly shook her head. "Impossible. Charles will have a solution."

Margarette felt Father Marc's gaze on her quaking form as waves of fear deep within rose to the surface. There the two women sat— the mother shaking her head in perplexity, the daughter trembling in anxiety.

THURSDAY, SEPTEMBER 18, 1751—MORNING—AMSTERDAM

Franz and Louis carried the valises of Lord Sturzhelm while Hans and Delbert toted George's baggage. The six travelers made arrangements for the night at an inn where Lord Sturzhelm learned that a number of hopeful emigrants to America were stranded in Amsterdam. The trip down the Rhine had been more costly than any farmer, hoping to better the life of his family in the new world, had anticipated. Crafty charlatans, pickpockets, and thieves had dipped deeply into the pockets of the unsuspecting. Many were too proud and protective of their families to risk indenture. They gathered in parks, on church lawns, and near the docks holding signs asking for honest work.

Lord Sturzhelm saw an opportunity. After talking with several young men and women that afternoon, he hired ten to accompany him to Cassel. If they worked well, he guaranteed them a lifelong position. The additions to their party required Lord Sturzhelm's hiring two more coaches, but he reasoned the new laborers would prove a good investment.

FRIDAY, SEPTEMBER 19, 1751—EARLY MORNING—AMSTERDAM

The company departed by stagecoach early in the morning. Barring bad weather, they would be in Cassel in one week.

George thought the hiring of the aspiring emigrants a compassionate gesture as well as a sound financial move. For a moment he reasoned that he had been too harsh on Lord Sturzhelm.

But that was a fleeting evaluation.

Nearly all of George's waking hours, Lord Sturzhelm talked about the March wedding, the success George would have in Togo, the opportunity this enterprise was bringing to George and his family, and the addition of the new employees being a boon to George and Charlotte in Togo. But these were minor incursions. The towering threat that loomed over George nearly every sentient moment—sometimes while he dreamed—was of being in a marriage without love.

George's tired brain recalled a professor in Marburg who had been dramatizing a scene from *Julius Caesar*. The wiry academician had leaned forward toward the class, squinted his fiery eyes, and nearly whispered the warning. "Beware the Ides of March!"

Chapter 6

TUESDAY, SEPTEMBER 23, 1751—MORNING—DARMSTADT-GIESSEN

Will Duffy caught his breath after entering the foyer of his home, waving *die Zeitung*. "Papa, the stagecoach will be leaving shortly." Will received no response. He stuck his head into the parlor. Neither his sister nor his father had on their cloaks.

Margarette sat on the edge of the sofa as Papa stood with his right arm resting on the wooden mantle piece. Mama, kerchief in hand, looked on from the entryway to the kitchen.

"Papa, why are you doing this to me? I have been a good daughter. I *never* stole from Lord Hempleman. You know that I would never jeopardize my position or bring discredit to our family. Allow me to go back to Scotland. I could live with Grandmama. That would mean fewer responsibilities for Aunt Mary. Grandmama is advancing in years. No doubt Aunt Mary needs extra help for her care. Please, Papa."

Papa heaved a heavy sigh, stooped to gather his valise, then took his scholar's cap and cloak off the coat rack. He said not a word. Mama now leaned against the wainscoted wall in the parlor, looking first at her husband, Charles, then at her daughter, Margarette, then at her son, William.

"Time to go," Papa announced. "Margarette, Will says the stagecoach will be leaving shortly. You can either travel with me or seek your own life outside these doors tonight. Make your choice."

"Papa, please," Margarette begged, falling to her knees. "All my life I have obeyed you. Please hear my heart."

"It is because of your heart that I make this decision, daughter." Papa took Margarette's elbow and brought her to her feet. "Once you are in your new environment, you will become accustomed to the routine. You will be a better person because of it."

Margarette looked with pleading eyes toward her mother. Mama gathered her apron in her two hands, covered her face with the coarse muslin fabric, and ran from the room.

Margarette thought, *Of course she must obey Papa. She always has. Mama. Kind Mama. Such a big heart. Such a warm touch. But confrontational? Never. That was not in Mama's character. But why is Will so distant? Does he believe that I am a thief? I could never think that of him. Why is everything so confusing?*

Avoiding Will's angry glance and Papa's riveting stare, Margarette raised her chin, stiffened her narrow shoulders, and picked up her valise and cloak. Never again would she be able to cross this threshold. Her future closed around her like a mountain fortress. But deep within, her spirit rose to levels where she found purpose. Margarette resolved to dwell on pleasant memories, and, when the real world became too cruel, to create situations where she lived transcendent above her circumstances, unpleasant though they might be. With God's help, she determined to remain strong.

The stagecoach rumbled over the cobbled streets of Giessen, Germany—swaying, rocking, jolting like a young mother trying to comfort her disconsolate child. Merchants opened their doors and peddlers set up their wares while constables stationed themselves strategically to scrutinize the gathering marketers. The rising sun flashed on the left side of the coach as Margarette squinted to gain a last look at the Duffy timber-framed home. *When will George be back? Will I never see him again? Will my memories satisfy? Will God hear my prayer? Will He override society's and man's will? The priest said that God is sovereign. Yes, my God is sovereign. I have to place my trust and my faith in Him.*

Three strangers joined the Duffys in the stage, a man in a military uniform and an older couple. The military man sat with Will and Papa in the forward seat, making a confederate of three. Margarette avoided their every look, instead fastening her eyes on the autumn landscape and trying to avoid physical contact with the plump lady by her side. At noon the stagecoach driver stopped at a way station to water and feed the horses. Papa led Margarette and Will to sit on the grass beside the River Giessen and unwrapped the lunch his wife had packed. Forcing himself to be light-hearted, Papa began his recitation in a quiet, private voice.

"Hesse and Darmstadt have been good for us. When you were only eight years old, Margarette, and Will just five, the ruling margrave agreed to allow us to settle here because I am a teacher and a tutor. It was a relief to your mother and me because of the conditions in Scotland. The talk was that Bonnie Prince Charlie would be coming back to make things right in Scotland. The Highlanders could have enticed Charles and Hank to join them, tempers that my elder sons have! Your mother and I saw the writing on the wall. A group of Highlanders against the mighty British army! We could never win. It was not worth losing your two brothers and having a bloody battle on our doorstep. Just as your mother and I expected, the revolt broke out three years after we settled in Hessen. Now Bonnie Prince Charlie is our neighbor in France after leaving his fellow Highlanders to the swords of the British."

Taking bites of cheese and bread, then washing them down with fresh cider, Papa carried on the course of his logic. "Now, my Charles is alive in Giessen with his lovely wife and children. He makes a good living working with his father-in-law. Hank feeds his wanderlust by boating up and down the Rhine and Ruhr. He may never settle." Papa paused, wondering first about Hank's future, then about Margarette's. He shook his head. "No matter. We had better go back to the stage."

Her curiosity roused, Margarette questioned, "What do you mean by 'no matter,' Papa? Everything matters. Each event in our life is of significance. We are either walking in Christ's footsteps or out of His footsteps. So, explain to me what is of *no matter*."

"You were my best student, Margarette. Always had your face behind a book when you were not helping your mother. I knew you often listened while I tutored. You are my bright little Margie. I love you, daughter."

"So why banish me so completely, Papa?"

"I puzzled over your future when you arrived home disgraced. How would we Duffys rise above it? After Father Marc left, I spoke to your sister, Susanna, and her husband. I counseled with Charles' in-laws, Hans and Anna Fownes. Your mother and I prayed about your situation again and again. Then it came to me quite suddenly while I was listening to one of my students reading *Hamlet*. My mind was not on the Bard's words but on you, Margie. My heart was consumed with your future. Then Unger, my student, read the passage that solved my dilemma."

"Oh, Papa, I know what you are about to say. It is the part where Hamlet is distraught, believing those closest to him are evil. In his despair, Hamlet rejects his true love by telling her—"

"'Get thee to a nunnery.' Yes, that is what Unger read, and it all made sense. Shakespeare repeated his advice to Ophelia four more times."

"Papa, Shakespeare is not Holy Writ. He also said, 'To thine own self be true.'"

"I know. I know. But the advice regarding the nunnery is so fitting. You will be exonerated by your chaste life. The Duffy name will be cleared of all scandal. Your sister and brothers, your mother and I will be able to live free from wagging tongues once again. It is the only way, Margie, the only way."

Margarette looked at Will, imploring him with her soul to come to her aid. Will shrugged his shoulders and looked away, pondering,

Maybe Papa is too dramatic in this instance, but Papa has made good decisions before. No one has come to Margarette's defense regarding the emerald necklace. Everyone has a weakness, Will concluded. *Perhaps Margarette's weakness was not really the love for a nobleman but the lust for material things. What will my future hold if I have an unmarried sister pining away and neighbors discussing her past, her present, and her future? Papa is right. To the nunnery with Margarette.*

The six passengers and coachman stayed in a fairly pleasant inn that evening in Alsfeld. The food was modest but nourishing, the sleeping area clean and cramped. Before the sun rose that Wednesday morning, all six passengers sat tucked in their seats, hugging their cloaks tightly around them. Conversation? There was none.

Margarette strained to see out the window. Farmers swung their broad scythes in the rising sun while children bundled the harvest into shocks. Carts, sumpters, and whirlicotes laden with wheat, barley, oats, apples, and grapes passed the cumbersome stagecoach. God was not stopping the movement of His universe because of Margarette's anguish.

She began to think. *Maybe I could make my own way in the world. Perhaps then I could locate George. I could always find work as a cook, a maid. But my story might already be public knowledge. How could I defend myself against a lord, a distinguished military veteran, a Cassel constable? George would not want me with the stigma of thievery hanging over me! Oh, my dear Lord. Help me. Love me. Comfort me.*

The Smythes, the surname of the couple seated beside Margarette, left the company at a lane leading to a rather large farm on the outskirts of Fulda. Immediately, Will filled in the empty space beside Margarette. An odd change in social atmosphere occurred when the party of six became a party of four. Just as a child released from standing in a corner with his nose pressed against the wall, the man seated beside Papa relaxed. He spread his long arms above his head, slouched in his seat, and yawned in pleasure.

"It is good you did not share any of your lives with those two. I wonder what they were doing in Hesse-Rheinfels-Rotenburg.

Probably up to no good. Dangerous couple!" He stared momentarily into the distance before asking, "So, where are you folks headed?"

Papa answered with a smile on his thin lips, "Are you one we can trust?"

The young soldier laughed heartily and extended his hand to Papa. "Lieutenant Garvey here, sir. I am on my way from visiting my parents in Mentz. I am due in Cassel by September 27. Who knows where I will be sent from there? It seems there is always a border squabble, what with over 350 German states plus the rumblings we hear across the borders into Austria and France. First the margraves and princes are bitter enemies, then they align to form a united front against some other foe. It is hard to remember who is whose enemy, or friend, for that matter."

"You sound more like a philosopher than a military man," Papa commented.

"My father is a professor in Mentz. *Wie der Vater, so der Sohn.*" Lieutenant Garvey laughed again.

"I, too, am a professor, or was one in Scotland before we moved to Hessen in 1742. Now I am a tutor. But Hessen and Darmstadt have treated our family well. Our forefathers did not convert under John Knox."

Smiling broadly, Lieutenant Garvey inserted, "Neither did your lively queen, Bloody Mary, if you will pardon the descriptive adjective, sir."

"We Scots never claimed that Mary. She was a British queen of Welsh and French stock, the daughter of Henry VIII and Catherine of Aragon. The one we Scots hold dear is Mary, Queen of Scots."

"I stand corrected, sir." Lieutenant Garvey nearly blushed because of his error.

"No matter. Both were ruled by their passions and manipulated by men. Personally, I could never understand fellow Christians spilling blood when we are under one covenant, one Lord Jesus Christ," Papa shook his head as if he were lost in the waves of history pouring over him.

The three youths in the carriage respected Papa's reverie with silence. The coach clattered on.

By mid-afternoon, the driver pulled the horses to a halt at the base of a mountain. On the summit of the rocky terrain stood a *kirch* with two wings branching off to the north and south.

"Mr. Duffy," the driver called. "Here is your stop."

Papa shook hands with the friendly lieutenant before stepping down from the stage. Then Papa took Margarette's hand to help her down. Will followed, clambering out by himself.

So the pretty young thing is going to become a nun, Lieutenant Garvey reflected. *I wonder what her story is. That accounts for the tight-lipped trip we had with the Smythes.*

Outside the coach, the driver instructed Mr. Duffy, "The abbey is right up that road. There is a guesthouse within the abbey walls for travelers. I am sure you will be given a place to stay. I will be making a return trip tomorrow. Watch for my stage by mid-afternoon. Good day to you, sir."

Chapter 7

WEDNESDAY, SEPTEMBER 24, 1751—LATE AFTERNOON—ABBEY NEAR FULDA

The stone walkway rose gradually to a flattened mesa where the triune complex rested behind a towering stone wall.

Margarette gasped, *It's a prison!* She looked around. *Perhaps running right now would be my best option. But where would I run? Who do I know?*

Will carried not only his own but also Margarette's valise. Mr. Duffy carried his own traveling bag. As Will observed the somber surroundings of stone, overhanging trees, and neatly clipped shrubbery, he began to miss his sister already. A small doubt clouded his mind about his sister's guilt. He had never known his sister to take what was not hers. In fact, Margarette was generous to a fault. How many times had he talked her out of half of her sweetened *Reibekuchen*? He also remembered the time when some neighborhood children were taunting little Claudia, the blacksmith's daughter, for wearing her father's kerchief as an apron. Margarette had soundly scolded her friends, taken Claudia to the side, and given her the apron Mama had made especially for Margarette, the apron with a dainty ruffle around the edge.

But Margarette was not perfect either. She had given Will a sound pounding when he had taken her book of poetry and written a not-so-kind poem of his own.

Big sister Margie, nose in her book,
Thinks she will avoid Mama's very stern look.
Dishes still dirty, sitting in the pan
Mama cut a switch and away Margie ran.

Will could not suppress a giggle at the memory of his own bad rhyme despite the seriousness of the moment. There they were, the three of them, mounting the walkway to approach the abbey, and Will was lost in a childhood memory. What woke him up was Margarette's jabbing Will in his ribs.

"Ouch! What was that for?"

"What was your laugh for, you heathen?"

"Papa, did you hear what Margarette called me?"

"I did, and I agree. This is not a time for laughter."

"But I was remembering something funny, something that I did long ago, and Margarette pounded me for it."

"Your sense of humor needs refinement, brother," Margarette sided with her father.

Will sighed. "Oh, well, even so, Margie, I do not think you are a thief. I am going to miss you terribly. If you ever get a chance to write, please send me a message."

Papa cautioned, "I do not believe she will be able to communicate with us for quite some time, Will."

Margarette saw the opening. "Papa, it is not too late. We could go back. You could use my dowry to send me to Scotland. Grandmama and Aunt Mary would be glad to see me."

"I have not changed my mind, daughter."

The trio approached the main entrance where massive gates yawned open. Hesitantly, Papa led the way on the path that led ever upward toward the abbey proper.

The baroque church acted as sentinel between the convent and the monastery, as a doting father often stands between his daughter and her suitor. Margarette saw the compact cloistered walkways surrounding the grey edifice as a tiny ray of hope, a movement toward the expanse of freedom and the unknown. But she also saw fastened wings projecting at right angles on each side of the church which gave the appearance of a series of houses clamped together by a giant's vise.

Papa looked from the main structure of the church to the left, then to the right. "Stay here. I will check to see which building we need." Walking through the entrance of the church abbey, Papa called, "Is anyone here? I am Charles Duffy from Giessen. I believe you are expecting me."

Soon a stranger's voice, that of a male, responded. Muffled conversation followed before Papa emerged with a caretaker who led the Duffys through a cloister toward a south wing that butted against the left side of the church.

"You will find Mother Louise to be a very kind woman, sir," the caretaker said before leaving the family in front of the only entrance to the convent.

The convent occupied a three-storey rectangular building, also of stone. *How many nuns live here?* Margarette wondered. *Or I should be wondering, how many nuns die here?*

Every place that Margarette looked she saw stone barriers. Even the baroque dome, which covered the church sanctuary and rose loftily toward heaven, offered no solace. Margarette had no wings. She was earthbound. Her soft chin quivered and tears streamed down her peach-flowered cheeks. Her feet clung to the ground, as if anchored by weights.

"Oh, Papa, please. Take me home. I will die in there. I was made for motherhood. I love the open countryside, the folk dancing, laughter, life. Papa, please, do not make me go in there. Do not leave me here. I will die. I know I will die."

Papa reached for the rope beside the gate and pulled decisively. A clear bell resounded.

Papa then pulled the rope a second time. He set down his valise and took Margarette's hand, fearful that she might bolt. For a moment he struggled with his emotions. *What kind of a father am I?* Then he allowed his head to rule his heart. *I am a good father. I have my family's best interest ever before me. I am doing this for a greater good. Margarette will adjust. This convent is devoted to prayer, study, and good works. These have all been part of my daughter's life from the time she was five. Life is never easy, but we manage. We make the best of what comes our way. We do our best. Margarette will adjust.* He took a deep breath, squared his shoulders, and stared directly ahead at the formidable wooden-hinged barrier that would soon engulf his daughter.

Footsteps could be heard on a stone walkway. There was a rattle of keys, then the insertion of the select key into the lock. The hinges groaned as the single block of oak swung inward only a brief way. In the late afternoon sun's glow stood a middle-aged woman in a black habit. Barely any part of her was visible except for her gnarled hands, which held a ring of keys, and her round face, which had somehow sneaked out of the darkness of her garb.

Margarette was surprised that the rigid woman bore a voice that sang like a lark. "Are you the family Duffy we are expecting from Giessen?" asked the portress.

"Yes. I am Charles Duffy, and this is my daughter Margarette."

He motioned proudly to Will. "This is my son William who is traveling with us."

The aged nun nodded and opened the gate wider while stepping back to watch the strangers as they entered. The small enclosure into which they stepped was a garden. The wall on the south side of the structure sported huge openings to allow the sun and fresh air an entrance. Margarette glanced upward and saw balconies on the second and the third floors of the convent. Were those faces peering behind dark draperies?

The silence was interrupted by a spoken melody, as stark a contrast as the grey stone walls were against the fall flowers growing around their edges. A petite woman with a perfectly oval face, nearly cherubic, floated across the stone pavement. She spoke to the portress, "Thank you, Sister Helene. You may return to your duties." The abbess, with hands folded as if in prayer, addressed Charles Duffy.

"I am Mother Louise. Please follow me this way to my office.

This should not take long. Evening vespers will start soon. While Margarette joins us for worship, Mr. Duffy, you and your son will be escorted to the travelers' house where you will be fed and bedded for the night."

"I understand. That is as the priest in Giessen informed me."

"Father Matthew?"

"The same."

The processing center was only a few steps away. Mother Louise located the correct key, unlocked the door, and bid them enter. She walked behind a large desk and invited the three Duffys to be seated on an open bench in front of her work area before she sat down.

"I will take your valise, Margarette," the abbess said. "You see, there are so few things from your home that you will need here. Let me look." She opened the case, deftly running her fingers through Margarette's belongings. Smiling, Mother Louise looked at Margarette. "You have packed sparingly and well."

The nun then turned her gaze toward Margarette's father. "The dowry?"

"It is all here." He reached for a leather pouch under his cloak, unfastened it from his belt, and placed it on the abbess' desk.

Picking up a small bell on her right side, Mother Louise summoned the cellaress who came through a rear door passage.

"Please take care of this donation, Sister."

The shorter, stouter sister took the bag, then left the room.

"She will return your pocket shortly, Mr. Duffy. You will have a written receipt. I thank you, in the name of our Savior, for your generosity." Mother Louise stood, "Now, let me show you the chapel where we will be having vespers shortly. We must move hastily."

Papa rose and motioned for Will and Margarette to follow. "I appreciate the tour, Mother Louise."

The black habit swept the stone flooring in a mesmerizing dance as the Duffys trailed behind the nimble-footed woman who had chosen solitude from the world in an embrace that was decisive and satisfying for her.

"This chapel is only for the nuns. The monks have their own

private chapel. Only when the parishioners attend services do both the nuns and monks enter the church sanctuary, and then we sit on separate sides and in different locations. We have no communication except for weekly confessionals, which are done in our chapel under my supervision and except in emergency situations. Your daughter will be well protected and supervised, Mr. Duffy."

"Father Matthew assured me that would be the case, and I thank you for the comfort," Papa responded.

Mother Louise opened one of the two doors of the chapel. Stone walls held a series of sconces. The candles breathed with the movement of the air and emitted the fragrance of roses. Rows of wooden benches faced toward the altar, which bore a golden crucifix between two candlesticks resting on intricately embroidered white linen.

"Plain but functional." Mother Louise smiled. "Now, let us return. You men must be on your way. So, scoot, scoot, scoot." The nun's fingers flew through the empty air, and Margarette was almost certain Mother Louise could take flight if she had so desired.

Chapter 8

FRIDAY, SEPTEMBER 26, 1751—LATE AFTERNOON—CASSEL

The marble flooring in the entranceway and grand ballroom had been waxed until it mimicked the river Fulda's translucent currents. Chairs were in place around the intricately carved oaken dining tables awaiting their white linen coverings. The relentlessly polished silverware and candelabra sparkled. Rows of dishes, cups, and crystal goblets stacked under linen waited on sideboards, ready for the homecoming.

Scarlet and gold banners hung from the walls celebrating the commencement of George's career in Togo. Similar accolades heralded Lord Sturzhelm as the primary benefactor of the venture. Massive crystal chandeliers held newly dipped candles that emitted the aroma of musk in the cavernous rooms. Richly ornamented scarlet and gold swags decorated the balustrade.

Lady Hempleman, with Siegfried in her arms, surveyed the preparations from the second-storey landing.

"Mama," Hayley called from her and Celia's room, "would you please come here? I want Marie to alter the dress I am wearing for George's homecoming banquet."

Anna walked in slow, careful steps into the girls' room. Day by day, hour by hour, she was weaning herself from wine. George would be home soon. She wanted more than anything, even wine, to make the homecoming of her eldest a treasured event. Anna felt rewarded for her self-discipline when she saw the effervescent Hayley standing on an ottoman modeling her dress for both her seven-year-old sister Celia and Marie Yarger, the household stewardess who was also doubling as a seamstress. *How many special moments have I already missed in the lives of my children?* she chastised herself.

"See, Mama," Hayley extended her arms. "The sleeves are too long. I am being swallowed alive by them."

Anna nodded. "I agree. Marie, do you think you could take up the hems, say, three-quarters of an inch?"

"I can do that without a problem, ma'am," she smiled, "if only I can persuade Hayley to step out of the gown for a few minutes."

Lady Hempleman returned the smile. "Dear, you must change into your everyday wear while Marie gets this garment sewn to your satisfaction."

Hayley curtsied dramatically and made her way behind the changing screen while Celia tugged on her mother's arm, which was supporting Siegfried, "Mama, what will I wear for George's homecoming? I want to look pretty, too."

"You are always pretty, my dear." Anna knelt to look her daughter straight in the eyes. "But you will not be attending the banquet. When you are a young lady like Hayley is, you may attend all the banquets we have in this home. But for now, you must confine yourself to sneaking one quick peek with Marie before she puts you in bed. Understood?"

Celia nodded her head. Anna kissed her daughter's light brown hair. "But for right now, we could all go downstairs and pretend that the banquet is just for you. How does that sound?"

Celia ran toward the steps and fluttered down them, singing, "The banquet is just for me, just for me, just for me!"

Lady Hempleman turned to Marie. "You know that you are indispensable to me right now. We are looking for a replacement for Margarette, and I truly appreciate how you are taking on so many extra duties until we can find someone we can trust."

Just then, the two women heard a scream. It was Celia's.

FRIDAY, SEPTEMBER 26, 1751—LATE AFTERNOON—ABBEY NEAR FULDA

Margarette looked at the plate of food in front of her. It had no appeal. For two days she had not had any appetite. She methodically did as she was told, keeping her mind fixed on a fantasy. For the moment, she was at home in Giessen helping Mama finish the evening dishes. George would come calling soon. Papa sat in his favorite upholstered chair in the parlor reading aloud in German *The Nibelungunleid* to the family. Will lay on his stomach on the rag-woven carpet with his hands propped under his chin. Anthony sat on the armrest of his father's chair gazing at the German language, which unfolded a drama unmatched in German literature.

Papa began chapter five. When he came to the part where Gernot urged King Gunther to present their sister Kriemhild to Siegfried, Margarette let her hands rest in the dishwater, not wanting any splash to drown out a word.

But not only Margarette's hands, her locks also felt wet. She reached atop her head, only to realize Novice Annette had just sprinkled a portion of her water on Margarette.

"Margarette!" Annette whispered. "Dinner is over. It is time for us to return to our room and prepare for evening vespers. I did not know how else to bring you back."

Margarette focused her eyes on the reality around her. She was not in her home with her family. She was not in a castle in Worms. She was not about to spend the evening with the love of her life. She was in the sterile, gray dining hall lined with plain wooden tables and benches. Women in black habits walked serenely out of the room in perfect piety and harmony. Now one of those women walked toward her.

Mother Louise gently put her hand under Margarette's elbow. "We must prepare ourselves for vespers, Margarette. And you must begin to eat. You have had nothing but water since you have come here. After vespers, I want you to come with me to my office. We must talk."

Margarette searched the kind lady's eyes and nodded agreement. She walked with Novice Annette to their room and both knelt on separate meditation stands. Annette immediately began to lift up adulation to the Triune God. Margarette knelt, pressed her hands together, and bowed her head. A tear formed in her eye, then two, making their way down her cheeks. Soon her shoulders were shaking, yet Margarette uttered not a sound. She sniffed quietly so as not to disturb Annette, but the tears kept emerging from the welled-up dam of her soul. Soon she slumped over in sobs. Quietly she sent up her supplication. "I am trying, God. I really am. But I cannot forget him. I know You are my first love, but I have never seen You. I have never heard Your voice. I have never felt Your touch. I have never smelled the fragrance of Your Presence."

Annette handed Margarette a clean kerchief and knelt beside her. "I am here because this is the one place in all the world where I want to be. But you, Margarette. Where is it that you want to be?"

Margarette lifted her vacant red eyes to Annette.

"I have no home but this, Annette. This is my home now, and I must learn to accept that reality. Forgive me for disturbing you." She heard the bell sound. "It is time for evening vespers. I will be all right. I just need to adjust."

FRIDAY, SEPTEMBER 26, 1751—LATE AFTERNOON—CASSEL

When Lady Hempleman and Marie Yarger, followed by a shoeless Hayley, reached the bottom of the staircase, they saw George on the veranda swinging Celia around and around as she squealed in delight.

"Oh, thank God! George, you are safely home!" Lady Hempleman smiled with her heart as her eyes and lips cooperated in the expansive crescendo.

George gently set his young sister on her two feet and rose to embrace his mother and baby Seigfried. Hayley was next in line. Soon Lord Hempleman joined the celebration along with Maurice.

"Good to have you home, Son," his father said, taking George's hand and vigorously shaking it with both of his. "Good to have you home. Come in. Come in. Marie, please tell the staff that Master George is home, and we will be wanting refreshments in the parlor." Turning to George, he asked, "Have you had your evening meal? It is in the making right now."

"I can smell the cooking, Father. It smells like roast pork. Am I right?"

Everyone laughed. George had correctly identified the main course for that evening.

The family walked to the parlor. Soon servants supplied the garrulous family with trays of cheese, biscuits, garden vegetables, and fresh cider. George glanced at each servant who entered, but he did not see the smiling face he most coveted. Yes, he was glad to be with his family after such a long separation. But Margarette was more than family. Margarette was his life. Yet, in his own home, he could not even ask the whereabouts of the one he loved most.

Chapter 9

FRIDAY, SEPTEMBER 26, 1751—LATE EVENING—CASSEL

George masked his emotions during the evening meal although his appetite was curtailed by Margarette's absence. It was obvious she was no longer employed by his family. He answered each question his family members asked about Togo, the sea voyage, the trip overland, and the prospects of the plantation. Lord Hempleman appeared well satisfied. Lady Hempleman was just pleased to have her firstborn home.

Since the evening was still warm, the older family members retired to the courtyard outside the parlor. George's mother had tucked Siegfried in bed immediately after dinner. Celia was also now slumbering in the girls' room. So only Maurice and Hayley joined their parents in extending George's homecoming. The fragrance of fall flowers and greenery, the cooling waters from the fountain, and the chirping of wrens provided an ambience of tranquility. But no tranquility resided within the spirit of George Hempleman. Even sitting in the courtyard brought back memories of stolen moments George and Margarette had had in this very place. To George, Margarette's presence dominated the courtyard even now.

In the past, on a pretext to be near Margarette's side, George had requested that she trim back some iris stems or rose bushes. Oftentimes he would have her cut fresh flowers to give to his mother. George's vibrant memories drew Margarette back into the courtyard humming a tune, telling a tale from her childhood. One story he particularly liked was how her older brothers once tricked her into eating poison ivy.

"You will never get the poison again, Margie, if you just eat these few leaves," her brothers had told her. So under coercion Margarette had eaten the leaf-of-three.

But the trick turned inside out. The leaves Margarette ate never affected her hands, her lips, her mouth, or her throat. But her brothers had a nasty case of poison ivy on their arms and hands for a week.

George remembered that Margarette had added to her story, "The remedy does not work. I can still catch poison ivy." Then she could not contain her melodious laughter, which wrapped around George and enraptured him more. He wanted to take her in his arms and hold her forever, but that could not be, not now at least. Margarette was a servant and a proper Christian girl. George thought of Margarette's laughter and the pleasure that sound brought to him. *I wish that someone sometime would invent a device to capture that laughter so I could keep it forever with me.*

George's father yanked his eldest back into the moment. "Tomorrow will be the homecoming banquet. We have made arrangements for music, speeches, good German cuisine, and dancing. Charlotte will no doubt be a vision of loveliness to your eyes."

George caught a quick look from his mother. "No doubt, Father," George agreed. Changing the subject from the woman he wanted to avoid, he said to his sister, "What will you be wearing, Miss Hayley?"

Hayley laughed at his formality. "I have a rose floor-length gown. It is beautiful. I feel like a princess when I am wearing it."

"You look like a princess, too, darling," her mother interposed.

George stood up, bowed deeply to his sister, and said, "May I have the first dance of the evening, Miss Hayley?" She tittered appreciatively. Then George quickly fisted Maurice's strong shoulder. "How about you, brother? Are you going to look like a prince?"

"I do not care if I look like a prince," Maurice said returning the fist hit. "I just want to be as rich as a prince."

"Well said," their father applauded.

As the evening wore on, the family heard the sound of approaching hooves on the stone streets of Cassel.

"Oh, no," Lord Hempleman groaned. "Business. Why can a man not have the opportunity to spend some time with his family once in a while?" He rose to face the inevitable even before Raymond announced the lord had a visitor.

After his father left, George turned to his mother and asked, "Could I please have a word with you privately, Mother? It is rather important."

Happy to have her son to herself, Anna rose ever so slowly to steady her legs. "Let us step into the parlor." She cast a warm smile toward her son, nearly heralding that she was trying ever so hard to refrain from wine, though the task was extremely difficult.

George waved a friendly warning to his brother and sister, "No fighting while I am gone." He double stepped to catch up to his mother.

In the parlor Anna seated herself near a small marble table on which an oil lamp glowed. George settled himself on the couch nearest to his mother.

Anna waited for her son to begin.

"Mother, I know that Father made a commitment to Lord Sturzhelm several years ago regarding Charlotte and me, but honestly, Mother, I am finding myself more and more in turmoil over this decision. I know a marriage to Charlotte would help our family in many ways, but I am not in love with Charlotte. In fact, I am in love with another woman, a woman with whom I could happily spend my entire life, even if I do not inherit father's title." George waited for a reaction.

Anna stared unswervingly at her son. "Mothers and sons have close connections, George. I have known about this for some time. I do not choose to go through life blinded to my children's needs. I have recently been reading my Bible. It has given me much strength.

In one verse, it says that we are to rear up our children in the way that they should go, and when they are old, they will not depart from it. This passage means more than choosing Jesus as Savior and Lord, although that is the most important decision you could ever make, and I rest assured that you, George, have already made that commitment. But the passage also means that God has a chosen destiny for you, one that your father and I need to respect. We, in our many frailties, have limited vision whereas God knows the end from the beginning. I do not pretend to be a scholar, but I know that God who created the heavens and the earth and who knows not only our ways but also our thoughts is much more capable of guiding you than I am. The Bible says that He knew us in our mother's womb. I certainly did not know you, George, until you arrived in this world. Then I watched as you grew and developed into manhood. You are uniquely different from anyone I have ever known, as is Maurice, Hayley, Celia, Siegfried, and your father. So, no, I am not shocked that your heart has been won by another. Perhaps she is the person God has chosen for you. Do you believe that yourself, George?"

"Mother, I only know that I cannot live without her." George then employed logic. "Besides, marrying Charlotte would be such a disservice to her. She deserves to have a husband who can love her as I love Margarette."

His mother smiled knowingly. "Your father also realizes that Margarette has captured your heart. You have made that rather obvious, even though you thought your stolen moments went unobserved. George, never underestimate the curiosity of a parent."

"So where is she, Mother? Where is Margarette?"

"It is a long story and quite a different one than what you might hear from your father. Do you want my version or his?"

George said, "I would like to hear both."

"So be it. But I must rush because I do not know how long we will be undisturbed. Nearly a fortnight ago, your father accused Margarette of stealing my emerald necklace and sent her back to her home. Just trust me when I say that Margarette never stole the necklace, but it did come up missing. Nevertheless, Margarette was the one your father wanted out of our household before you returned. He does not want the plans he has for your life to be thwarted."

"What about the plans *I* have for my life?"

"Son, you know that means very little to him. Not that your father does not love you. His thinking is that money is success, and the more you accumulate, the more successful you are."

"I have known that about Father for a long time, Mother. But I am different."

"I have known that for a long time too, George."

"So what am I to do?"

"What do you want to do?"

"I want to marry Margarette."

"That means that you will lose your father's title."

"So be it. Did you hear what Maurice said tonight? He wants to be as rich as a prince. The family title will not be lost. Lord Sturzhelm does have two other daughters."

"Think of the consequences of your refusing to marry Charlotte, George. Your father could disown you, put you out on your own. That would not be easy for you or Margarette. A woman likes security."

"I am strong and adaptable. I will do my best to provide for her."

"There will be a scene if you tell your father of your decision."

"So what do you suggest?"

"I have given this much thought since Margarette's dismissal. Your father is a headstrong man, yet I am equally headstrong. Forcing you to marry a woman you do not love is not something I want for you, George. I love you. I want you to have a fulfilled life. What I am suggesting is that we enter into an honorable deception, pretending that plans for your life are going forward but devising new plans so that you can marry the love of your life."

"What do you mean, Mother?"

Anna studied her son's reaction before asking, "Have you asked Margarette to marry you?"

"I have, but she gave me no answer, except to say that it would be impossible."

Anna smiled and stood. "You need to be guided by God, George. I do not work with the impossible, but God does. Let us go back and join the family. Tomorrow we will be having your banquet. Lord and Lady Sturzhelm will be here with Charlotte and her two sisters, as well as many of our family members and guests. You and I have a lot of acting to practice. Are you up to the challenge?"

George smiled broadly and nodded. Lady Hempleman returned the smile with a wrinkled brow. Many fairy tales originated in Hessen-Cassel, but not many had their basis in day-to-day life. Fairy tales, Lady Hempleman knew, were fantasies that helped people overlook the difficulties and challenges of life to momentarily live a dream that would never have substance.

Chapter 10

SATURDAY, SEPTEMBER 27, 1751—EARLY MORNING HOURS—FULDA CONVENT

Mother Louise was on her face before the Lord. It was nearly three o'clock in the morning and her aging bones and muscles were screaming for relief. Yet she was not going to rise from the cold pavement in her room until she had peace regarding the newly arrived novice. Mother Louise knew that only God could give the wisdom that she needed. The situation with Margarette was out of control.

Moaning in agony, Mother Louise supplicated into the night. "Dear Heavenly Father, You created this child that You have put under my protection. Please show me how I can reach her. Please show me what You have planned for her life if that will help me direct her correctly. I pray that Your Kingdom come and Your will be done in my life and in the life of this child, Margarette. Lord, I know that I cannot manipulate You. So I humbly ask You to show me Your plan. This young lady appears to want to do what is right. She says she will conform, but I know that You want people to serve You with love. Do you have a different life for Margarette outside of this convent? Please, Heavenly Father, Holy Spirit of the Living God, Jesus my Savior, guide me. Guide Margarette. Show us Your way, Your plan, Your purpose for her life."

The first radiance of light penetrated through the nun's narrow window. The sunbeam flickered on the wall and became brighter, longer, more pervasive. Mother Louise reached toward the beams chasing darkness from her room. "Yes, Lord Jesus, You are the Way, the Truth, and the Life. You are the Light of the world. I must follow Your light as You lead me moment by moment, day by day. Help me to hear Your voice clearly, to know Your thoughts and Your ways. I accept the wisdom with which You are saturating Me. I declare that Your Kingdom come and Your will be done! Amen."

SATURDAY, SEPTEMBER 27, 1751—CASSEL

Guests began arriving in late afternoon. On a dais in the grand ballroom, the musicians playing harpsichord, flute, and violin reproduced masterful concertos by Bach and lively overtures by Handel.

Lady Irene Sturzhelm took the hand of her husband and stepped from the Sturzhelm pleasure coach onto the glistening stone walkway. Followed by their three daughters, the couple glided up the wide entry steps into the Hempleman entrance hall where Lord and Lady Hempleman stood with George.

"Delighted to see you again, Lord Sturzhelm." Lord Hempleman vigorously shook his benefactor's hand. "I see that you are carrying your violin. Will you be playing us a tune tonight?"

"I always come prepared," Lord Sturzhelm responded with loud laughter.

Lord Hempleman bowed and gently kissed the gloved hand of his benefactor's wife. "Always a pleasure to greet you, Lady Sturzhelm."

Lady Hempleman then welcomed them to the grand homecoming. George stiffened as he saw Charlotte directly behind her parents. What had his father said last night? *Charlotte will be a vision of loveliness to your eyes?* She was certainly eye-catching in a satin French dress that exposed her ample cleavage in the empire-waist long flowing gown. George had difficulty focusing on Charlotte's face as he greeted her. Her sister Rhonda, two years younger than

Charlotte, also wore a French gown. Ten-year-old Gertrude, who should have been home in bed, followed in a similar dress, but her anatomy was as flat as the coastal region surrounding Hamburg.

Lords and ladies, relatives and friends rapidly filled the grand ballroom. The Sturzhelms were led into the lively arena by the Hempleman chamberlain and his wife, who seated the noble family near the dais.

Peering around at the lavish decorations, Lord Sturzhelm began tapping his fingers on the arm of his chair, mastering the rhythm of the small orchestra. Recognizing "Concerto in E Major" by Bach, Lord Sturzhelm observed to his wife, "Poor taste to be playing music of the recently deceased. Poor taste, indeed."

"Not poor taste at all, dear husband," Lady Irene corrected him. "A tribute. Playing his magnificent music is a tribute to the brilliant composer. Musicians may be playing his works for hundreds of years, no doubt."

"It is still poor taste in my mind," Lord Sturzhelm resisted.

Soon an overture by George Frederic Handel filled the air.

"That is more like it," Lord Sturzhelm said loudly while fastening his thumbs in his vest pockets. "Handel is more appropriate for this occasion. Too bad the English stole him from our coast. Those Brits. Always generous with the arts."

"We are very fortunate to have Handel's music, dear," countered Lady Irene. "Let us just enjoy the banquet. Why, look! There is a banner hanging from the balustrade with your family crest, dear. The Hemplemans have certainly looked well to your pleasure during this homecoming."

"Humph!" Lord Sturzhelm grunted, then took his wife's hand. "Shall we?" Lady Sturzhelm rose and the couple began to dance to the strands of Handel's *Minuet*.

As dancers filled the grand ballroom, George heaved a sigh of relief that his duty was greeting incoming guests. Otherwise, Charlotte would be demanding his attention. Even now she was seated on a couch with her two sisters, looking about the room and occasionally stealing glances toward George.

When the last of the guests had arrived, Lord and Lady Hempleman walked to the dais hand-in-hand in court fashion to begin the formal proceedings.

As the applause subsided, Lord Hempleman announced, "I am delighted to have all of you celebrating with us. We shall begin our festivities with an invocation by the Reverend Konrad Willis."

Having lingered in the empty foyer, George was about to step out of the vestibule into the ballroom to hear the prayer when he heard leather boots on the stone entry steps. Lieutenant Garvey peeked tentatively through the entrance.

"William!" George said as he strode to greet his dear friend from the military. "What brings you here?"

"The streets are filled with talk about your homecoming. I could not resist getting in touch with you. I have some news that you may want to hear."

"Say on. I hope it is good, because most of what I have heard since I have returned has not been to my liking."

"Excuse me if I am intruding too deeply into your private life, George, but I remembered your telling me while we were in training together that you had become interested in one of your servants, the daughter of a professor in Giessen."

George nearly shook the information out of William. "Yes? Yes?"

"Don't man-handle me, George. I am your friend, remember." William smiled yet stepped back to safety.

Energetic music from Lord Sturzhelm's violin flowed into the foyer.

"Sorry," George apologized. "It is just that Margarette is gone. My father sent her home under a false allegation."

"Why am I not surprised?" William quickly assessed the situation. "Anyway, when I was traveling back from Mentz to Cassel, I was in a stagecoach with a professor, his son, and a very attractive strawberry blonde."

"You think it was Margarette? Do you know where she is?"

"The driver of the coach stopped in front of a monastery and nunnery on the western slopes outside of Fulda. I heard him use the name *Duffy* in addressing the professor."

"They have put her in a nunnery! My Margarette is in a nunnery!" George began pacing back and forth with his hands clasped behind his back. "The western slopes, you say?"

"Yes. As far as I can tell, there are five monasteries outside of Fulda, but the one the Duffys entered was on the western slopes," William said.

Raymond Yarger cleared his throat as he stepped into the entryway. "Master George, your father is announcing you. It is time for your report on Togo."

Lieutenant William Garvey put a steady hand on George's shoulder. "I hope to be seeing you soon. If there is anything I can do to help—"

"Thanks, William. You have been a godsend."

The two friends shook hands. With that, George assumed his role as an obedient son and entered the grand ballroom like a seasoned actor about to take center stage. He nodded to his mother who had taken her seat beside Maurice after Reverend Willis' prayer. She smiled at her eldest son with pride.

As George made his way to the dais, he stopped for an instant to whisper to Hayley, "Please run upstairs to get me one of your shawls."

Hayley smiled knowingly. "I understand. I have seen her too."

Thunderous applause followed George Hempleman's report on Togo and its prospects for enriching the Hessen-Cassel state. Lord Hamler and Lord Wolff gave similar reports. But the standing ovation was reserved for Lord Sturzhelm. That was what was expected, and that was what was delivered.

With the speeches concluded, the men on the platform, led by Lord Sturzhelm, gathered their wives and walked to their reserved seating. Hayley handed George a lovely woven shawl before he reached Charlotte. Prior to taking his betrothed's hand to guide her to the dining table, George slipped the covering over Charlotte's shoulders and whispered, "You embarrass me. I will not be seen with any woman who exposes herself in public. Wear this tightly around you." He smiled masterfully as Charlotte clutched the fabric and attempted to hide her embarrassment at being openly shamed in front of the entire gathering.

For the rest of the evening, Charlotte knotted Hayley's wrap around her to avoid irritating her future husband. George felt he had scored a major victory. Like his father, he was one who intended to win every dispute.

The evening had been strained, as George had wished it to be. Charlotte would have much to sort through in the days ahead.

At last the guests left. The musicians gathered their instruments and their pay. The family retired to their chambers. All was quiet except for George's active mind. Instead of climbing into his bed, whose comfort and security beckoned him, he walked onto the balcony overlooking the courtyard. Gripping the wrought-iron railing, George ran through his options. It would be difficult but not impossible to get Margarette out of the nunnery. If his father proved too resistant, he might sail to Togo with two women: one his wife in name only, the other his wife in God's eyes. *After all,* George reasoned, *God looks at the heart. Margarette and I could have our own ceremony and be married in God's eyes. Charlotte could live in the grandeur to which she is accustomed and die a virgin. But Margarette and I could have a house full of children. Who would come to Togo to visit us? Charlotte would be too embarrassed and proud to reveal the affront. Perhaps Margarette and I could be married by a minister in Togo. Somehow I will make this work!*

While George considered his future, Lady Hempleman was actively doing the same. She took her scissors and cut a small slice in the linen pillow casing. Reaching her small hand into the down, she located the loose satin glove that held her emerald necklace. She set the heirloom on her satin comforter and moved to the chest at the foot of her bed. Inserting the key, Anna quietly lifted the lid and took out a small flexible pouch that contained money she had saved for years. All her financial needs had been met for a lifetime; she had no need for what she had saved. She shoved the emerald necklace into the pouch with the money. *Oh, I really need to insert a note.* Anna sat down beside her small table, opened a drawer, and took out paper, ink, and quill. She soberly considered that this might be the last communication she would ever have with her firstborn. She wrote from her heart, then surveyed the room. On her table lay a copy of the Bible that had given her so much strength recently. *George and Margarette need more than physical provisions!* Picking up the Good Book, she slipped out of her room, through her husband's chamber, and down the steps.

Anna made her way to the back entrance where George typically kept his saddlebag. Emptying its contents and laying them on a nearby cabinet, she slid her heart's tokens into the bottom of the satchel before piling the originals back into place.

Chapter 11

SUNDAY, SEPTEMBER 28, 1751—LANDECKER LAND

George rode through the night, yet was not the least bit weary. Before dawn, his mount needed water and hay. Looking to the east of Waldecker Land in the emerging sunlight, George spotted shocks of hay in an open field near the river road he had been traveling. Being a nobleman, he had never felt constrained to ask permission to help himself in the past. This time was no exception. Dismounting, he took out a cloth to wipe down his horse before allowing *Beleuchtung* to drink from a rivulet and then eat the fresh timothy mixed with clover. In the meantime, George pulled out some pork and pastries he had taken from the Hempleman pantry. The food tasted better than it had at the formal banquet the night before.

Filling his canteen with fresh water from upstream, George remounted *Beleuchtung* and continued heading south.

SUNDAY, SEPTEMBER 28, 1751—EARLY MORNING—CASSEL

The September sun shone through the windows of the Hempleman master bedroom. Johann smelled the heavy fragrance of bacon and a lingering aroma of coffee. He stretched widely before casting his long legs from underneath the elaborate quilt, which bore his family crest, onto the cool flooring.

Taking a deep breath, he sighed in satisfaction. Last evening had gone ever so well. He had struck a good bargain with Lord Sturzhelm four years ago. Soon the money would start flowing into the Hempleman coffers. It was a good day to be alive.

Having heard their lord awaken, Norman and Ernst entered, Norman with fresh clothing and Ernst with a tray of steaming coffee and a creamer filled to the brim.

"Ah, my good men, welcome, welcome. It is a beautiful morning. Is the family at the breakfast table?"

"Maurice and Celia are, sire. No one has heard a stir from anyone else," Norman replied.

"Let the ladies sleep. Hayley must have danced holes through her slippers last night." Lord Hempleman chuckled. "Let us get me groomed and downstairs, Norman. Ernst, check with Hans and Delbert to awaken George and get him to the table. He must be military about his rising from now on. He is soon to become a married man, a landowner, heir to my title. Industry begets success."

After his matinal ablutions, Lord Hempleman clicked his heels down the staircase and made his way into the dining hall, now cordoned off by tall fall-colored screens. Behind the farthest partition, he heard Celia.

"I tell you, George is not here. His bed is made. I sneaked into his room this morning to pour some water on his head. You know, how we used to?"

"Must you remind me?" Maurice grunted.

Lord Hempleman swept through the enclosure's opening. "What is this you are saying, Celia?"

"George is gone, Papa. I went to his room this morning and he was not there."

Lord Hempleman immediately picked up the bell that always remained on the family dining table and rang while shouting, "Raymond! Come here at once!"

Hustling at his usual crisp pace, Raymond was quick in answering his lord's summons.

The head of the Hempleman household assigned Raymond to locate the lord's eldest, the one on whom the fortunes of the family rested.

Without delay, Raymond Yarger scoured the premises and asked staff members the whereabouts of young George. Meanwhile Lord Hempleman poured himself a cup of coffee, without cream, and paced.

Not wanting to be disturbed in his thoughts, he ordered, "Children, eat your breakfast."

Lady Hempleman hesitantly joined her family, her attention piqued by Celia, who was rolling her napkin into a cylinder, then lifting it to unravel. Maurice had followed his father's advice and, with a mouthful of bacon and breakfast roll, glanced up at his mother.

"Bad news, dear," Johann explained to his wife. "Celia could not find George in his room this morning. She said that his bed is undisturbed. Raymond is conducting a search. Our son cannot just disappear."

Anna sank into her customary seat while raising her delicate hand toward her cheek. "Where could he be, Johann?" She paused. "He must have taken an early-morning ride. He has a lot on his mind. He probably wanted some time to himself."

"Well, he should have left a note. But that doesn't explain his unmade bed. No, he is up to something. Just when all my pieces were fitting so snugly together." Johann continued his pacing as one of the household servants entered to pour Lady Hempleman a warm cup of tea.

Upon returning to the dining room, Raymond verified Celia's earlier report. "None of the staff, including Hans and Delbert, has seen Master George today. His horse is gone too." Raymond hesitated. "Also, sir, if I may be so bold?"

"Speak up!"

"Right as the cleric was delivering his prayer yesterday,

Master George was conversing with a young lieutenant in the entranceway."

Lord Hempleman stopped his pacing and laughed. "Of course. He is probably out carousing with some of his military friends. He knows he will not have much freedom after his March wedding." Johann immediately regretted his *faux pas* and looked sheepishly at his wife, who pretended not to have heard.

Relieved by his wife's grace, the lord questioned, "Raymond, did you catch their conversation? Anything at all?"

"Only briefly," Raymond admitted. "Something about a nunnery."

"A nunnery. That makes no sense! A name? Did George use a name?"

"Yes, your son called the lieutenant *William*."

Lady Hempleman picked up her napkin and began fanning herself. Where was her son? Things were getting out of hand quickly. She lifted up an unspoken prayer, one that only the Lord could hear.

Meanwhile her husband barked, "Have someone check the military barracks, Raymond. I am sure George is around someplace. But if he is not, have Colonel Giesler interrogate all the lieutenants under his command. Raymond, you may have to identify the lieutenant named *William* in a line-up, if it comes to that."

Raymond bowed briefly and tended to his lord's request.

No word had been heard from George by mid-afternoon. The commander at the military command post had not seen the young nobleman. Every lieutenant on the premises had been questioned, but not Lieutenant William Garvey. After he had reported in late yesterday, Garvey had been immediately dispatched with his platoon to the Hesse-Darmstadt border due to a small uprising regarding property rights. The lieutenant had been instructed to stay at the border until order was restored.

Lord Hempleman extended his search. In addition to George's

horse being gone from the stable, his saddlebag was also gone from the nook in the rear entrance of the home. He had left no note so far as anyone knew, but George never left notes.

As the day wore on, the family learned that George Hempleman had not been sighted by any relative or friend of the family in the vicinity. By early evening, Lord Hempleman called in his deputy.

"Scout the area, Wolfgang. Use all the men you need. There will be a hefty reward for whoever finds him."

Wolfgang Gunther was pleased to be involved in the search for George Hempleman, whom he considered to be a spoiled young nobleman.

"Born with a silver spoon in his mouth," he muttered as he mounted his steed. "More like a golden spoon, if you ask me. Yes, *Donnerschlag*," he patted the shoulder of his standardbred, "we'll bring Master George Hempleman back into the ring, tethered and dragged, and I will be the richer because of it."

SUNDAY, SEPTEMBER 28, 1751—LATE EVENING—CASSEL

Leaving his study, Lord Hempleman mounted the main staircase slowly. His heart beat rapidly. He felt an intense pain at the base of his skull. His left arm went limp. His left leg barely held his weight. By an act of his strong determination, Lord Hempleman pulled his tall, stout frame to the top of the staircase, then steadied himself by placing his right hand on the wall. His vision blurred. Still he slid one foot in front of the other until he located his doorway on the opposite side of the hallway. *I can make it*, he vowed. With his good right leg, he took a step toward his bedroom door, grabbing the handle to steady himself. The handle slipped from his grip.

"Anna!" he called. "Anna!"

Lord Hempleman collapsed with a mighty thud onto the dark floor.

MONDAY, SEPTEMBER 29, 1751—ROAD TO FULDA

Night travel was slow and hazardous on the rocky steep river roads leading to Fulda. Heavy vegetation blocked much of the rays from the moon and stars. George decided on a slow, steady walk for *Beleuchtung* rather than risk injury to his horse. As the day emerged, it was not a matter of visibility slowing him down. Whenever George heard a passer-by or an oxen cart on the road, he guided his colt into the forest and waited in silence. Despite the delays, he completed nearly twenty-five kilometers in a matter of fourteen hours.

By mid-afternoon, he could no longer stay awake. He entered the forest, tethered his horse near a stream where broad green grass thrived, and removed the colt's saddle, blanket, and his own saddlebag, using these items to make himself a bed. Then he stretched out his tired body and napped.

The sun was low in the sky when George awoke. Upon opening his eyes, he saw the massive oaks towering above him. The cool September evening crept over the forest. The friendly cries of birds and beasts, which were pleasantries during the daylight hours, sounded threatening and encroaching as illusions chased dark shadows. George reached into his jacket pocket and pulled out his round watch, a gift he had received from his parents after he had finished his studies at Marburg. From the emerging moonlight, he read the face of his timepiece. Eight fifteen. He hoped there would be no cloud cover tonight and that the light of the moon and the stars in the heavens would illuminate his travel.

George ate the remainder of his provisions. *By Wednesday night I should reach the convent. For food along the way, I will pick fruit and gather nuts in the forest. Hopefully no mother bear with her cubs will be around. Maybe I will risk stopping a peddler or a farmer going to market. I have most of my pay from the military and a partial payment from my father and Lord Sturzhelm for the recent trip to Togo, but I want to save most of that for when Margarette is traveling with me. I will not expect her to live off the land. I will keep her in hiding until we sail for Togo next March. Then somehow I will devise a way to get her on board the ship. Hopefully she will see the pragmatism of the situation. This will all work out.*

MONDAY, SEPTEMBER 29, 1751—EARLY EVENING—CASSEL

Lord Hempleman rested in his massive bed, his wife at his bedside. Raymond entered the master bedroom periodically to see if either of the Hemplemans needed assistance. The doctor had prescribed sleep, no visitors, and a bland diet of tea, toast, fruit, and vegetables with no salt or gravy, and plenty of water for Lord Hempleman. Anna herself had no appetite except for warm tea and dry toast.

Tears rolled down the cheeks of Anna's husband. She took her own clean handkerchief to wipe them away, then took a laver cloth, dipped it in a basin of cool water, and wiped her husband's warm brow. For the first time in years, Anna felt compassion, even a spark of love, for the man she had passionately loved in the first few years of their marriage. She groped to understand these invasive foreign emotions.

"Uorge," Johann called. "Ann, yit Uorge. So surry. So surry. Yit Uorge."

"It is all right, Johann. George will be in to see you as soon as he gets home."

"So surry. My ault, Ann. So surry," he slurred.

"Rest, Johann. All will be well. Just rest." She raised a cup of water to his lips. Johann turned his head away, staring pointlessly at the wall.

"So supid of me. So supid."

Chapter 12

WEDNESDAY, OCTOBER 1, 1751—TWILIGHT—NEAR FULDA

Dulcet thin lengths of musical harmony ebbed from the open shutters of the convent. Bold strands of tenor and bass broke forth from the monastery. The two separate floating melodies met in a dance that lilted into the valley below the abbey.

Margarette lifted her sweet soprano evening sacrifice with only a few tears. Annette squeezed Margarette's hand softly, a tactile encouragement for the steady progress her roommate had made in one long week.

A quarter of a mile away, George Hempleman nested in a wooded area planning his next move. Surveying the religious complex, he thought through strategy after strategy, discarding parts of each. He knew that tomorrow he would have to make his move.

WEDNESDAY, OCTOBER 1, 1751—DUSK—CASSEL

The political wheels began to turn, slowly but ever so effectively. Lord Sturzhelm learned of Lord Hempleman's condition and decided to supervise the search for George. Charlotte was close to driving her father to distraction with her tears and unending complaints.

Partially to release his own frustrations and partially to reassure himself that he was in command, Lord Sturzhelm shouted so loud that everyone in the Sturzhelm mansion heard him summon his chamberlain. "Maxwell, get in here *now!*"

Only a few steps away from his lord's office, Maxwell knocked briefly while announcing, "Maxwell here, sire."

Behind closed doors, Lord Sturzhelm spoke in the quietest tone Maxwell had ever heard from his superior. "See here, Maxwell, I am rather in a tight spot right now. George Hempleman has evidently been kidnaped or left the area voluntarily. His father is no longer able to perform his duties as constable, so I want you to have Deputy Wolfgang Gunther brought here immediately. I intend to direct the search for young George until he is found. Gunther will have all the information I need to take care of this matter in an expeditious manner. Understood?"

"Understood, sire."

"And, Maxwell, send for Johann Hempleman's lawyer. What is his name?"

"*Herr* Jerome Gibbons."

"One more thing. Prepare an official paper relieving Johann Hempleman of his post as constable. He is to receive no further assignments or pay. Naturally, he and his household will have to vacate their living quarters. Hempleman is useless to me now," Lord Sturzhelm concluded.

Maxwell Braun left Lord Sturzhelm with a light step. Rubbing his hands together with pleasure, the chamberlain determined to use what contacts he had to aid in the search. Lord Sturzhelm was loosening the fast ties between Gibbons and Hempleman. Braun felt that Lord Hempleman deserved to be brought to ruin. Had he not brought disgrace upon Maxwell's sister years ago, then abandoned her with a child?

THURSDAY, OCTOBER 2, 1751—CASSEL

Lieutenant Garvey returned from the Hesse-Darmstadt border with his platoon before dawn and reported that the Darmstadt border uprising had been quelled. The land dispute had involved disarming two contending parties, not an easy task. Rather than receiving an expected commendation, he was immediately arrested and placed in solitary confinement with no explanation as to why he was interned.

William sat on the cold stone floor for several hours in a darkened room on the west side of the barracks. The only light entered through a twelve-inch square opening near the top of the ten-foot-high ceiling. He was given no meal, no water, no reason for his isolation.

"So much for a hero's welcome," he muttered, reflecting on the irony of the successful completion of his assignment and the cell in which he now resided.

By daybreak, William heard the crisp click of several boots approaching his cell. A key clanged in the lock. The door opened. Lieutenant Garvey rose to his feet in military fashion. Four soldiers carrying muskets stepped into the room. Two stationed themselves on each side of the doorway. The other two took positions in opposite corners. Corporal Giesler followed with what looked to be a constable's deputy and an elaborately clothed man who defied the current vogue by wearing a white wig to cover his pate. Garvey reasoned the man must be in the employ of some powerful nobleman.

Corporal Giesler cleared his throat. "Lieutenant Garvey, this will be as simple as you wish to make it. We have word that you spoke to George Hempleman on Saturday, September 27, in the foyer of his home. Is this correct?"

William looked puzzled yet replied compliantly, "That is correct, sir."

"We also have word that you spoke to this same George Hempleman about a nunnery. Is this correct?"

"Correct, sir." William wondered where this was leading.

"Could you identify this nunnery?" Corporal Giesler pursued.

William told the corporal the approximate place where the Duffys had gotten off the coach without mentioning any names before adding, "I do not know the exact name of the facility, sir."

"Understood." The corporal looked toward the nobleman's subordinate and asked, "Any questions from you, sire?"

Maxwell Braun, whose thumbs hung smugly in his tight-fitting waistcoat, shook his head and turned to go. The sentry unlocked the door for the corporal, deputy, and nobleman's liege to leave. The military men backed out of William's cell with their muskets at the ready. Soon the door shut, the key performed its task, and William was left to consider his fate.

THURSDAY, OCTOBER 2, 1751—OUTSIDE THE ABBEY NEAR FULDA

George was up by dawn. He walked *Beleuchtung* to a fresh stream. Before allowing the horse to drink heartily, he tipped his canteen into the sparkling water. Then George guided the animal to an area where tall grass had survived the harvest.

"You are eating better than I am, my friend," he said as he stroked the strong neck of his colt, thankful that his mount was not the color of lightning. The midnight sheen of *Beleuchtung*'s hair blended in well with the dense vegetation. His steed was faster and stronger than any horse he had ever ridden or seen. He felt a rising gratitude toward his father for having a good eye for the best in equine stock.

While *Beleuchtung* feasted, George scouted the area until he located some wild berries and fallen walnuts. He even found a well-laden chestnut tree. "Oh, for a chestnut pie!" His thoughts and appetite wafted to times past. With his vivid imagination in play, he convinced himself that his meager breakfast was actually quite satisfying.

George placed the blanket, saddle, and saddlebag on *Beleuchtung* and patted him affectionately.

"Now, boy, I am going to fasten you loosely with a lot of leeway in your tether. Just be ready to go. You will be carrying a double load when I return."

George threw a last handful of currants into his mouth. He crept to the edge of the forest, thankful for the plentiful trees and shrubs leading up the hill where a stone wall and a baroque structure dominated the summit. Somewhere inside, his lady-in-waiting sought release.

THURSDAY, OCTOBER 2, 1751—EARLY MORNING—CASSEL

Lord Hempleman was awakened by the shouting in the main entryway of his home, but he could do nothing about it. He looked around his bedchamber. Beside his bed sat Anna, who had apparently spent the night watching over him. Johann's pleading eyes bore toward his wife.

"Raymond will report to us in a moment, dear, if the doctor approves. I recognize Lord Sturzhelm's voice and Maurice's. Neither sound too happy, do they, dear? We will wait and see." Anna patted Johann's paralyzed hand in comfort.

Soon the shuffling of feet was heard on the staircase. Three taps struck the door.

"Waymon," Johann whispered.

"Yes," his wife agreed. "Come in, Raymond. We have been expecting you."

A rather ruffled Raymond entered the master suite, shut the door behind him, and waited to be addressed. Lady Hempleman nodded for Raymond to begin.

"As you might have surmised," he looked at Lord Hempleman first and then the lord's wife, "Lord Sturzhelm is wanting to arrest both you, my lord, and George for breach of contract. He says that Charlotte is frantic and has taken to her bed. He has Deputy Gunther and Corporal Giesler downstairs with him—"

THURSDAY, OCTOBER 2, 1751—EARLY
MORNING—ABBEY NEAR FULDA

Because the gates of the abbey had not yet been opened for the day and because George wanted to enter the compound undetected, he located a long oak log, rolled it up against the side of the stone wall, and anchored it into the ground. It held fairly steady as he crawled the fifteen feet to the apex of the wall's restrictive barrier. Looping a rope around the log's girth, he then eased himself down and inside the abbey grounds. He reasoned that when he returned with Margarette, he could climb up the rope first, then pull her up afterward.

Dashing from tree trunk to tree trunk, George progressed toward the abbey. Finally he hid in a row of bushes near a cloistered walkway. All the while George wondered what the chances were of his getting a monk's robe and cowl.

The abbey would most likely be filled with activity early in the morning. George considered this to be in his favor. With monks moving about, it would be less distracting for another hooded figure to join their ranks.

About to begin circling the north side of the structure to find access to the interior, George trashed his plan as he saw a solitary monk leave the north wing enclave and advance toward the church complex. George slipped off his boots, drew out his pistol, and circled behind the man who wore the garment he needed. Careful to stay close behind the bushes while gaining distance on the unwary man, George began whispering.

"Help me, brother. I have injured my leg. Help me. Have pity."

The monk stopped and looked around.

"Pity me. I need your help, brother," George feigned weakness in his voice.

The monk walked toward the plea that had summoned him.

"Oh, thank God that you have come. God has sent you, Brother. Thank God."

As the monk stepped between two shrubs, George leaped to his feet behind his quarry and held a loaded pistol to the startled man's head while using his other hand to hold him in an arm lock. "I do not want to hurt you, Brother," George whispered. "I just need to know your name and where you are going."

"Brother Michael," the cenobite garbled. "I am on my way to hear confessions at the convent. Do not hurt me. I will cooperate."

George loosened his grip on the man's arm slightly. With that, the wiry monk shoved his free left elbow into George's ribs and wrapped his left leg around the left leg of his captor, tumbling George to the ground. George's pistol fell beneath a dense shrub beyond his reach.

Quick to recover, George lassoed the legs of Brother Michael, throwing him to the ground. Mounting the burly brother, George located the man's left and right carotid arteries and applied pressure while managing to pin the monk's left arm with his own knees. To muffle the cries, George plunged his head into the monk's mouth and held it firmly in place despite the teeth that clamped into George's forehead. Blood flowed.

I've got me a real black bear, George thought as his adversary's free right arm pushed against George's chest, flailed toward his long pigtail, desperately trying to gain a hold. But the pressure on the man's neck ebbed his strength until he succumbed to unconsciousness. Just to make sure of the saint's inertia, George did the unthinkable and slammed his own bleeding, throbbing forehead into that of the monk.

Shaking off dizziness, George stood up, wiped the blood from his own forehead, and stripped the monk of his robe, cowl, and soft-soled shoes. He tied the hands and feet of the limp form, clad only with a long linen undergarment. To keep Michael quiet, George pulled off his own right stocking and stuffed it into the man's mouth, then anchored the gag in place with a kerchief George had used on his ride to Fulda.

Directing his attention to the black attire, George wrapped the robe around himself. The shoes were a bit large, but George was satisfied with the fit of the garment and head covering. He rummaged beneath the foliage for his pistol and tucked it in his belt under the holy robe.

Mimicking the gait of Brother Michael as best he could, George drew the cowl closely around his face as he walked to the church's main entrance. A rather husky custodian emerged from the church narthex. He looked George over rather suspiciously before saying, "Ah, Brother Andrew, you are a bit late this morning."

So the monk's name wasn't Michael! George wondered if there was a second act of deception taking place and exactly what the custodian had seen and heard prior to his greeting.

George mumbled a reply, "Matins were longer this morning."

"Yes. Yes. Of course." The guardian gazed long and hard at the hooded figure before him. "You do not sound like yourself this morning, Brother. Are you okay?"

To end the scrutiny George patted the man on his back and gently guided him toward the south wing, which was apparently the nunnery.

"I am fine. Shall we go?"

The custodian walked with George to the convent and pulled on a rope, which rang a bell on the other side of the wall. With no hesitation, the gate opened.

Mother Louise smiled knowingly to the hooded figure in front of her. "Welcome, George. We have been waiting for you. But you need not have been so rough with Brother Andrew. He is quite a kind fellow."

George felt his injured ribs and the throbbing of his forehead. "Of course!" he said.

THURSDAY, OCTOBER 2, 1751—EARLY MORNING—CASSEL

Lady Hempleman directed her piercing eyes toward Raymond. "Why the shouting?"

"Lord Sturzhelm wanted to come upstairs to talk with your husband personally. The doctor and Maurice would not permit him to advance one step toward the staircase."

"See law'er, Anna," Johann ordered his wife. "Welease Uorge. Welease Wolf, too."

"You want me to contact *Herr* Gibbons, our lawyer, to have him start proceedings to release George from the betrothal contract? Is that what you are saying, Johann?"

The lord nodded and lay back on his pillow. "Wes. Welease Uorge. Welease Wolf, too."

Lady Hempleman turned to Raymond. "What does he mean by *release wolf?*"

"I believe your husband had ordered Deputy Gunther to locate Master George, ma'am."

Lady Hempleman raised her eyebrows in comprehension before responding, "Raymond, tell Lord Sturzhelm that we will be contacting him shortly. Nothing will be done today. Perhaps next week we will have a response. Also, tell Deputy Gunther to wait downstairs. But do not tell him why he is being detained. "

Raymond smiled, pleased with the decisions, clicked his heels, and turned to deliver the messages.

Lord Hempleman admirably surveyed his wife in wonder. *The woman is quite capable. Why did I never see that before?*

Chapter 13

THURSDAY, OCTOBER 2, 1751—EARLY MORNING—ABBEY NEAR FULDA

Mother Louise did not invite George Hempleman into the nunnery. Instead, the young nobleman first heard and then saw a group of hooded clerics running through the cloister toward the convent's entrance. At the forefront was Brother Andrew in his nightshirt, sporting a dark purple bruise the size of a baby's fist on his forehead.

Within seconds two monks grabbed George by both arms, pinning them behind his back while a third quickly twined George's hands with the rope George had used to bind Brother Andrew. Then an older man threw back the pilfered cowl, frisked George, lightened him of his pistol, and proceeded to walk around the tall prisoner. Military inspection had never been so intrusive.

"We are here to help you, young man. I think you were asking help from Brother Andrew before the attack. Correct?"

George's shoulders slumped. "Correct, sir. I am sorry for the trespass. I just wanted to see Margarette."

"That will happen in due time. But first let us get you fixed up. That injury on your forehead could become infested if not taken care of quickly." The older man turned to Mother Louise. "If you and two sisters could bring a basin of clean water and other essentials, I think we can get down to business in the nave of the abbey."

Mother Louise nodded and disappeared in a whisk behind the door of the nunnery.

George was jostled about to face the direction of the church. A monk on each side of him held his bound arms steady, but not too gently. All followed behind the cleric giving the orders.

THURSDAY, OCTOBER 2, 1751—EARLY MORNING—CASSEL

Lady Hempleman listened to the muffled voices of Raymond and Lord Sturzhelm. Next came the sound of the entry door swinging open, leather boots on marble, then on stone pavement. A horse was mounted and a *Droschke* pulled away from the Hempleman home followed by the clatter of hooves. The entrance door closed with finality. Anna heard Raymond speaking, then another man's voice responding.

Footsteps scampered up the staircase. Raymond's familiar tapping on the bedchamber door told Lady Hempleman it was time to address the deputy. She smiled kindly at her husband, gave him a kiss on the forehead, and tended to the matter at hand.

Anne explained to Wolfgang Gunther that Lord Hempleman no longer wanted his son pursued; the deputy simply nodded and passed Lady Hempleman an official paper. He left before she read the content of the message from Lord Sturzhelm.

THURSDAY, OCTOBER 2, 1751—MIDMORNING— ABBEY NEAR FULDA

Once George was seated on a wooden bench near the narthex of the church, the two monks acting as officers bound his feet and removed Brother Andrew's footwear, which they handed to the owner, who had somehow located a replacement robe. Carefully,

Father Benedict removed the stolen cowl and returned that to Brother Andrew, who held it in his hands.

Two nuns cleansed George's head wound and swabbed it with ointment. Mother Louise gave him a fresh drink of water. Brother Andrew located George's boots in the shrubbery and set them in military fashion beside George's feet. His left foot sported a silk stocking, but his right foot remained barefoot and rested on the cold stone flooring of the church.

Brother Andrew pulled out a rather damp piece of cloth from under his robe and dangled it in front of George's nose. George threw back his head while turning to one side. "Whew!"

Brother Andrew commented, "My sentiments exactly!" He dropped the sock beside George's empty boots.

Father Benedict positioned himself in an upright chair to face George so that it was impossible to avoid eye contact. "Where shall we begin?" He waited for a response. None came.

Scooting back his chair, he rose to his feet declaring, "I guess he does not want to talk now. Put him in solitary."

"No. No! *No!*" George protested, wanting no delays in reuniting with Margarette. "I will begin." He looked cautiously at his audience. Could he win them over? He vowed to try. "I found out from a friend that Margarette was in a nunnery outside Fulda. I came here to rescue her."

"Did she say she wanted to be rescued?"

George looked astonished. "Why, no. But I am sure she does not want to spend her entire life here. I want to marry her."

The elder cleric sat down in his seat once again. "Does she want to marry you?"

"Of course she does."

"Did she tell you that?"

"Yes," George affirmed.

The elder cleric looked askance.

George reconsidered. "Well, not exactly. But I know she does."

"How do you know that?"

"Well, a man can tell when a woman loves him."

"How is that?" Father Benedict urged.

"He just does." George realized his logic was no match for the cleric's. He changed his strategy. "I will take good care of Margarette. She will have the best."

"Do tell me what kind of life Margarette will have with you, George. Tell me about her first year she would have with you."

"Well, I am going to manage a cotton plantation in Togo, Africa."

"Excellent. When do you start?" Father Benedict asked.

"Next March. After the wedding."

"You are going to wait until next March before you marry Margarette, but you want to *rescue* her from here—let me see— six months before the wedding?" A sarcastic smile crept onto the cleric's lips.

"I can explain. You see, four years ago my father betrothed me to a woman I do not love."

The cleric's eyes widened in mock amazement. "So you are betrothed to another. Did you know those agreements are binding?"

"Yes, sir. That is why I wanted to hide Margarette away for six months."

"Where will you put Margarette, George?"

"I will find her a pleasant flat. She will want for nothing," George defended.

"Tell me where that *pleasant flat* will be." Father Benedict crossed his legs, leaning back as if hearing an open-ended fairy tale.

"It will be in Cassel. I have friends in Cassel who will help us."

"So Margarette will stay locked up in a flat and see only you or those you send to her for six long months. No fresh air. No visiting neighbors. No shopping. Let me review. You came here to rescue Margarette, but you do not know if she wants to be rescued. You are going to marry her, but she has never told you that she will marry you. She will have the best, but she must stayed locked up in a flat in Cassel for six months. Then you will move her to Africa with a wife you do not love. Tell me, George, what will your two wives think about this arrangement?"

"I know it sounds crazy, Father, but it will work. I will never consummate the marriage with Charlotte. In God's eyes, Margarette will be my only wife. We will be properly married in a church, before God and man."

Father Benedict stood. "George, I can agree with you on one statement that you have made. This plan of yours is crazy." The cleric looked around at all the witnesses who had heard George's wild explanation. Smirks, sneers, and shaking heads confirmed agreement.

Throwing his head back with a sigh, Father Benedict addressed Mother Louise. "I think we need to hear what Margarette thinks of all this."

Mother Louise swept through an opening in the nave and quickly reappeared with Margarette. The elderly nun held Margarette's trembling hand.

George gasped. He had wanted to tell her his plan in private, explain how everything would fall into place.

THURSDAY, OCTOBER 2, 1751—MIDMORNING—CASSEL

Lieutenant Garvey regretted not having eaten before arriving at the Cassel command post. Hours ago he had heard the men in his platoon heading off in the direction of the commissary. The scent of fried sausage, hot biscuits, and steaming coffee in the air taunted Garvey's sensibilities.

"Right now I would be happy with a cup of water," he spoke to the rancid air around him.

Garvey marked the time by watching the variations of light hues stealing through the narrow square at the top of his cell. The exchange of fresh air from that opening lessened the stench of the seldom-used stone chamber in which he now sat, but he could still

detect the smell of stale urine and body odor encased in mold cling-
ing tightly to the stone walls and pavement. What he could not
detect was why he was here. Apparently, it had to do with George
Hempleman and Margarette Duffy. Why would the military be
concerned about these two? It must have to do with the man in
the white wig who was in the room earlier, probably an emissary
of a high-ranking nobleman. But anyone with any sense did not
cause a nobleman any grief unless that person happened to be the
margrave.

When aromas of the noon meal began to infiltrate William's
cell, he heard the fast clip of military steps in the outside hallway.
Again a key was inserted, turned. William stood up as the same
four guards took their positions. Colonel Giesler entered with the
same deputy that had been present earlier. This time there was no
nobleman's lackey. Instead a middle-aged gentleman with an officious bearing accompanied the colonel and deputy.

"My staff confirmed the existence of a Fulda convent," Colonel
Giesler began. "That will go well on your record. Now we need
additional information. You will walk out of here with us if you
cooperate fully. Understand, Garvey?"

"Understood, sir," William replied.

"Did George Hempleman tell you that he was about to leave
the area?"

"No, sir, he did not."

"Did he give any indication of his future plans?"

"No, sir, he did not. But Hessen-Cassel was filled with news of
his plans to go to Togo next year. That was no secret, sir."

"Yes, we know that!" Colonel Giesler grumbled impatiently.

The deputy stepped forward. "May I, sir?"

The colonel stepped back. "Certainly."

"There has been talk of George Hempleman having a liaison or
attachment to one of the Hempleman servants," Wolfgang's dark
narrow stare searched deep within Lieutenant Garvey's psyche.

*I was right. George has gone in search of this young servant and
sacked his future!*

Wolfgang continued, "Did your friend mention a Margarette Duffy to you on Saturday?"

Garvey wondered why they were questioning him when these men already had the information that they needed.

"He did."

"She is the daughter of a Scot, a professor in Giessen?" Wolfgang pressed.

"That is what I understand, sir."

Wolfgang leaned into William's face. "Being such a good friend of George Hempleman, you felt it your duty to ruin his career, cause his father to lose his health, and destroy the hopes of a young noblewoman who has been betrothed to your friend for four years—in a binding legal contract?"

"I never intended any ill will, sir."

William knew his commission was lost. He would be sent home to Mentz disgraced if he were allowed to leave the barracks at all. He stood immobile, waiting for the conclusion.

Colonel Giesler ripped the lieutenant insignia from his uniform, slapped the young man in the face, all the while glaring intently, and robbed William Garvey of his integrity and his will to resist.

The officious gentleman in the shadows stepped forward. "There is a way you can regain your commission."

Hope crept back into William's empty vault. "Regain my commission?"

Herr Gibbons had found William's Achilles' heel. "That and more!" the crafty lawyer proceeded. "Help us track George Hempleman. Being that you are his friend, you will be able to approach him, reason with him, and bring him back to his family. You will be rewarded generously. You can make your decision right now and walk out of this cell with us."

When William did not give an immediate response, the austere *der herr* said, "We will return in the morning."

THURSDAY, OCTOBER 2, 1751—MIDMORNING— ABBEY NEAR FULDA

Although she was dressed in a plain novice uniform, the sight of Margarette shattered George's normally self-assured composure. Embarrassed by his own appearance, he tried to sit straighter on the wooden bench. He wished he could push back his hair, cover his wound, untie his hands, fall on his knees to plead for her forgiveness, and ask for her hand in marriage.

Mother Louise released Margarette's hand.

Margarette's quiet dignity and tear-filled eyes captured the attention of very person assembled in the cavernous nave as she walked slowly toward George, holding him in captivity with her challenging blue eyes.

Stopping an arm's length in front of him, Margarette stared deeply into George's soul while she addressed another. "Mother Louise, would it be possible for the brothers to loosen George's bonds?"

Father Benedict questioned, "Will you behave yourself, George?"

Without taking his eyes from Margarette, he answered, "I will." The solemnity of the moment reminded the senior cleric of many a marriage ceremony he had performed.

The two officer-monks were given the go-ahead, and soon George was standing in front of Margarette, their eyes continuing a steady embrace.

"Do not mistake my tears for weakness, George," Margarette's soft voice echoed.

"I would never do that, Margarette."

"So you are planning on shutting me up in a flat, your own Rapunzel."

"I did not mean to take you from one captivity to another. I would take care of you, Margarette, always. You will have the best."

"May I help plan my future, George?"

George dropped his head, unable to continue eye contact. "Of course. I just did not know how to talk with you ..." His head still bowed, he glanced at Margarette hesitantly. "I did not know how to smuggle you out of here and keep everyone in Hessen happy until we can begin our married life in Togo."

"What if I do not want to go to Togo?"

"Well, uh—"

Margarette interrupted, "What if I want to be your one and only wife?"

George lifted his head, gazing into the blue, penetrating eyes. "I am listening."

Margarette's shoulders held firm, her composure steady. "I will not enter the drama that you have been creating. I need to live openly, freely, with my head held high. I need to be your helpmate, not something you help yourself to at your convenience."

"Margarette, I never intended—" George took her hands in his.

"Let me finish, George."

"Of course."

"I thought I knew you, and I thought that you knew me." Margarette paused. "George, I will always strive to live a chaste life. I do not want to live with even the remotest appearance of evil. I never want to give people the occasion to think evil of us. I want us to be able to stand together before God and man with no shame. George, I will never be your mistress, your whore. I will never live in hiding. If you cannot claim me as your one and only, I will stay here in the abbey for the rest of my life."

"Margarette, I want the same life for us that you want, but things have become so complicated. How can I marry you now? I do not have an income to provide for you. My father and Lord Sturzhelm will not allow us to live in peace in Hessen-Cassel or any German state. I know them well."

"Perhaps we should ask for advice, George, good advice. A repository of wisdom surrounds us. Mother Louise understands my love for you. Your daring in trying to rescue me indicates your love for me. Most would not have risked what you have risked, George. For that I admire you, but I want a settled life without so many risks. Shall we ask for some much-needed advice?"

George stared steadfastly into Margarette's unswerving eyes but spoke not a word. Silence screamed in the still stone space where they stood. All waited for George's response. Slowly a wry smile crept upon his lips and a twinkle lit up his dark eyes. He turned to Father Benedict and then to Mother Louise. "Would you be willing to guide us? I, for one, need a lot of wisdom right now."

Mother Louise laughed in relief.

The senior cleric from the monastery stepped forward with a slant smile, put one arm around George, and extended his right hand. "I am Father Benedict, and I thought you would never ask."

George dropped one of Margarette's hands and eagerly shook the hand of the older cenobite.

Chapter 14

Roosters crowed in the compound. Water splashed in *das Badezimmer*. Aromas stole through the corridors as light rays cavorted on the horizon announcing a new day, an unspoiled day, a day of new beginnings.

It had been twenty hours since William Garvey had been stripped of his rank, thirty-six hours since he had last eaten, and twenty-five hours since he had last touched water to his lips. Huddled in a corner of the isolation cell, which contained absolutely nothing except four cold stone walls, he felt bereft of his human dignity. He would continue to feel like this for four more hours.

The decision William was asked to make would mold his character, probably forever.

William could justify siding with the establishment; laws were in place to be obeyed, and obedience to his superiors would reinstate his commission, return esteem to his family and himself. However, he could also justify aligning with his friend because loyalty and betrayal are antithetical. No personal integrity could be maintained if he acted treacherously toward his friend.

William's dilemma was deciding on a manageable solution in which he could juggle both duty to the state and fidelity to a friend. Of course, this acrobatic feat involved trickery, but William rationalized the spinning of deceitful acts in mid-air more acceptable than betraying a friend. His task would be to keep the people for whom he was performing so fascinated on his surreptitious chicanery that they could not see the deception. He began to wonder what the deception was himself.

FRIDAY, OCTOBER 3, 1751—EARLY MORNING—ABBEY NEAR FULDA

George woke with a fierce throbbing headache. In the abbey, no hint of human activity seeped into his room. Even the early October rain fell in a whisper. George's clothes still lay on a chair where he had placed them last night. He grabbed his kerchief, dipped it in a laver of water, and held the compress on his forehead.

Doors began opening and shutting. George bathed with the remainder of the water in the basin, donned his clothes, and waited for his small cell—which held only a bunk, washstand, straight-backed chair, and prayer stand—to be unlocked.

During matins, George sat between two brothers. In fact, he was surrounded by black robes and hoods in the refectory, in the chapel, in the hallway, everywhere he went. This was a jarring anomaly for him.

Now sitting in the abbot's office opposite Father Benedict, George was keenly aware that two hooded creatures stood outside the door of the archimandrite's study. Additionally, Brother Andrew stood behind the abbot as George's instruction began.

George was grilled and drilled on God's and society's expectations of a husband and father, on a wife's expectations and needs. George soon wondered if any man should ever get married except under compulsion or for the passion that love or money brought with the bond.

He was to love Margarette as Christ loves the Church. That meant that he must be willing to die for her. He was to love, comfort, honor, and protect her in sickness and in health. Before God and man, he was to pledge his solemn promise that he would forsake all others and keep himself only for her as long as they both lived.

The imbroglio was learning how to love, comfort, honor, and protect.

"Volumes have been written on each of these four subjects," Father Benedict said. "I have very little doubt that you love Margarette, George. My main concern is that you live the love. Then the comfort, honor, and protection will easily follow. When you put two people in one room, two opinions emerge. How will you resolve your marital differences, young man?"

"I was of the opinion that the husband makes the decisions and the wife obeys them."

"Most men would like to believe that, but marriage does not work that way. God did give Eve a brain and self will."

"See where that has led!"

"Adam sinned too," the cleric reminded George. "All have sinned except Christ. But may we stay with the process? I have observed in my many years of ministry that the happiest marriages are those where the husband leads and protects the family while listening to the concerns of his wife. Do you know what concerns Margarette?"

George was stumped. He thought about her family. "Family seems to be a concern for everyone. I know that my family is important to me, just not as important as Margarette is. I have seen a brief interaction between Margarette and her father. They seemed happy, light-hearted, so I guess that he must mean a lot to her. Mostly I know about the Duffys from Professor Duffy himself. You see, he taught my brother and me for three years and told us bits and pieces about his sons and daughters. The family seems to be close-knit."

"So, Professor Duffy is a faithful family man. Margarette will be accustomed to that quality in a man. Go on."

"Margarette said she wanted a settled life without many risks. I will work toward that end, but I cannot give that life to her right now." George paused to remember he was not entirely lacking in meeting Margarette's need. "Sir, I definitely have abandoned the idiocy of having two wives. What was I thinking?"

The cleric smiled. "So now that you are thinking more clearly, George, please continue."

"Margarette is well-learned for a woman. Her father taught her well. She has a love for books. I noticed that when she worked for our family that she would spend some of her earnings in *die Buchandlung* and sometimes quoted passages from books."

"Some men cannot live with a woman who loves learning. Would you grow jealous of her books, George?"

"The truth is that I am jealous of anything that keeps her from me."

"So you want to be the center of her life."

"Well, yes. Is that not what a wife is all about? Being a helpmate?"

"Let us define *helpmate*. You start."

"I thought that you had all the answers and I was the student."

"Being a teacher means leading a student to clarify, to think, to recognize truth."

George was beginning to like this instructor. By the end of the first session, George began to realize that he did not want Margarette to change in the least. He wanted Margarette exactly the way God had created her. He did not want a lifelong companion who was a mindless replica of Lady Sturzhelm or a cunning copy of his own mother. He wanted the original, untarnished model.

"Father Benedict, I must admit that when God does the molding, the finished vase is quite beautiful. But when people start tampering with the mold—"

Father Benedict smiled and stood. "Lesson one complete."

George's head was still throbbing, yet there was one other important matter on his mind. "Father, my horse. It has been tied up since yesterday morning. Could I—"

"No, you may not. But tell me where your horse is, and I will have it brought into the compound."

FRIDAY, OCTOBER 3, 1751—ROAD
FROM CASSEL TO ALSFELD

The troubled, reinstated Lieutenant William Garvey kept pace with Deputy Wolfgang Gunther as their horses alternately walked and trotted the distance to Alsfeld. Garvey had been given back his rank but not his status. Gunther barked out orders and kept *Donnerschlag* a few paces ahead of William's *Schatten*. Additionally, it was Gunther who kept in his possession the official papers that legalized their search for George Hempleman.

After pushing his weary standardbred and Garvey's thoroughbred to finish the seventy kilometers in a taxing daytime trek, Gunther reined in *Donnerschlag* in front of the local barracks. Fortunately, William sighted a few of his comrades in the compound and began to feel less of a social misfit.

Wolfgang nestled with his companions sharing beer, dice, exaggerated stories, pornography, and foul jokes. He felt right at home.

Chapter 15

SATURDAY, OCTOBER 4, 1751—ABBEY NEAR FULDA

Margarette read again the verses Mother Louise had told her to commit to memory regarding humility, pride, and judging. Yesterday Mother Louise had chastened Margarette for emasculating George Hempleman and then judging him for being theatrical when Margarette herself played to the audience during her entire dialogue with George. Without being aware of it, Margarette had fallen into the same sin of which she had accused George.

As she recited the verse about removing the beam from one's own eye prior to taking the speck from the eye of another, Margarette heard Annette clear her voice.

"Aren't you expected at Mother Louise's teaching this morning?"

Margarette picked up her Bible and scrambled toward the door. "Thank you, Annette. When I start reading and studying, I lose track of time." Margarette was halfway down the hallway just as Mother Louise turned the corner.

"Did you forget our appointment, Margarette? I do hope you will not develop a pattern of tardiness." The elderly nun held out a receptive hand and sheltered Margarette under her arm, guiding her to the abbess' office.

After a prayer, Mother Louise directed Margarette's attention to verses on purity and illustrations from the Old Testament and

New Testament of people who had committed sexual sins and of the consequences the guilty parties had paid for those sins.

"The Bible has a lot to say about keeping our vessels clean," she told Margarette.

Thinking that the mother superior was accusing her, Margarette defended, "George and I have not sinned in that way."

"I am sure you have not. But you will have your share of temptations if you insist on becoming husband and wife."

"Why can we not be married here?"

"It would not be safe. Father Benedict and I are convinced that a search will be made for George. If he is apprehended, he will be taken back to Cassel and forced to fulfill the marital agreement that his father struck four years ago."

"What are you saying, Mother Louise?"

"I am saying that if you and George want to become wife and husband, you will have to emigrate out of the reach of Hessen-Cassel's long arms." The abbess clapped her hands and then drew them in a long stretch as she accentuated *long arms*.

Margarette began rocking forward and back, as though the movement would cause thoughts to churn into wisdom. "Mother Louise, I have a grandmother and other relatives in Scotland."

"But, child, how would you get to Scotland? Father Benedict and I both agree that neither you nor George is ready for marriage. You both seem to be ready for passion, but not marriage. If you were to flee this territory, you and George would have nearly impossible obstacles to overcome. You could end up hating each other very quickly. Close proximity creates a bond between people, either a good bond or a bad bond. Bonding has a way of yielding to passion. Yet, stolen passions steal your identity."

"Steal my identity?"

"Yes, dear. When you were born, you were immediately identified as the daughter of your parents. George was identified as heir to his father's title. As you grew, your God-given identities became known. Additionally you were creating yourselves identities by your responses to life. The Good Book says that even a child is known by his ways.

"As society judged you, you began to hear things about yourself that others spoke. 'She's lovely.' 'Isn't he the handsome one?' and so on. You took hold of these words and incorporated them into your identity. Then you might have also heard statements like 'She's a scholar, that one,' and 'He was first in his graduating class.' All these positive statements gave you and George self-confidence, helped you to see who you were. God is pleased when you and others see the fine attributes He has given to you or the qualities you have developed from the good seed He has planted within you.

"But there are others in our world who do not want you to have a God-centered identity. When Lord Hempleman called you a thief, you said that you were humiliated, depressed. Because he lied about you, he began to steal your identity. Some in Cassel will always think of you as a thief. So it is with George. When he was informed that he was expected to marry a woman that he did not love because it would enhance the family fortune, he began to see himself as a commodity and not as a person. He lost part of his God-given identity. As George began to cooperate with the false identity his father was giving him, he began to become less of a free agent that God had created him to be and more of a pawn on his father's chessboard. When this happens, people may become angry, depressed, compliant, rebellious, and so on.

"Father Benedict and I have discussed your situation, and we agree that much of your aberrant behavior is caused by people trying to steal your God-given identity. When that identity is restored and affirmed by those you hold dear, then your behavior will become more God-like. You will be free to be the one and only unique person that God has created to live in this place at this time."

"It is painful that our parents have not affirmed our identities."

"Of course it is. But they may be changing right now. God is the potter. We are the clay."

"What are you suggesting, Mother Louise?"

"I am suggesting the ideal. Yet I know that it sometimes takes a lifetime to achieve an ideal. So let us look at some alternatives in a fallen and broken world."

"It is frightening, but I am listening."

"You say that you love George and want to marry him. He says the same about you. The Lord God in His infinite wisdom said that when a man and woman marry, they become one flesh. You will no longer be Margarette Duffy but Margarette Duffy Hempleman, wife of George Hempleman. George will be known, because he is both protector and provider, by his profession but also as the husband of Margarette. Your identities are enhanced by the marriage.

"But it may be a long time before you can be lawfully married. How strong are you? How strong is George? If you seal the union before the marriage, something uncanny happens. Part of your identity is gone, especially for the woman. Some women, and even some men, spend the rest of their lives searching for that lost identity. Jewish tradition emphasizes that the act of marital consummation is so sacred that newly married couples must sleep on a clean white cloth. The blood from the union of husband and wife serves as a type of covenant into which the husband and wife have entered. That blood covenant is to last until death. God honors a blood covenant!

"If the couple steps prematurely into a sexual relationship, the woman particularly feels as if she is unprotected. The sexual act is the most intimate of all relationships. Two people are becoming one. The mix of identity inside the marriage bond makes the couple stronger, more resilient, more expansive. But outside of marriage, the mix of identity can cause confusion. The man who was to be the woman's protector has become a thief, stealing her security, her self-esteem. The man begins to wonder if this woman he has violated would also yield to another so easily. Then the mind games begin. The blaming starts. Drunkenness, wantonness, promiscuity, even frigidity and other abnormal behaviors can emerge. The relationship that God wanted to bless and multiply is filled with distrust. No marriage can achieve happiness that is not built on God and trust."

"There is always forgiveness," Margarette argued.

"I agree, and many marriages work through this identity crisis successfully. However, harsh words spoken and thoughts running amok are not good building blocks to place on any foundation. Jesus wants to be the foundation for your marriage, and His ways always produce victory. Nowhere in the Holy Book is permission granted to consummate *before* you vow before God and man to love, comfort, honor, and protect in sickness and in health and till death parts you."

"I knew couples who tampered with the order, Mother Louise, and they are still married to this day."

"This is true. But do you know the inner struggles, the doubts, the regrets? Margarette, God, in His infinite wisdom and love, has given us commandments to keep so that we can live freely, with our heads held high. I believe freedom is one of the values you mentioned to George yesterday. Christ gives us freedom so that we do not have to be entangled in sin, in bondage. Guilt is a killer!"

"So, you are not opposing our marriage. You are opposing sexual sin."

"Exactly. As I said, it will not be easy for you and George to obey God. It never is. But to obey is in your best interests. Promise me, Margarette, that you will remain chaste and *only* be united in marriage to George as a virgin."

Margarette thought of the expanse of her vow before answering, "I promise, Mother Louise."

"When temptation comes, I want you to remember that promise. In moments of temptation, ask God to help you keep that promise. That promise is really not to me, but to Him. Margarette, God desires only good in your long and successful life."

SATURDAY, OCTOBER 4, 1751—ROAD FROM ALSFELD TO FULDA

Lieutenant Garvey realized that he and Wolfgang were making too much progress too quickly. When the two men stopped to rest at mid-day, William picked up a small sharp stone in the stream where he and Wolfgang were filling their canteens. Although his container was not filled, William capped his vessel and walked idly over to *Donnerschlag*, placing the stone under the saddle while Wolfgang was still stooping over the rushing water and dabbing a handful of its refreshment over his face. Wiping off the excess, Wolfgang replaced his hat while strolling arrogantly toward his horse.

"Garvey, when we get to the abbey, I will stay hidden while you make the first approach." Wolfgang grasped *Donnerschlag*'s reins with his left hand and the cantle with his right. "Do not be stupid and try anything that would hinder the capture." Wolfgang placed his left foot in the stirrup while giving William a warning glance. Springing up to stand in the left stirrup, Gunther swung his right leg over his horse's back. "I will have my gun sights on you." Placing his right foot in the stirrup, Wolfgang cautioned, "Accidents happen." Then he settled himself in the saddle.

The two riders began with a walk. Then Wolfgang used his sharp rowels to command *Donnerschlag* into a trot. Dissatisfied with the pace, he struck *Donnerschlag* sharply on his flanks with a riding crop. As his horse broke into a gallop, Wolfgang's weight pushed heavily on the saddle. In an instant, *Donnerschlag* reared his front legs high into the air. Wolfgang tightened the reins and crouched closely to his horse's body. But as the horse settled his front legs on the ground, Wolfgang's body was pushed into the saddle exactly where the stone dug into the horse's flesh. *Donnerschlag* shook his owner before again rearing with his front legs, then with his back legs. The tortured horse continued the jostling until Wolfgang lost his grip and fell forcefully to the rocky ground.

William slid off *Schatten* and reined in *Donnerschlag*. Wolfgang lay quietly on the ground. Watching for signs of Wolfgang's recovery, William removed the stone from beneath the horse's saddle. Wolfgang was as still as frozen blood. William took some cool water from his canteen and poured it over the unconscious man's forehead.

Momentarily Gunther tried to focus his eyes on William. But now there were two Williams. No. Three, four, five Williams bent over him.

"What happened? Where am I?"

"You had a nasty fall," William explained. "When you whipped your horse, he just started rearing and never quit."

"Pour some more of that water on my head. My horse is here, right? He did not run away, did he?"

"No, he is tied up over by that sapling."

"I will whip him good when I get on my feet." Wolfgang tried to focus on the real William in the midst of the several duplicates floating in front of him. "I never thought I would say this, but thanks. I am indebted to you."

William smiled as Wolfgang lost consciousness once more.

Chapter 16

SATURDAY, OCTOBER 4, 1751—MID-AFTERNOON—ABBEY NEAR FULDA

Father Benedict concluded the session on sexual purity before marriage. "George, men are sexually driven. If they do not control their passions, they will wreck havoc on women, themselves, and society. Sex inside of marriage is honorable, but not outside of marriage. Moderation is primary. The woman you love could end up hating you for your constant nagging for sex. Your wife will want you to nurture her and meet her needs. Then she is more than willing to satisfy your desires. Before marriage, a woman may submit to a man because she wants to be loved, but your appetites could drive the love she craves from you and the love she is willing to give to you farther and farther away. Women are social creatures. It is all about relationships, intimacy, and feelings with them. That is why you see women stroking fabric. A man looks at fabric. A woman wants to touch it."

"How do you know so much about women, being a celibate?"

"I have kept my eyes and ears open while disciplining myself not to sin. The Bible warns us to guard our hearts. Believe me, it has not been easy, but this is the life I have chosen. I am God's servant, George. So are you, as a believing Protestant. We just serve God in different capacities, with different doctrines.

"As God's servant, George, you are to seek His will in all matters and obey at all costs. You must preserve Margarette's chastity. She has been rejected and falsely accused by your father, judged and abandoned by her father. Margarette needs a man who will protect her and the values she holds dear. She could easily compromise her ideals because she does not want to lose another important male relationship, but you must remain strong. I want you to take a vow. I want you to vow that you and Margarette will not consummate your relationship until after a legal and binding marriage ceremony. Will you do that?"

George considered the seriousness of such a vow. He was thankful that the good priest had not tried to convert him to Roman Catholicism but had respected his Calvinist rearing. The cleric, George observed, was a man of integrity who valued the integrity of another, believing God could do a better work than he himself.

Feeling secure in his relationship with Father Benedict and knowing his own parish reverend would approve of the cenobite's counsel, George willingly vowed, "I will preserve Margarette's honor. We will not have sexual relations until after our wedding vows, which we will declare before both God and man."

Father Benedict leaned back in his chair and breathed a sigh of relief.

George himself gulped. *Becoming a man is not an easy task!*

As the two rose and shook hands over the abbot's desk, Father Benedict said, "Bad news, George. The brotherhood could not find your horse anywhere. I am sorry. I know that a horse means a lot to a man."

SATURDAY, OCTOBER 4, 1751—LATE AFTERNOON—ROAD TO ABBEY NEAR FULDA

Wolfgang Gunther sat on a log holding his head between his hands while resting his elbows on his knees. Now that his senses were clearing, he was convinced that Garvey must have had something to do with *Donnerschlag*'s throwing him. He just needed evidence.

Wolfgang decided to use Garvey's services until Hempleman was trapped. *I will make sure the trap I set is large enough for both.*

Evaluating his prey, Wolfgang said, "We need to get going. Douse the fire with the rest of that coffee. I have had all that I want for the day."

Garvey obediently emptied the liquid. He wished that putting out the fire of hatred in Gunther could be so easy.

SATURDAY, OCTOBER 4, 1751—NIGHTFALL— ABBEY NEAR FULDA

The session that Mother Louise had with Margarette played and replayed in the nun's mind. The subject had been too intimate, too personal. She wanted to retreat behind higher, thicker, more fortified walls. She wanted to be alone. She wanted to be protected.

Daddy, why are you here? Daddy, what are you doing? You are hurting me, Daddy! Stop!

Momma! Daddy is hurting me! Please help me! Help me! Help me!

But Daddy did not stop. Momma did not come. It happened over and over and over night after night after night. Soon it became normal to the nine-year-old child. But it was not so normal that she could talk about it.

She grew shy, timid, and self-conscious in the presence of adults. She knew that she had to protect herself from adults because adults were not safe. She was thankful when Sunday came and the family went to church to pray, listen to the music, and sit attentively while the priest spoke.

When she was of confirmation age, she asked if she could become a nun. Of course, her parents were relieved to have the soiled creature disposed of, and the church was glad to have a new member in its order. Her papa was now entering her younger sister's bedroom. She herself was too old to be violated.

The young girl took her vows, never allowing anyone to know that she was not chaste, that she was not worthy to become a holy woman. For forty years, she had kept the secret. For forty years, she tried to reclaim her identity, her dignity. Without sharing the secret, she had read the Scriptures, studied to show herself approved unto God, unashamed, rightly dividing the word of truth.

Mother Louise was a whole person, a free person, a forgiven and forgiving person, a new creation, a child of the King. But the memories still hurt. The nightmares still haunted.

All was calm in the abbey. Vespers had been sung. Lights had been extinguished. Mother Louise went to the clothes pantry where used clothing waited for paupers and beggars. *Now where is the winter clothing?* She rummaged through the articles stacked neatly on the shelves. When her hands felt the homemade fabric of woven linen and wool, she selected two of the turtig smocks. Then she chose two flat broad-brimmed hats, two sets of leather trousers with belts, several pairs of socks, two lightweight cloaks, and two pairs of walking shoes. Each set was remarkably different in size. She packed them in a gunnysack.

Her fleet feet carried her to the room where Annette and Margarette slept. Slipping in quietly, Mother Louise gently put her hand on Margarette's shoulder and whispered, "Get your belongings, all of them, and quietly come with me."

Bedazzled and half asleep, Margarette obeyed.

In the shadowed hallway, Mother Louise put her forefinger to her lips, grasped Margarette's elbow, and led her to the kitchen.

"It is time for you and George to leave. I know for a certainty that there will be a search. You must not be here. George must not be here. You must keep your vow, but you must leave. Are you all right with that?"

Margarette nodded as fear crept near her soul, fear similar to the terror she had felt when the stranger had attacked her in Cassel.

Mother Louise took loaves of bread, dried fruit, meat, and containers for water, placing all in a wicker basket that could be worn on Margarette's back. "This will help you for a while."

Seeing that they were quite alone, Mother Louise said, "Now for your transformation. You will not be known as Margarette until you are safely in Scotland. We talked about identity this morning. Tonight I am giving you a new identity. You will be known as *Marc*." She pulled clothing from a sack. "Slip out of your nightwear and put these on. We will practice how men walk on our way to get George."

Mother Louise pulled Margarette's strawberry blonde hair back into a pigtail the way most men wore their hair. With the turtig shirt and smock, leather trousers and belt, broad-brimmed hat, male cloak, and men's work shoes, Marc looked non-threatening yet convincing.

"Will George know who I am?"

"Of course. What I am hoping is that he will not care how you look until you get to Scotland. Now, we must go. Pick up your belongings and put them in the sack with the costume for George. Here. I will hold the backpack while you slip it on." She paused and took out a leather pouch from beneath her habit. "Here is your dowry. You will need it on your way. Spend wisely." Mother Louise tied the leather pouch to Margarette's belt.

As the two crossed the arcade, the abbess instructed Margarette in the male swagger.

SATURDAY, OCTOBER 4, 1751—JUST BEFORE MIDNIGHT—ABBEY NEAR FULDA

Wolfgang asked, "Are you sure this is the right abbey? There are five abbeys around Fulda."

"This is the one that I remember," Garvey replied. "But I do not think it is wise to be beating on a closed gate this late at night."

"Do as you are told! It is nearly Sunday, and we do not want to be here when parishioners start rambling around."

Lieutenant Garvey, in his impressive officer garb, pounded on the wooden gate. Deputy Wolfgang Gunther stood behind with a pistol aimed at Garvey's back.

"What was that?" Margarette asked Mother Louise.

"That, Marc, is what I feared. We must move quickly."

Father Benedict was the next to hear the disturbance. He called for Brother Andrew and Brother Joseph. The two of them were instructed to find out what was astir and report back, but no gate was to be opened unless the elder cleric approved.

George heard the bombardment from his second-storey room. Just then, a small rock flew through his window opening. He rushed to the window ledge and saw the silhouette of Mother Louise standing beside a young man outlined by the light from the full moon. Mother Louise put her finger to her lips. With her other hand, she motioned for George to look in his room. George picked up the rock, which had a note secured with twine. He held the note to catch the moon's rays.

Get your belongings. Tie your bedding together and use it as a rope. Eat this note and bring this rock with you.

Within three minutes, George stood on solid ground with his mouth full of paper. He handed the rock to Mother Louise.

Brother Andrew shouted over the gate, "State your business."

"Official business. I need to speak to the abbot. I have papers to arrest George Hempleman. If you have any information about this person, you must cooperate fully. Now open this gate!" Garvey yelled the message, hoping that if George were in the compound he would have sense enough to leave.

"I will take your message to Father Benedict." Brother Andrew replied. "Brother Joseph will wait here until I return with a reply."

In the darkness, Mother Louise led George with one hand and Marc with the other to the rear of the abbey grounds where she unlocked a small narrow gate hidden behind ivy and brush. "It is time for you to go. Live wisely. Do not forget your vows. Trust God and He will protect you." She briefly hugged Margarette and then took hold of George's shoulders with her hands.

"Protect your future wife, George. Your life with each other begins now." With that, she shooed the young fledglings out of the abbey grounds into the wild, vast world.

Margarette laughed as she looked up at George. "I am Marc from now on, and I have an outfit for you which will make you look as homespun as me. Here." Margarette handed him the clothing. "Go behind the shrubs and come down to my level, Master Hempleman."

George emerged a changed man. He took the brim of his hat in his right hand, being careful not to cause further injury on his forehead. Then he took the brim of Margarette's hat with his left hand and pulled their faces together so that their noses touched.

Margarette smiled. "What do we do next, Brother?"

George was relieved with her light-hearted manner. "Well, I am going to fetch my horse, *Bruder*. I do not expect you to walk the full distance to the river road."

George put his fingers to his lips and blew a piercing whistle.

Beleuchtung raised his ears at the familiar sound, whinnied, and raced toward his owner. Neither shrubs, trees, rocks, nor the two men standing in front of abbey's entrance gate impeded his gait.

"What was that?" Wolfgang asked as the black thoroughbred, prodigy of *Godolphin Barb*, streaked over the landscape.

"I think it was a one-horse cavalry," Garvey responded.

Wolfgang dismounted *Donnerschlag* and began beating his fists on the abbey gate. "Let me in! Hempleman is probably escaping right now! Let me in!"

With a modulated tone, Brother Joseph retorted, "Easy! I think I see Father Benedict coming down the path. Yes, it is the abbot."

"Well, open the gate! He is the one that I need to speak to."

Father Benedict called over the gate. "Could this wait until Monday? Today is the Sabbath."

"We have been given strict orders by Lord Harry Sturzhelm himself that George Hempleman is to be brought back to Cassel with no delay. *With no delay* means exactly what it says! I take it that Hempleman is in your abbey. That was his horse, was it not?"

"I saw no horse. Also, I have seen no official summons." Father Benedict called over the gate before turning to Brother Joseph with the order, "Open the portal and stay alert."

Wolfgang pushed with his shoulder against the wooden gate just as Brother Joseph let the hinge slide free. The deputy's arm hit a sharp rock on the sloping mountain as he landed at the feet of Father Benedict.

"There, there, man. Easy. Brother Joseph, help the man up," Father Benedict chuckled.

Wolfgang rubbed his bleeding elbow as Father Benedict took the deputy's good arm and led him to the monastery. Garvey followed, trailed by Brother Joseph.

Chapter 17

SUNDAY, OCTOBER 5, 1751—SHORTLY AFTER
MIDNIGHT—OUTSIDE THE ABBEY NEAR FULDA

George fastened the sack with their belongings to the saddlebag, mounted *Beleuchtung,* and then pulled Margarette, complete with rucksack, up behind him.

"Hold on!"

Margarette's slender arms wrapped around George's strong chest. Embarrassed, she loosened her grip.

George took her hands and clasped them together. "You must hold on. I do not want to lose you on some dark path." He pushed his feet down in the stirrups and *Beleuchtung* broke into a trot.

Father Benedict took a long, slender wick from a repository mounted on his study wall. Leaning over the fireplace, he caught an ember and moved toward his desk where he lit a candle.

As he straightened his fragile, aging body, the archimandrite spoke with authority. "Let us introduce ourselves and get to the business at hand. I am Father Benedict. Brother Andrew and Brother Joseph are my associates." The cleric stood immobile with his hands behind his back, not giving his customary handshake in welcome.

Gunther moved forward while taking a rolled sheet from beneath his cloak. "I am Deputy Wolfgang Gunther, emissary of Lord Harry Sturzhelm of Hessen-Cassel. I have been ordered to arrest George Hempleman and take him back for a hearing and possible trial."

Perusing the document, Father Benedict asked, "Who is the lieutenant with you?"

"Lieutenant William Garvey. He was to assist in this undertaking, but he has fallen far short of fulfilling his commitment." Gunther glared at Garvey, who feigned innocence by casually studying the contents of the room.

Father Benedict rolled up the paper and returned it to Gunther. "Everything seems to be in order." He turned to Joseph. "Bring young Hempleman in here."

Brother Joseph clipped off the steps to the second storey and down the hallway. Bursting into the now vacated room, which was richly washed in moonlight, Joseph saw bedding tied to one leg of the bunk and stretched out through the open window. Curious, he peered out and found no movement except the wind stirring the leaves.

Hurrying back, a puzzled Brother Joseph asked to speak to the elder cleric in private. Father Benedict motioned for Brother Andrew to join their conference just outside of the abbot's study.

"He is gone, Father. He apparently let himself out of the window with the bedding," Brother Joseph reported.

Father Benedict nodded to Brother Andrew, "Check with Mother Louise. Perhaps the girl is gone too."

When the abbot and brother shared the information with their uninvited guests, Wolfgang grabbed Garvey by the throat. "You slowed me down! He was within my reach! I will have your rank. I will have you in solitary. I will have you in stocks! Or maybe I will just shoot you right now!"

Brother Joseph easily loosened Wolfgang's stranglehold. Garvey gasped for breath as his adversary shoved him out of the abbot's office while beating him with the butt of his pistol.

Beleuchtung carried George and Margarette to the river road where George halted the colt. George glanced back toward Margarette, asking in a wry grin, "Where do you want to live for the rest of your life, my lady? Prussia or Sweden?"

"I was thinking Scotland would be a safe place."

"So yah want me to be a shepherd, do yah?" he mimicked the Scottish brogue.

"Your Scottish accent is pretty good for a German," Margarette laughed.

"Quiet, girl. We do not want to alert the natives. I am on a most-wanted list."

"I threw that list away when I captured you." She gave him a quick hug.

George unclasped Margarette's left hand and lifted it to his lips. "I am going to have to keep my wits sharpened around you."

Gripping the right rein, he pressed his left knee against *Beleuchtung* and headed north.

William had managed to dodge the majority of Wolfgang's strokes. To ward off further injury, as soon as the two men were outside the perimeter of the abbey, Garvey turned on Wolfgang.

"I do not defile a holy place. But I do deform an ugly face!"

Wolfgang felt the strength of Garvey's quick right fist on his left jaw, then the full fury of the lieutenant's lightning fast knuckles on his right jowl. Wolfgang staggered to regain his equilibrium while he thrashed his own knotted fist toward Garvey.

Garvey turned his head to let Wolfgang's first jab roll off before thrusting a right fist into Gunther's stomach. As the deputy bent in recovery, Garvey dove into his opponent's legs and brought him face down to the ground. Putting his knee on Wolfgang's mid-spine, Garvey pinned both of his arms in a lock and took hold of Gunther's hair. Like a smith with a hammer, Garvey struck the man's head against the stone pathway until the deputy lost consciousness.

Using rope tied to *Donnerschlag*'s saddle, William secured Gunther and his mount to an ancient oak. He then rifled through Gunther's saddlebag for a gag. Grabbing the soiled cloth used to wipe sweat and foam from *Donnerschlag*'s taxed body, Garvey stuffed some of the fabric into Wolfgang's gaping mouth, though much dangled off to the sides. Then William ripped his adversary's scarf from his neck and tied it securely around the bobbing head of his foe. Garvey chuckled as he tested the tightness of the fit. *That will hold!*

SUNDAY, OCTOBER 5, 1751—PAST MIDNIGHT—CASSEL

Lady Sturzhelm led Charlotte back to her bedchamber.

"Will Father keep his word? Will he bring George back to me? Oh, Mother, I have been shamed. The servants are whispering. The townspeople are gossiping. Lord Hempleman will probably enlist *Herr* Gibbons to annul my betrothal to George! It is all over Cassel! And I cannot sleep."

Lady Irene patted her daughter's hand. "We do not know for certain that a procurator is involved."

"But that is what Father said."

"What your father said is that he *thought* that Lord Hempleman would employ *Herr* Gibbons to arbitrate our conflict. It has only been one week, Charlotte. Your father is developing his strategy. Two mornings ago your father dispatched men to bring George back. These things take time, dear."

"Well, I want it done *now*, Mother. I am awake all night. During the day, I have no energy. I am so embarrassed to even face a servant. A *servant*, Mother! I am Lord Sturzhelm's daughter, and yet I am timid around servants!" Charlotte burst into another convulsion of tears.

Her mother slowly sat down on the edge of her daughter's bed, gently seating her daughter beside her. Lady Irene rocked her seventeen-year-old daughter until the girl had no more tears. Then she eased her down onto the feathered bed.

"Mother," Charlotte whispered, "I resolve to give my father no rest until George Hempleman fulfills his contractual agreement."

SUNDAY, OCTOBER 5, 1751—PAST MIDNIGHT— OUTSIDE THE ABBEY COMPOUND

Since the days had shortened and the weather had cooled, warning man and beast to prepare for a long winter, two flying squirrels heeded their instincts and busily gathered strips of bark from their sturdy oak. However, they also needed leaves. This required countless trips down the oak, sorting through leaves on the ground, and scampering back up the tree to their shared den. The furry-tailed animals had stopped their activity when two men began wrestling on their turf. Once the turmoil ceased, the noisy creatures ventured toward the ground. Near the bottom of the tree trunk, sharp claws dug into human flesh at the base of the giant oak.

Wolfgang yelped. Then a second critter coursed over his body. As Wolfgang's mind cleared, the deputy realized that Garvey had tied him straddled to a tree, a tree apparently shared by forest *Eichhornchen*.

Gunther's face hugged rough bark. Pain screamed from his frontal lobe, which William Garvey had struck repeatedly on hard pavement. His wrists and ankles cried to be released. His own horse's sweat cloth prevented him from crying out; the stench and taste nauseated the normally resilient Wolfgang.

Rather than weaken his resolve, Wolfgang's predicament hardened his determination. He was accustomed to frequent beatings as a child. His impervious stance to repeated blows had caused his father to accuse him of having a head thicker than that of a bear. Although his father had meant the comment as an insult, Wolfgang had turned it into a compliment and prided himself on his ability to withstand abuse.

Slowing moving his hands and wrists in rhythmic motion, he weakened the knot of the rope. Soon he was able to use one hand to stretch the hemp while he folded his other hand into a narrow stem. At last, his hands were free. He quickly untied his feet, untethered *Donnerschlag*, and mounted.

Gunther had seen Hempleman's horse heading toward the rear of the abbey. The deputy reasoned that Garvey would join his friend.

Checking his weapon, he decided that there were no restrictions regarding Garvey, so he was as good as dead. But before Garvey's death, Wolfgang wanted to have Hempleman unconscious and tied to a horse. Maybe he would even tie a couple of squirrels around Hempleman's neck on the return trip to Hessen-Cassel. Garvey's corpse could lie on the forest floor for predators feasting in the wood.

George began to doubt his ability to keep his vow as he felt the warmth of Margarette's body close to his. It was easier to resist her when he saw her before him disguised as a man. But the constant movement of her soft body through the turtig smock brought incredulous desires. These were heightened by Margarette's feminine fragrance, which intoxicated his mortal mind. The next time that he read Homer, he would not be so quick to judge the Argonauts sailing near the sweet voices of the Sirens. Father Benedict had cautioned that George must not give Margarette any reason to distrust him. Yet George felt the need to satisfy his own pleasure.

A thunderous crash reverberated through the foliage. Hooves thudded against the hard ground and wild snorting jettisoned from wide equine nostrils.

Rescued from his desires, George gripped Margarette's hand and spurred *Beleuchtung* into a full gallop.

SUNDAY, OCTOBER 5, 1751—DEAD
OF NIGHT—CASSEL

Lady Hempleman awakened with a start and sat up in her bed. The nightmare was horrifying. She wanted protection, comfort. For the first time in many years, she wanted the arms of her husband around her frightened body, even when one of those arms was paralyzed.

Burying her pride, she tiptoed into the master bedchamber, slid under Johann's covers, and wrapped her arms around his burly chest. How satisfied she felt lying close to him without having to smell cheap perfume.

The husband and wife rested in comfort. Then Johann gasped in staccato breaths.

"What is wrong, dear?" Anna loosened her arms and sat up, rubbing Johann's shoulders gently. "Shall I send for the doctor?"

"No, no, no. I fine. Fine. I learn ssss-looow. You good wife. Good mutter. Love you, Anna. So surry."

Anna lay back down and wove her arm under the arm of her husband and hugged him tightly.

"Me, too, Johann. But we do learn. We do learn who is important in our brief lives."

"Anna, weet Anna," Johann stroked the warm arm of his wife with his right hand. With some effort, he turned over and embraced his wife with his right arm. "Good wife. Good life."

Nestling closer to her husband, Anna asked, "Will George be all right?"

"Uorge 'ill fine 'is way, Anna. Uorge 'ill be fine."

"And us, Johann? Will we be all right?"

Johann tried to dispel his wife's anxiety by drawing her closer and kissing the crown of her head. Yet Anna's fears would not leave her. So many uncertainties taunted her, and she did not dare to trouble her husband due to his health.

Herr Gibbons had not responded to her request to discuss the matter of the betrothal. It was, indeed, odd because Jerome Gibbons had been the family's legal consultant since Johann had left his family's land holdings in southern Hesse to become constable in the state's seat of power.

Then there was the matter of Lord Sturzhelm's issuing Johann a dismissal. Of course, Johann did not absolutely need the job of constable. Six years ago, Lord Sturzhelm had approached Johann saying that he wanted someone he could trust in Cassel. Johann had agreed to accept the position due to Lord Sturzhelm's higher nobility ranking, which offered obvious gratuities, both socially and economically. The office also had provided a cosmopolitan atmosphere for the family.

However, the true wealth of the family lay in the Hempleman manor in southern Hesse even though the production on the land had not been particularly lucrative in recent years according to the *Vogt* who managed the demesne and hectares. Of course, Johann had double-checked the statistics, surveyed the land, and talked with nearby lords. All the information had pointed to one fact. The dwindling family income needed a boost. For this reason, Johann had entered the Togo venture with Lord Sturzhelm.

With Johann's poor health and George gone, Anna felt overwhelmed. It was all very confusing. She knew she must be strong, at least until Johann regained his health, if he *did* regain his health. But for now, she rested in her husband's arms, wept quiet tears, and allowed sleep to come.

Chapter 18

SUNDAY, OCTOBER 5, 1751—DEAD OF NIGHT—OUTSKIRTS OF FULDA

Beleuchtung sensed the anxiety of his owner and plunged into the dark terrain with a ferocity that equaled his name. Yet the horse trailing behind closed the distance. George realized that *Beleuchtung* carried too great a load to continue the marathon much longer. Seeking to foil his pursuer, he decided to use the steep incline outlined in the darkness ahead to his advantage.

Dipping over the top, George reined *Beleuchtung* into the forest, found a mound of massive brush, and tightened the reins in his right hand. As Margarette flipped forward because of the sudden halt, George steadied her with his left arm and yanked her back on the forward croup of the horse. Their pursuers raced by.

Even in the darkness, George recognized the outlines of the two men who rode the same horse. He spurred *Beleuchtung* forward.

"What are you doing?" Margarette asked through clattering teeth.

"That was a friend of mine, and Brother Andrew is with him."

As *Beleuchtung* raced after *Schatten*, George shouted, "Garvey! Come back here! Garvey! Brother Andrew! It's me, George! You just passed me!"

Brother Andrew was the first to hear the cry.

Garvey double-backed. Within minutes in the shadows of

Waldecker Land, the two male parties laughed, dismounted, and began slapping each other on their shoulders while Margarette waited atop the very tall thoroughbred, wishing to be on *terra firma* too.

Coming to her aid, George held out his arms and received her with the joy he often received his sister Celia. He swung her around and around, elated to be in the safety of friends.

William ended the levity when he said, "Brother Andrew and I were chasing you down, George, but Wolfgang Gunther may be on our trail in short order." William explained his arrest, his compromise, and the abandonment of his compromise.

After a quick chuckle, all four quieted and listened. Only the soft October breeze, the harsh hooting of owls, and rustling movements from the forest interrupted the night.

Brother Andrew whispered, "We need a plan. I have been given an assignment by Father Benedict, so we will have to work the assignment into the plan."

"What is the assignment?" Garvey wanted to know.

"I am to stay with George and Margarette until they are properly married."

"What?" George asked in astonishment.

"You heard correctly. After Father Benedict learned that your room was empty, he suspected that Margarette might be gone too. He sent me to Mother Louise. There was no answer at the convent for the longest time. Through floodgates of tears, an aide of the abbess spoke to me from behind the convent door informing me that Mother Louise had passed away in her sleep."

Margarette gasped in unbelief. "Mother Louise? Dead!" Margarette did not hear the rest of Brother Andrew's explanation as she processed the news. The good woman who had spent much time talking with her, giving her guidance—dead! Biting her lips to keep back the tears, Margarette wondered why. *Why?* She heard no answer, just the hollow words streaming from Brother Andrew.

"Not to be deterred, I asked Sister Claire if she could please check the room where Margarette Duffy stayed. In a few minutes, she confirmed what Father Benedict had suspected.

"By the time I arrived back at the monastery, Gunther and Garvey were gone. Father Benedict told me that you two, George and Margarette, were not to be left alone. He told me to pack. He gave me provisions and sent me out."

Garvey interrupted, "That is where I come in. As I rounded the rear of the abbey wall, I saw Brother Andrew scrambling down the path toward the river road. I told him that I was a good friend of yours and asked if he wanted a ride."

George took up the narrative. "That is when I panicked. I thought my father had sent someone to take me back to Cassel."

Brother Andrew hurried the discussion. "I am to travel with George and Margarette to supervise them along the journey." He stopped to address his new assignments. "Do you two know where you might be headed?"

"Scotland?" Margarette proffered.

"Scotland?" Brother Andrew drew in his breath. "Why Scotland?"

"Margarette has relatives there," George advised. "My father has no connections in Scotland that I know of. We should be safe."

Garvey interrupted, "You are not there yet. Remember, there is a madman looking for both of us." The pulsating from his injured parietal bone reminded William of Wolfgang's unlimited brutality. "I know he is under orders to take you back alive, but I cannot be guaranteed of the same."

"Is he a killer?" Margarette asked.

Before Garvey could answer, George queried, "Who is he?"

"Deputy Wolfgang Gunther," informed William.

"He is on my father's payroll," George expressed with amazement.

"*Was* on your father's payroll. Lord Sturzhelm has taken over the search. It is a long story." William did not want to tell George about his father just yet.

"So the wolfhound is tracking stray sheep," George remarked.

He put an arm around Margarette's shoulders. "And, yes, he is a killer."

Brother Andrew removed George's arm from around Margarette and offered a partial solution. "The abbey has a boat anchored nearby. Father Benedict suggested that we travel the river. Who would suspect two country bumpkins and a monk of foul play?"

"I will overlook the insult, Brother, but you speak good sense. What about you, William?"

"I will throw Gunther off your trail by making it look as if I am you on your horse."

"I have to give up *Beleuchtung*?" George was incredulous.

"He will not fit on the boat, George," William argued with a chuckle. "I tell you what. I will take your horse back to the monastery before I travel south."

"That is too risky," Brother Andrew cautioned. "Could you travel with two horses, William? If you and George ever reunite ...."

George was still engaged in an inner struggle over losing *Beleuchtung*. The thoroughbred had been given to George on his fifteenth birthday. *Beleuchtung* was a symbol of his manhood, his independence, his mobility. His identity was tied to the sleek black colt. How could he explain the great loss that he felt?

Garvey punched George on the shoulder. "Are you listening? Do you have a map of southern Europe?"

George returned his attention to the escape. "Yes. Sure. I have several maps in my saddlebag. Why do you need one?"

Garvey explained, "We want to throw Wolfgang off your trail, right? Right! If you mark a route in your own handwriting on your own map, I will drop it on my way south before I turn west toward Mentz. I have enough relatives in the Rhine region who can put me into hiding until I plan what to do next."

"If you take a liking to the Highlands, you can join me outside of Braco, Scotland, where I will be tending sheep." George laughed.

George's attempt at joviality quickly turned to remorse as he loosened the saddlebag from his horse. He stroked the colt's neck and nose. He wished he had a nosebag full of oats to give this treasured animal. But he had nothing to give except his affection.

Reaching into his saddlebag, George's hand slightly scraped across the leather pouch—which contained his mother's emerald necklace, her note, and money—before he touched the familiar maps he always carried. Then he dug deeper into the satchel to locate some charcoal. *Was that a book in the bottom?* He never remembered putting a book in his bag. *And what was that leather object my hand brushed? Probably a glove.*

He motioned for Garvey to walk with him to a spot where the moon shone through the trees. Kneeling on one knee, George placed the map on the ground and charted a course from Fulda, southeast to Bamberg, then through Nuremberg to Regensburg. Looking over George's shoulder, Garvey enjoyed the fictitious excursion. He pointed toward the Mediterranean, so George continued routing through Bavaria to Munich into Innsbruck, Austria. From there he spotted the Brenner Pass, ending the markings in northern Italy. Then he placed a large question mark on the map.

"Good enough?" he asked his friend.

"Superb!" Garvey snatched up the map.

As the two friends parted, Garvey put his hand on George's shoulder. "I am really sorry to tell you this, and I do not have a lot of information. It seems that your father took ill after you left, at least that is what Wolfgang Gunther let slip. I do not have any details. I am truly sorry, George."

SUNDAY, OCTOBER 5, 1751—DEAD OF NIGHT—BEHIND ABBEY NEAR FULDA

Wolfgang Gunther held his mount in readiness behind the abbey outside of Fulda wondering which direction his prey had taken. Rubbing his sore wrists one at a time, he considered returning to Cassel to ask for more manpower. But this idea assaulted his ego. He took a piece of hard tack out of his saddlebag but first rinsed his mouth with water from his canteen. He swirled the liquid around in his mouth, hoping to get rid of the taste of the dirty sweat cloth.

Just then he thought he saw two horses moving along the river road some distance away, one with no rider. No sooner had he spotted them than they were gone. *Were they an apparition?* Wolfgang did not believe in apparitions. He lived in the real world, the world he touched, saw, heard—and yes, smelled and tasted. "Yuck!" he said as he recalled the all-too-vivid smell and taste of his own horse's sweat.

Spewing the water out of his mouth, Wolfgang stuffed the hard tack between his jaws and chomped down as he squeezed both of his legs against *Donnerschlag's* sides.

SUNDAY, OCTOBER 5, 1751—OUTSKIRTS OF ABBEY NEAR FULDA

Brother Andrew and his charges trudged back toward the abbey to the shallop bobbing in the Fulda River currents. The trio stored their belongings in the boat, then settled themselves.

"I will take the first hour," Brother Andrew volunteered as he centered himself with oars in hand. "If the wind picks up, we can raise the sail. George, you guide the scull at the stern. Have you sculled before?"

George answered defensively, "Naturally. I have lived next to the Fulda all my life."

Margarette took the seat at the bow and stretched her spine, relieved she no longer bore a basket on her back.

As the small vessel glided north, George scanned the shores for any sign of human activity. It was still hours before dawn, but he began to feel the heavy burden of protectorate. "Margarette," he whispered, "when we are with people, I will introduce you as my deaf brother. Your voice would unmask you immediately."

"So is this your plan for having a peaceful voyage?" Margarette smiled even though George could not see her visage.

"It could work that way," George returned. He too smiled, which she could sense in her heart.

Brother Andrew agreed. "Brilliant. It could have obvious advantages. People are quicker to speak around someone they believe is deaf. You, Margarette, could pick up all kinds of information that neither of us could. By the way, where did you two get those outfits?"

George evaded the query immediately. "My brother Marc had them, but he is not telling me where he got them."

Brother Andrew realized he was not going to get any answers. "So your brother is christened Marc, eh? That will work."

SUNDAY, OCTOBER 5, 1751—BEFORE DAWN—SOUTH OF FULDA

Lieutenant William Garvey needed to keep a safe distance from Gunther, yet not so far away that the deputy lost Garvey's trail. When the lieutenant saw the eastern horizon clarify details in his surroundings, he stopped on the gravel road, had the two horses trample around in a few circles, then left in an obvious gallop before dropping the map a few dozen meters beyond.

Wolfgang had sight as keen as that of an eagle. Even in the early daylight hours, he sighted *die Landkarte* that had blown off to the side of the road. Dismounting *Donnerschlag*, he picked up the scrap of paper.

"Italy and beyond?" he said aloud. "I need to catch Hempleman before he gets through Austria. I never negotiated Brenner's Pass."

Quickly remounting, Wolfgang spurred his hungry and thirsty horse into a gallop.

SUNDAY, OCTOBER 5, 1751—MORNING— NORTH OF FULDA

The upper flow of the Fulda accelerated the progress of the three companions. Although it was Sunday, they were stopped at every state border for the customary toll. If they did not have papers proving that the toll had been paid upon entry, customs officials charged an exit fee. Right beside these state officials were customs officials for the next German state wanting an entrance fee. The landgraves' hunger for money never ended. Although Brother Andrew transacted the matters since he knew many of the officials, Margarette, George, and the monk each took turns paying the toll.

Sunday night the two exhausted men slept on a hard shore while Margarette curled up in the cold shallop. Consumed by thoughts of his ailing father and the loss of his horse, George slept little. The sleep he did get was tormented with shadowy ghastly images that sought to fetter him with their persistent clanging hovering manacles.

Chapter 19

MONDAY, OCTOBER 6, 1751—BANK OF THE FULDA RIVER

By morning all three were shivering in the cold. Margarette pulled out the last of the bread, dried meat, and fruit, eating only a morsel of bread herself while the men hungrily devoured the jerky between bites of dry bread. The dried apples they shared with Margarette who had little appetite. The death of Mother Louise weighed heavily upon Margarette's fragile emotions.

"We are going to live off the land, fellows," Brother Andrew announced after breakfast with a twinkle in his eye as he routed through a small chest for fishing tackle. Thus, while he and George manned the boat, Margarette cast a line and hook into the Fulda River.

MONDAY, OCTOBER 6, 1751—CASSEL

Charlotte tapped softly on the door of her father's bedchamber.

"Father, I must talk to you ," she spoke in hushed, urgent tones. "I know this is early, but I must speak to you. Please, Papa. This is important."

Rapidly running down the hallway toward their master's suite,

Franz and Louis devised ways to keep themselves from being blamed by the impropriety.

"*Fraulein*, what may we do to help you?" Franz began the approach.

"I must speak to my father," Charlotte sneered, offended that servants, underlings, dared to interrupt her.

"He is still sleeping, *Fraulein*," Louis whispered.

Charlotte began to see the folly of her actions and did the unspeakable. She wept in the presence of servants.

"Now, now, *Fraulein*—"

Franz never finished his reasoning. The bolt lifted and the door opened. Standing in nightshirt and headcap, Lord Sturzhelm thundered, "What are you doing waking me up this early in the morning? Can you see that the house is not astir? Get back to bed! *Now!*"

Convulsing into an avalanche of tears, Charlotte hid her red nose and puffed cheeks with her large hands and dropped to the floor.

Lady Irene put a gentle hand on her husband's shoulder. The man knew when he was defeated. "Franz and Louis, go back to bed. Charlotte, come in. We will keep this a family matter."

Lady Irene helped Charlotte to her feet, wrapped her arm around her daughter, and guided her into the bedchamber, seating her on a cushioned chair overlooking the balcony and gardens beyond. Avoiding eye contact with her parents who sat opposite her on a small couch, Charlotte lamented, "It has been one long week. That is seven long days, and nothing has been heard from George." Charlotte looked imploringly at her father, who actually listened to her lament. Emboldened, she continued, "Father, you have contacts in most of the German states. Could you please expand the search over a larger territory?"

Surprised at his daughter's shrewd initiative, Lord Sturzhelm moved forward to sit on the edge of the couch. With his elbows resting on both knees and his hands cupping his broad jaw, he said, "I agree. The deputy and the lieutenant have proven to be incompetent. I will speak with Maxwell this morning and commission a larger search with more resources. I will spread a massive net, a tight net over every part of Germany. I will catch that fish and reel him in."

"Oh, *mein Papa*! I love you so much." Charlotte ran to her father, giving him a huge hug and equally huge kiss on his cheek. Then she gave her mother a quick peck on the forehead before darting out of the room, stumbling over her own feet before she was out the door.

By noon Lord Sturzhelm had a team of twenty men combing the surrounds of Hessen-Cassel. Maxwell Braun, second in command under his lord, ordered each of these men to return before nightfall with at least three recruits each. The new recruits would be trained and sent as envoys into neighboring states. Each of these recruits would also recruit. Thousands would be infiltrating the Germanic territories in only five days. Lord Sturzhelm had the funding. Many a man needed a job.

MONDAY, OCTOBER 6, 1751—FULDA RIVER

Two small fish lost their freedom. They were the main menu that evening over a campfire at the confluence of the Fulda and Eder rivers. After the meal, George went scavenging and located an apple tree near the river. He packed all the red fruit that lay on the ground in his cloak. Meanwhile Brother Andrew located a small stream to replenish their dwindling water supply. When the two men returned to the camp, Margarette cooked several of the apples on skewers over the open fire.

"You're becoming more valuable to me every day, *Bruder*," George commented to Margarette as he sank his teeth into the dessert.

"Not bad. Not bad at all," Brother Andrew said as he reached for another roasted treat.

For the first time since Margarette had been abandoned by her father, she relished the taste of food. Looking at Brother Andrew and finally at George, she pronounced, "Good company. Good appetite." She too reached for a second helping.

The evening meal helped to keep body temperatures normal, so Margarette in the boat and Brother Andrew on the bank slept fairly well that night. However, at the back of everyone's mind was the river passage tomorrow past Cassel. George, unable to sleep at all, planned his next move.

MONDAY, OCTOBER 6, 1751—DARK OF NIGHT—HESSEN-CASSEL

The initial twenty recruits fanned out. A man was stationed at each gateway into or out of Cassel. Others took up residence in and around taverns, inns, coach stations, churches, customs, market plazas, everywhere a thoroughfare existed. A handsome reward had been placed on George Hempleman's capture. Rix-dollars exchanged hands for information. Promises floated on the air like fireflies swarming the landscape on a warm summer night.

MONDAY, OCTOBER 6, 1751—BESIDE FULDA RIVER

In the deep of night, George quietly lifted his saddlebag out of the shallop where Margarette slept. He also tore off the top of the gunnysack, fashioned two slippers for his feet and bound them with rope. He set off. Within a mile of the camp, he spotted a barn. A cottage nearby lay in quiet tranquility.

The animals stirred and chicken feathers flew when he lifted the latch and crept into the barn. Despite the noise, George was actually glad to hear a whinny and moved toward the welcome sound. Rubbing his hands along an upright beam, he located a bit and bridle. Invading starlight aided George in fastening the headpiece.

"Don't worry, fellow. I will have you back before dawn," he said as he stroked the Percheron's neck and led the draft horse from the shadows into the penumbra beyond the stall. After closing the barn door, George continued on foot for several meters beyond the barn before mounting. Familiar with the terrain, horse and rider adapted quickly to the night ride. By two in the morning, Cassel emerged on the horizon like a single chiseled grey stone. Tall, closely assembled structures blocked the passage of any stranger. A few stubborn revelers stalked or stumbled on the city streets. This was usual. What was also usual was the shadow of two armed guards standing at the foot of the long stone bridge supported by multiple culverts.

Dismounting, George tethered the "borrowed" horse. He reached into his saddlebag for a small flask. When the guards saw the scruffy young man approaching, they pointed their muskets. Calmly George mimicked a country accent. "How long till I can enter the town? I need to see Lord Wolff about his lands in western Hesse."

"Thunder and lightning!" one guard exclaimed. "I thought I had caught me that young Hempleman who has a bounty on his head."

"I heard about him," George answered. "Any leads?"

"None that we know of. He has been missing for a week," replied the second guard.

"What about my chances of speaking to Lord Wolff? I have some papers from his *Vogt*."

"You will have to wait till dawn when we open the gate. Orders!"

"Do you mind if I sit with you till then? You can catch me up on the news," George feigned.

The guards lowered their guns and sat down on an open bench, allowing enough room for George to sit also.

Unable to stop spilling out the gossip of the town, the guards told of the romantic scandal that had initiated a search.

"Rumors are all over the area, aren't they, Floyd? Of course, I try to sort out the truth."

Floyd continued the story. "It does seem that Lord Sturzhelm and Lord Hempleman are no longer in league. Sturzhelm's daughter is running the search, it sounds like to me. Right, Leo?"

Leo reflected, "Now that would be a woman to live with!" He slapped George's shoulder in jest. "Never a dull moment with that *Fraulein*! Too bad she isn't pretty."

George did not answer but slowly pulled out the glass flask and uncorked the bottle. As he placed it near his lips, Floyd asked, "Do you have one of those for me and Leo? We get mighty thirsty out here on this long watch."

George handed the flask to Floyd who took a long drink before handing the pint to Leo. Leo finished the contents. Within minutes the guards were slumbering peacefully with their backs against the guardhouse, their chins resting on their chests, and their guns lying on their laps. Cautiously taking the gate key from off Floyd's belt, George then crossed the bridge, whose one and two-storey houses held no light but cast a rigid gloom over his path. At the end of the long passage, he unlocked the gate, stepped into the town, and locked the iron barrier behind him.

Because a constable must be on call at a moment's notice and needed quick access to the city's exit and entrance, George had a short walk to the Hempleman house. Going to the side entrance of his home, George inserted his key into the courtyard gate. The lock cooperated; he stepped into the enclosure.

Taking two steps at a time, he hastened up the staircase to the balcony and tapped lightly on his mother's bedroom door while dropping his broad-brimmed hat on the balcony floor.

"Mother, open the door. I have come home."

Within scant seconds, the door flung open. Anna pulled her son into her room and clasped him by his shoulders. "Thank God you are safe. I have been so worried."

Inspecting her son in the shadows, Anna caught her breath in astonishment. "George, you look like a commoner, and you have an injury!"

He laughed softly. "I could not very well come back to Cassel dressed in my usual apparel." Rubbing his forehead injury gently, he grinned, "Just a scratch, Mother.

"But first allow me," he said as he leaned to give his mother a kiss on her cheek. It was then that George noticed that there was no odor of wine on his mother's breath.

"Mother, you have stopped drinking."

"I had to, Son. I did not want to spoil your homecoming. Then your father took ill after you left. I am in the midst of preparations to move the family back to our manor. Did you know Lord Sturzhelm dismissed your father?" Anna took George's hand and led him to a chair near her table. "Enough about us. Please sit and tell me why you have come back. You must know that there is a bounty out for you."

"I just heard. Nevertheless, Mother, the reason I have come back is to see how father is doing. I heard from three sources that he is not well. Now I am hearing the same from you. What is wrong?"

Anna tried to sound cheery. "Your father is gaining strength every day. He is still weak on his left side, and it is difficult for me to understand his speech, but he is much better. The good report is that his mind is still keen. I am grateful for that."

George rose from the chair, went to his mother, lifted her to her feet, and wrapped his strong arms around her. "I am so proud of you, Mother."

With that, a cascade of tears that had welled up since October 27 broke silently onto George's shoulder. However, within moments, Anna straightened. "Forgive me, Son."

"Forgive me," George corrected. "I am the one who has caused your stress."

Shifting the focus, Anna informed her son, "George, your father called off a search for you after he became ill. He is so sorry for arranging your life and trying to force you into a marriage you never wanted."

"May I see him, Mother?"

"Let me check." Anna stepped into her husband's bedchamber. Shortly she called, "Come in, George. Your father will see you."

George hesitated before entering. A small candle burnt on a table near his father. George glanced toward the man lying amongst comforters on the massive bed. His father's countenance was somehow different. Yes, there was a pull on the flesh, but there was something additional: a tender glance, an inviting slanted smile. Taking his father's strong right hand into his own, George bent over the man who had sometimes boasted and blustered over this eldest son of his, at other times, had badgered and baited him. On rare occasions, the elder Hempleman had seen his eldest as a man and bantered in conviviality. But never had Johann wanted to banish George. He had only wanted a son with backbone, and that is exactly what he received.

"Uorge, good see you."

"Good to see you, too, Father. I was concerned when I heard you were not well. I am sorry that I have caused you so much grief." Tears gathered in George's eyes.

"Am surry, Uorge. My ault." Johann squeezed his son's hand.

"You were just doing what you thought was best for our family, Father. I understand."

George's father fought back gathering tears. "*Danke schon.*"

"Father, I cannot stay long. I came because I wanted to see how you were. I also wanted to tell you that I plan to marry Margarette Duffy. A monk is supervising Margarette and me until we become husband and wife. I would be so grateful if you would bless us in our marriage."

"*Ja*," Johann nodded his head and lifted his weakened hand to also clasp George's.

Anna observed with amazement, "Johann, you are getting stronger. You moved your left hand."

Johann smiled, took a deep breath, and looked steadily at his son. "Bless you, Uorge. Bless Mahgette too."

George wrapped each parent in a mighty embrace. "I always knew that I had the best parents in the world. I will send you messages. We, Margarette and I, will send you messages. Keep us in your prayers."

"Are you going to become a Roman Catholic, George?" his mother asked.

"Whatever church we choose, Mother, we will not forget to live God's primary commands."

Johann turned his face slightly to Anna. "I tole you Uorge be fine."

"Yes, you did," Anna kissed her husband on his forehead. "Yes, you did."

"I am so thankful that I have had these few minutes with you, but I must leave. I have borrowed a key and a horse."

"George, be careful." His mother gave him a last hug.

"And wise," his father added.

"I love you both. In a few weeks tell Maurice, Hayley, Celia, and little Siegfried I love them too. Until then, this visit is our secret. Okay?"

His father raised his right hand in affirmation.

His mother said, "Agreed. We love you, son."

George gave them each one last hug.

Chapter 20

TUESDAY, OCTOBER 7, 1751—BEFORE DAWN—BESIDE FULDA RIVER

Amazingly, George returned the key and the horse and arrived back in camp before anyone awoke. He settled his exhausted body on the ground and slept fitfully for about half an hour before dawn.

When Brother Andrew awakened, he sat up and reviewed his horrifying nightmare. Wolves had been chasing him. Others in his dream had also been fleeing the man-eating, snarling carnivores. He could not distinguish who the others were. However, he knew that they were friends, and he knew that all their lives depended upon outrunning or outsmarting the wolves.

Next, Margarette awakened with a scream. Brother Andrew ran to the shallop placing his wide hand over Margarette's mouth while saying, "You are okay. It is just a dream."

Margarette's round-eyed stare saw nothing around her. Her dream continued as an army of faceless men, who emanated an odor of stale tobacco, liquor, urine, vomit, and unwashed flesh, stretched out their gaunt arms and bony fingers toward her running, weakening, exhausted body.

Soon she relaxed, became cognizant of reality, and began to relate her dream.

George, who had joined Brother Andrew at Margarette's side, spoke with amazed hesitancy. "I had a dream too, Margarette. You and I were on a ship at sea. You were shackled in the hold of the ship. I wore weights and chains around my ankles and wrists and stood before Lord Sturzhelm and Charlotte in the captain's quarters. Charlotte wore a wedding gown of grey satin. Her hair hung in matted tangles. A civil servant entered the quarters with a signed document just as I heard your scream."

"I am not about to ignore these warnings," Brother Andrew said. "George, you are well known in Hessen-Cassel. Margarette, you also could be easily recognized. We need a plan to bypass Cassel. Any ideas?"

George ran his eye over Brother Andrew. "You and I are about the same size. Would you like to switch roles? A cleric's garment is highly respected, but the outfit that I am wearing will produce a lot of scrutiny. You will be able to withstand the scrutiny. When we row past Cassel, I will ride in the stern. If someone asks me a question, explain in a country dialect, 'The good brother has taken a vow of silence for the year.' That way I do not have to speak, and no one will recognize my voice."

"Capital! It appears as if you have been awake all night thinking about this."

"You might say that," George nodded.

Brother Andrew continued, "My reason for being in the boat with you will be that I am a wine merchant. We are sailing to Corvey to pick up a shipment for the abbey outside of Fulda." Brother Andrew winked before he added, "Incidentally, most wine merchants are educated, so I will not have to pretend to be illiterate."

"What about me?" Margarette asked.

"What about you?" Brother Andrew asked with a twinkle in his eye.

"Well, I am rather tiny, and I am good at keeping still, both physically and verbally."

"What are you thinking, Margarette?" George asked.

"See that gunny sack where we have our belongings and the rest of the apples that you found? I could climb in there." Margarette picked up the sack. "What happened? It has been ripped at the top. Was someone in our camp last night?"

Both Margarette and Brother Andrew stared at George's feet.

"Whatever were you doing?" Margarette questioned. "We need this sack."

George confessed. As Margarette listened to the tale unfold, she felt as if her insides were being torn out. Here was the man she was supposed to trust for the rest of her life, and he had left her out in the open countryside. Yet she understood the necessity of his returning to his parents. However, was a man not to leave his mother and father and cling to his wife? Also, did George not realize that his father had been the one who had sent her back to Giessen disgraced?

Margarette's flesh won over her spirit. "You left me! You left without telling me where you were going! How could you?" She started to stand but the shallop rocked with her movement.

George took her small hands snugly in his. "I had so little time, and I did not want you to worry."

"Well, I am worried now because I do not know if I can trust you in the future."

Brother Andrew interrupted with a chuckle, "Welcome to the prelude of married life."

George smiled his wry grin. Margarette studied both men with a scowl.

"I mean what I say, George Hempleman. Do not ever leave me again without telling me where you are going!"

George laughed in agreement and resisted the impulse to give her a hug. "Margarette," he said, "you are a tiger when you are angry!" Then George took his beloved's hand, raised her up, and helped her step safely out of the boat. With a long stride, he too was on land.

"Well, that is settled," Brother Andrew said as he sat alone in the shallop. "Now what is for breakfast?"

"Apples, I guess," Margarette said. "We need to eat as many as we can this morning. I plan on traveling in that gunny sack."

"So what will we do with our clothing and extras, Miss Captain?"

Margarette ignored her new nickname. "The backpack is totally empty."

George agreed. "I think it will work!" He turned to Brother Andrew, "*George*, we need to get changed. Margarette, you sort out what needs to go in the pack, eat some apples, and climb into the sack. That is, after you are back in the shallop. We will tie the knot when we get back." He paused before saying, "I wish!"

TUESDAY, OCTOBER 7, 1751—EARLY MORNING—CASSEL

Herr Maxwell Braun used his own key to open the Cassel gate before leading new recruits to relieve Floyd and Leo. When he saw the two slumped on a bench at the end of the long bridge, Braun urged his thoroughbred into a trot. The replacements followed indecisively, wondering what they had gotten themselves into by volunteering to aid in the search for George Hempleman. "What are you doing sleeping on your watch?" roared the newly installed constable.

Floyd felt burgeoning blows against his head and shoulders before he opened his eyes. When he saw that Maxwell Braun stood over him with a horsewhip, Floyd pleaded, "*Herr* Braun, stop beating me. I think I was poisoned last night."

With another swat of the whip, Braun awakened Leo, who hollered and began rubbing his head.

Standing over his deputies, Constable Braun placed the whip under his arm. "What do you mean? Poisoned? You look perfectly alive to me."

"Maybe it was a sleeping potion," Leo explained. " A young fellow wearing a broad-brimmed hat and country clothing approached us in the middle of the night. He said he had some information to deliver to Lord Wolff. We told him that the gate would not open till morning. He asked if he could sit with us. He must have poured some liquid down our mouths."

"Sure he did!" Braun understood the scenario exactly. "How was he supposed to do that without a fight? He had a flask of liquor, right? You both wanted some. He gladly shared, good fellow that he was. You incompetent ... Never mind! Get to your feet, both of you! I will have you in the stocks as a public spectacle! You two just let George Hempleman in and out of Cassel and lost a healthy bounty with your bungling. How tall was this young man?"

Floyd answered, "A bit taller than you, *Herr* Braun. Slender, broad shoulders. Dark hair from what I could see hanging down his back."

Braun felt the sting of the description. Hempleman was everything he had always wanted to be. Was Floyd mocking him? He grabbed Floyd by the nape of his neck, forcing the deputy to stand, albeit rather woozily. Braun turned to his newest recruits. "What you see cowered under my right hand is an example of what you must never become. Understood?"

"Understood, *Herr* Braun," the first new recruit said. "You can depend on me."

The second added rather nervously, "I have George Hempleman's description memorized perfectly. He will never get past me!"

Constable Braun bound the hands of Floyd and Leo, then gave them both a shove toward Cassel. Mounting his horse, he said to the new sentries, "I will send men to relieve you before sundown. Keep alert! Do not forget to send any prospective recruits to the barracks. You know how to use those muskets, do you not?"

"Yes, *Herr* Braun." To prove their competence, the young recruits grabbed the weapons left behind, stood at attention, and clicked their heels together in military fashion. Braun simply shook his head before yanking the chains of his catch as the two flipped and flailed behind the trotting horse. The two captives would be the main subject of conversation that evening in all of Cassel.

TUESDAY, OCTOBER 7, 1751—HESSEN-CASSEL

By midmorning, the twenty original recruits had filled their quotas. The newly enlisted men received their training. Colonel Giesler gave instructions to inform the amassing civilian army that Deputy Wolfgang Gunther and Lieutenant William Garvey were officially classified as deserters. Everyone knew what happened to deserters!

TUESDAY, OCTOBER 7, 1751
MIDMORNING—CASSEL ON THE FULDA RIVER

At the edge of Cassel's boundaries, customs agents flagged down boats traveling on the Fulda River. Each boat was charged a state fee for the privilege of using the river. Additional taxes were placed on goods brought into or goods taken out of the city-state.

Eric and Del stood nearby. They had just come from recruitment training.

"Me and my *Frau* could live on the reward money for a full year. Better yet, we could buy some land, and I could become *der Grundherr*," Eric reasoned.

Del responded, "If we catch this Hempleman together, you and me, we could split the reward. It would be *auf wiedersehen* to city life!"

Eric looked down the busy Fulda River traffic toward the south. "I don't plan sharin' the reward. It's whoever marches the man to Lord Sturzhelm that gets the rix-dollars. And seein' that I'm a lot bigger man than you—"

"It ain't the size of the man. It's the cunning that measures the man. I have you on that score," Del argued.

Eric took his companion by the collar. "Start usin' your wits, man."

The two exchanged blows as a shallop floated up to the custom station.

"What do you have there, Brother Monk?" the slumped-shouldered custom agent asked.

"The brother back there is not speaking, sir," Brother Andrew said. "He has taken a vow of silence."

"A vow of silence, is it?" the custom agent squinted to get a better look.

George continued to hide his face under the black cowl.

"Most peaceful ride I have had in many a day," Brother Andrew joked.

"I know what you mean," the agent grimaced. Spying the sack, he asked, "What's the cargo?" He took a long stick and struck the burlap bag. Margarette bore the injury on her head without moving a muscle or making a sound. George nearly jumped out of the boat to permanently injure the stooped, scrawny man.

Brother Andrew's voice stifled George's impulse immediately as he lied to the agent, "I am delivering a couple of smoked hams and a few pecks of apples to Corvey before heading back to Fulda with a wine shipment. What will be the cost for everything?"

The agent named the fee, which included a small tip for himself. Just as Brother Andrew handed him the rix-dollars, the agent glanced behind him.

"See those fellows over there? They are arguing over who is going to capture some poor *der Kerl* who broke his betrothal agreement. What men will not do for money!"

Brother Andrew responded, "Tell them to stay alert. You never know when that poor *der Kerl* might come through. Good-day to you, sir."

"Good-day to you, too, sir. Pleasure doing business with you." The agent pocketed the generous tip that Brother Andrew had included in the transaction.

TUESDAY, OCTOBER 7, 1751—MIDMORNING—
ABBEY NEAR FULDA

Sister Claire sat beside the body of Mother Louise. She stroked the carvings in the beautifully crafted coffin. Soon she would be addressed as Mother Claire. Reviewing the events of Saturday night, she resolved to keep her suspicions to herself and leave the memory of Mother Louise unscathed. Tomorrow the revered abbess would be commemorated and her lifelong dedication to the sisterhood extolled.

As the bell signaled a new hour, Sister Claire stood, faced the altar, and made the sign of the cross. Her light footsteps resounded in the sanctuary as she walked toward the open door where another sister was just entering to continue the wake. The two sisters nodded briefly as they passed. The cloistered life had been interrupted, but the indomitable life of holy living flowed over the disturbance with continuity, with resolve, with love that surpassed human comprehension.

TUESDAY, OCTOBER 7, 1751—MIDMORNING—
CASSEL ON THE FULDA RIVER

Using his left oar to push the scallop away from the embankment, Brother Andrew positioned the vessel back into the middle of the river.

"This cross wind will take us to Munden. When we are a few kilometers past the confluence of the Fulda and Werre, we can catch a bite to eat. I believe that apples are on the menu for today."

George wished the good monk would stop referring to food, even available food.

Once they were beyond the hearing range of customs, George fastened the scull with a rope, stepped past Brother Andrew, and knelt beside Margarette.

"I am opening the sack, Margarette. I will pretend to be getting an apple and I will also hand one to Brother Andrew. Are you all right?"

There was no answer.

"Are you all right?" George nearly ripped the fabric from its aperture to the seam at the bottom but, again, restrained himself.

A faint sigh answered him. "Oh, my head. What hit me?"

"That little *der Trottel* of a customs officer. I wanted to make mincemeat of him! But then we would have been caught. Please stay quiet for a while. I am sure no one can hear us, but anyone on either side of the river has full view. I will leave the sack open. Please be patient. Brother Andrew and I will get you out of there as soon as we think it is safe. I am sorry, Margarette. If I knew of a better way to treat you, I would."

"I will be okay. You had better get back to your sailoring, George."

Lifting an apple high above his head to show the agent on the bank what he had taken from the sack, George took a bite as he stepped past Brother Andrew, giving him a ripe apple as well.

Once the men had finished their apples and George had the scull in his hand, Brother Andrew lifted the oars out of the water and guided the boom to sail across the wind.

TUESDAY, OCTOBER 7, 1751—MIDMORNING— ROAD SOUTH OF FULDA

Because of the spurs repeatedly digging into his bleeding flesh and because of the lack of water and food, *Donnerschlag* slowed his gait.

"Good-for-nothing horse!" Wolfgang bawled. "Need some water! Need some hay! Need some rest!" Wolfgang guided the animal to a narrow stream. The horse drank heartily as Wolfgang crouched to sketch a map on the dusty ground with his finger.

TUESDAY, OCTOBER 7, 1751—LATE MORNING—FULDA RIVER

Within half an hour, Brother Andrew guided the boat to the bank of a forested area. George quickly helped Margarette out of the sack and applied cool compresses to her skull. She drank some water and ate an apple before they sailed on. Soon half-timbered houses came into view on both sides of the river. Munden lay directly ahead.

Neither George nor Brother Andrew suggested that Margarette go back into the sack. Yet without a male head covering, Margarette looked undeniably feminine. So with great caution Margarette put on the broad-rimmed hat, being careful not to touch the knot on her head. She pulled the brim as low over her face as possible.

"We have matching head wounds," she commented to George before she resumed her role as mute *bruder*.

It was nearly noon. Traffic on the river was heavy. The customs agents surveyed each vessel, barked out a fee, and received the payment. No change was given. Any poor fellow who did not give an agent the exact amount could lose up to a week of wages. He only lost it once! The next time he would be prepared.

Brother Andrew pulled out his money pouch before guiding the shallop to shore. The custom agent asked to see the receipt from their last toll. Brother Andrew handed it to him. The agent looked it over, placed it in a receiving box, and announced his fee. As Brother Andrew reached into his moneybag, a deputy strode up to the agent.

"Who do you have here?"

TUESDAY, OCTOBER 7, 1751—NOON—FULDA

Albert Smythe leaned over the sturdy oak table. "You say the abbess up on the hill is dead?"

"That's the word that I've heard. I was deliverin' a cart of oats to the abbey. There they was preparing for a funeral. So I ask who is in the coffin. They say it's the abbess. Died suddenly Sunday morning. Funeral's tomorrow."

"So how did she die? Old age?" Albert asked.

"So one would think, right?" the farmer said.

"Go on, man."

"I need to be movin' on. Got another delivery to make."

Smythe slid a rix-dollar across the table.

"That's more like it," the farmer snarled. "A scandal it is. Seems a couple monks were attacked the same night. Some nun is missing. So is the man who attacked the good brothers. A deputy from Hessen-Cassel shows up with a squad of armed men lookin' for the attacker, I hear. Word is that Brother Andrew is gone too. No one's seen him since that night. Probably took off with the nun. The boat behind the abbey is gone too. Strange goings on."

TUESDAY, OCTOBER 7, 1751—NOON— FULDA RIVER BANK

For a moment the Munden custom agent thought that the newly deputized officer was accusing him of false dealings. Then he saw the deputy lean toward the man who rowed the boat and held the purse. With a sweep of his hand, the recruit pulled the broad-brimmed hat from off the head of Brother Andrew. Standing back a bit embarrassed, he said, "I have mistaken you for someone else." Without apology he turned with disgust and walked away.

Brother Andrew settled the hat back on his head, paid the fee, and accepted his new receipt.

"The law these days!" the customs agent said.

Brother Andrew responded, "Just doing his job, I guess."

Once back into the main stream, the small shallop nearly skipped on the river current as the Fulda met the Werra in a confluence. The trio sailed north on the mighty Weser River. Margarette dropped the fishing line and hook into the water.

George smiled and said, "Bring in some big bass."

Brother Andrew said, "They almost did, *Bruder*."

Chapter 21

WEDNESDAY, OCTOBER 8, 1751—BEFORE DAWN—NEAR BAMBERG

After riding south for three days, Garvey reached the outskirts of Bamberg before daybreak. He knew he must not allow eyewitnesses to see him riding one horse and leading another behind him. Too many questions would be asked. The cobblestone road leading into and out of the city provided him the perfect terrain to alter his course west toward Frankfurt and Mentz without being detected.

WEDNESDAY, OCTOBER 7, 1751—LATE MORNING—FULDA RIVER

Margarette pulled in a sizeable perch. As the men licked their lips appreciatively, she held out her palm and asked, "Is that a drizzle of rain that I feel?"

George and Brother Andrew both protested.

"That explains the wind," Brother Andrew observed. "Let us eat that critter while we can still build a fire." He guided the shallop to the shoreline.

George started a fire with items from a tinderbox Brother Andrew had aboard the shallop. The drizzle turned into a gentle rain. Hovering over the precious flames with his hat, Brother

Andrew prayed as George gutted and scaled the fish before skewering it onto a stick. Margarette had three apples already over the fire when George put the prize catch close to the flames.

The small band stared at their lunch as their mouths watered. They were pulled starkly out of their fantasies when a gust of wind laden with rain extinguished the orange-yellow glow, which bowed way to dark thick smoke.

"We need to push on," Brother Andrew declared. "This river is swift-flowing and clean. We will eat the meat as it is."

They picked the bones clean, ate the semi-cooked apples, and ran for the boat as the rain pelted them without mercy.

WEDNESDAY, OCTOBER 7, 1751—LATE MORNING—BAMBERG

Wolfgang Gunther followed the map south into Bamberg. Scouting around, he located the town tavern where he handed the reins of his horse to a stable boy.

"Sir?" the boy asked.

"Give the mount enough to keep it alive."

Wolfgang himself enjoyed a full breakfast of sausage, eggs, bacon, coffee, and *ein Kasebrotchen*.

In speaking with the innkeeper, he learned that two horses had been sighted north of town before dawn. Gunther then went to the constable, who said he would be on the alert for any reports regarding George Hempleman. The constable wrote down a description and asked for the offense.

"Broken betrothal," Gunther explained.

The constable roared in laughter. "Perhaps I should give this young lad a place to hide."

Gunther cast a lightning-flash warning. "The betrothal was to Lord Harry Sturzhelm's daughter in Hessen-Cassel."

Immediately the Bamberg official straightened his posture,

hoisted up his trousers and belt, and replied. "Yes, *Herr* Deputy. I will keep my eyes open. You can count on it."

Gunther turned on his heel and left for Nuremberg. If he did not find Hempleman there or in Regensberg, he would have to return to Hessen-Cassel. His resources were nearly exhausted. Patting his stomach, he relived with delight his ample breakfast. However, he had grumbled at the stable hand for feeding *Donnerschlag* three pounds of hay.

WEDNESDAY, OCTOBER 7, 1751—LATE MORNING—FULDA RIVER

The broad-brimmed hats and monk's cowl only hindered the lashing cold rain, which found a target on the turtig cloaks and smocks. Margarette was the first to start shivering; soon all three could not stop their teeth from chattering as they shivered underneath their drenched clothing.

"We are making good progress!" Brother Andrew shouted above the storm.

As if to wipe out any optimism, the elements compounded their assault and nearly lifted the broad-brimmed hat from the monk's head. George hunched at the stern in hopes of evading some of the assault of both wind and rain. However, he kept his eyes riveted on the bow and Margarette. Because of that vigilance, he was the first to sight a phantom outline in the distance.

"Here comes another boat!" George warned.

Brother Andrew trimmed the sail to avoid a collision. Just then another streak of lightning flashed across the sky. Brother Andrew used this explosive noise to conceal the sneeze he did not want George and Margarette to hear.

The single occupant in the other boat yelled, "Fairer skies in the north!"

The encouragement strengthened the men's resolve.

As Margarette huddled into a tiny ball of humanity, the men

defied the mandates that the wind and rain issued. Margarette thought of hearth and home and, not infrequently, of heaving over the side of the shallop.

WEDNESDAY, OCTOBER 7, 1751—AFTERNOON— ROAD TOWARD NUREMBERG

On the road south of Bamberg heading toward Nuremberg, Wolfgang stopped every traveler that he met. No one had any information about a man on a horse that might fit the description of Hempleman. However, he was beginning to fit the puzzle together.

If I were a man in love and on the move, I certainly would not leave without the woman. So Hempleman must be traveling with the girl. Maybe that was the reason for the horse without a rider. He could have been on his way to get her. Or maybe he already had the girl. Maybe the rider that I am following is Garvey and the map I found was a ruse. Undoubtedly, Hempleman is headed north, not south!

Wolfgang tightened the lower reins abruptly. *Donnerschlag's* head dropped as the horse came to an unexpected stop. Wolfgang tightened the left rein and pressed his right knee against the horse until *Donnerschlag* faced north. The horse whinnied in agony yet obeyed the commands. Wolfgang sunk his spurs deeply into the horse's tortured flesh, forcing the animal into a full gallop.

WEDNESDAY, OCTOBER 7, 1751—EARLY EVENING—FULDA RIVER

Margarette grew accustomed to the cold chill and the wet clothing that tightened around her. The rain stopped and the dreary grey of day turned to darkening eventide. George was now manning the sail while Brother Andrew stayed with the scull.

Hour after hour, the dinghy crept northward. Left unsaid was the futility of stopping for the night. The bonus factor for continuing into the night was that the customs offices were closed.

Wolves and wild dogs howled in the darkness. Growls emanated from land-preying animals. Occasional screeches drowned out quieter sounds of the night. The noises blended into a macabre cacophony soaring, leaping, spinning on the threads of night. All the while, the ripples on the river gained force and attacked the sides of the shallop. The cold fierce wind never ceased its assault.

Numb and shivering, Margarette succumbed to sleep—or shock.

Brother Andrew persisted in muffling his coughs and sneezes.

WEDNESDAY, OCTOBER 7, 1751—DEAD OF NIGHT—OUTSKIRTS OF FORCHHEIM

So I've been foiled by the young nobleman and his friend. Well, the final story is not written.

Forchheim lay directly ahead. Wolfgang decided to stay the night in the inn. *Hay will not cost so much here as in Bamberg. Spies. That is what I need. I will ride back to Fulda and ask around to find who the local informants are. Word gets around. I just need to locate the right people.*

Chapter 22

THURSDAY, OCTOBER 9, 1751—EARLY
MORNING—APPROACHING CORVEY

At the confluence of the Weser and Nethe rivers, Brother Andrew said to George, "Port at the next inlet, George. We are almost there." The good cleric then suppressed another deep guttural cough.

The men began to see glimpses of trees swaying in the wind and thousands of leaves abandoning their branches. "It is snowing leaves," George remarked to himself. He had never seen such a gentle bombardment. On the left he sighted a manor with a timber-framed house surrounded by barns, cottages, and grazing animals. Rejoicing birds declared a new day.

"Wake up, Sleeping Beauty." George attempted to sound cheerful as he saw Margarette's curled form at the bow.

No response.

"Wake up, sleepyhead," he said more loudly.

Again, there was no response.

"Brother Andrew," George was close to shouting. "There is something wrong with Margarette! She is not waking up! We have to get her ashore immediately!"

"Corvey Abbey is right ahead," Brother Andrew deterred George's urge to stop at once. Stifling a sneeze and bent over in sheer exhaustion, the monk mustered a calm reserve and assured George, "Soon she will have the best of care."

"If she is alive," George answered. "Oh, God," he pleaded, "please keep Margarette alive. *Please keep her alive!*"

THURSDAY, OCTOBER 9, 1751—EARLY MORNING—FORCHHEIM

Rising early, Wolfgang ate a quick and light breakfast. Then he located the stable.

"I washed the bleeding off your horse last night and poured some ointment over the cuts," the stableman informed Wolfgang. "He's a beauty of a horse. You must be in quite a hurry to be spurrin' him like that."

"I have a job to do, and I aim to do it," Wolfgang defended. In defiance, he mounted *Donnerschlag,* sunk his spurs into the horse's flanks, and galloped toward Fulda.

When he was well out of sight of the stable hand, Wolfgang reined in his mount. Realizing that *Donnerschlag* could no longer withstand a prolonged canter, the deputy alternated between walking and trotting the horse. If he kept the horse watered and fed him well tonight at Fulda, Wolfgang reasoned, *Donnerschlag* should be able to last until Cassel. The mountainous terrain was wearing on both man and equine.

THURSDAY, OCTOBER 9, 1751—EARLY MORNING—MUNDEN

Over one thousand recruits searched public buildings and questioned private citizens, knocking on the doors of nobility and commoner alike. The deputy who had suspected that George Hempleman sat in the shallop at the Munden customs office began to have doubts again. For two days, Frederick Birkham had mulled the situation over in his mind.

He called to his apprentice, who was fashioning a hat with a plume for a nobleman in the vicinity, "Alex, I will be gone for a few days. I am trusting you to run the haberdashery honestly. I will have *Frau* Birkham check on you. She will close the shop at the end of the day. Understood?"

Alex acknowledged his orders.

Birkham went to the back of the shop, mounted the stairs, and called, "Sophia! I am going to make us rich. Hopefully, I will be back in a few days."

"What are you talking about, Frederick?"

"Remember that boat I told you about a couple of days ago?"

"Faintly."

"I think the man at the stern was George Hempleman!"

"Oh, Frederick, if it is, we will be rich! I will pack you a bag of food. This is so exciting! Fill up your canteen. But do be careful."

Birkham took the bag of food, kissed his wife on her cheek, and scrambled down the steps.

THURSDAY, OCTOBER 9, 1751—EARLY MORNING—CORVEY

Brother Andrew, coughing in deep, hoarse spasms, led the way to the abbey. George insisted on being the one to carry Margarette, who hung limply in his arms. As George studied Brother Andrew, he surmised that the monk was probably in his late thirties. Perhaps that accounted for the cleric catching a cold so quickly, an infection George did not want Margarette to contract. George reasoned, *Brother Andrew has been a good man. To think that we were in a vicious struggle the first morning I arrived at the abbey, and he has shown no indication of personal vengeance. He is more than stellar in character. Had it not been for him, Margarette and I would not have made it this far. God surely must have something special for all of us, that is, if Margarette ...* George looked at the fragile bundle he cradled in his arms.

Margarette breathed small gasps. Her face was flushed. Here

was a woman who needed to be protected, and he had done one poor job of doing just that.

Brother Andrew rang the bell at the side of the abbey gate. A voice called out, "Who is it?"

Brother Andrew responded, "It is Brother Andrew from Fulda, Brother Anthony, and I have a sick woman with me."

Immediately the gate opened. Surveying the three who stood before him, Brother Anthony ushered them through the gateway. "I will send someone to notify Mother Catherine at once." He called for a brother, whispered in his ear, and the monk left the premises. Brother Anthony continued, "Let us put the girl in the travelers' house. I have asked for an infirmaress to come with Mother Catherine." Walking through the colonnaded cloister, George wondered how long he and Margarette would be confined to this abbey. Since someone in Munden had been searching the boats coming through customs, and he judged that *he* was the focus of the search, it would not be wise to be on the continent any longer than absolutely necessary. *Dear Lord,* he thought, *let Margarette and Brother Andrew recover quickly. Keep all three of us safe.*

The travelers' house within the abbey walls had many rooms, each spotlessly clean and furnished with beds and scant furnishings. Brother Anthony walked into a room on the first floor, pulled down the bedding, and motioned for George to place Margarette down. As she touched the bed, her eyelids flickered momentarily. The monk then took off her shoes and removed her hat before covering her with the soft quilted comforter. Margarette yawned and curled into a tiny fetal position.

Father Francis had been watching from his study when the newcomers arrived in the abbey compound. It was his nature to wear a perpetual, genuine smile on his round, shaven face. However, his smile faded when he tracked the travelers down and saw Brother Andrew.

Amidst bouts of coughs, Brother Andrew greeted his friend and gave a brief recapitulation of their journey.

"Enough. Enough," Father Francis declared. "You need care."

He clapped his hands together and a monk entered. "Take Brother Andrew to the monastery infirmary."

Brother Andrew protested. "I will be fine. I just need some rest."

"You shall have your rest, dear brother. Now off with you." A fellow monk linked his arms under those of Brother Andrew and ushered him out of the room.

Meanwhile an elderly nun accompanied by two less officious sisters scurried into the room. The infirmaress touched Margarette's forehead and whispered a command to the second nun who immediately left. Father Francis took Mother Catherine aside and spoke with her briefly. The abbess glanced toward George and said, "She shall have the best of care."

Grasping George's elbow, Father Francis took his new guest to the refectory where he was served warm gruel covered with milk and honey.

"That is it until lunch, young man," Father Francis said. "Your stomach will be growling loudly by then, I can see by the looks of you. Now tell me your story. I have heard bits and pieces from Brother Andrew. Are you the young man who is trying to slip out of a betrothal?"

George did not know how to respond. *Could this priest be trusted? Priest? Ah! Perhaps he would be willing to perform the marriage ceremony. But that would go against Father Benedict's instructions.* George wolfed down the gruel while cautiously telling his story.

He concluded, "Father, I did not intend for this to become so complicated. I am in love with Margarette, and I do not want to live without her. To marry another would be treason to my heart. Thankfully, my parents now agree with me."

"Father Benedict is a wise and good man. I shall try to carry out his wishes. For now, I am thinking that you need warm, dry clothing and a bed." The cleric hesitated before breaking into a broad grin. "Perhaps you could have a warm *das Brotchen* and cider before you sleep. You look mighty thin to me."

THURSDAY, OCTOBER 9, 1751—EARLY MORNING—CASSEL

Even with the astonishing number of spies looking for Charlotte Sturzhelm's betrothed, results were nil.

Consulting with Maxwell Braun about the sighting of George Hempleman four days ago, Lord Sturzhelm concluded, "We do not need more spies. Stop the recruiting. It is nearly bankrupting me. The Togo venture had better be lucrative, with or without George, because I will need the additional income."

"What do you suggest?" *Herr* Braun asked.

"We need a man who will put his life on the line to capture George Hempleman."

"Who you are looking for sounds like Wolfgang Gunther, but he is wanted for desertion."

"That can be reversed," Lord Sturzhelm said. "Gunther went trailing off down south someplace, correct?"

"Correct, Lord Sturzhelm. Fulda to be exact. It has been nearly a week since anyone has heard from him. He left with Lieutenant Garvey on Friday, the third of October, to be exact."

"Send a couple scouts to spread the word. Military scouts, not any green recruits. Find Gunther and bring him back!"

"*Ja, der gnadige Herr.* Will that be all?" Braun felt a special affinity with Wolfgang Gunther, kindred souls that they were.

"Just bring him back!" Lord Sturzhelm commanded.

THURSDAY, OCTOBER 9, 1751—LATE AFTERNOON—CORVEY

When Margarette awoke, she thought that the last five days had been a dream. Beside her bed sat a nun embroidering. *I am back in the abbey outside of Fulda!*

"Oh, I see that you have awakened," said the sister. "I will inform Mother Catherine."

The nun put her embroidery on the chair where she had been seated and left the room.

Margarette looked around. *No, I am not in Fulda. Now I remember. Brother Andrew was taking us to Corvey. We have apparently arrived. But where is George? Where is Brother Andrew? And where is my male disguise?* Actually, she never wanted to see the disguise again, and the soft, clean cotton gown she wore felt like the attire that queens wear.

Mother Catherine rushed, if an abbess ever rushes, to speak to the new arrival. When she walked into the room, she found Margarette sitting on the side of her bed with blankets wrapped around her.

"I see you are strong enough to sit, dear. I have sent for warm broth and milk for you. How are you feeling?"

"Rather confused. What happened to me?" Margarette asked.

"You were faint when you arrived at the abbey. The weather had taken a toll on you. Brother Andrew is also down with a fever. Let me touch your forehead, dear." The nun reached toward Margarette. "Just as I thought. Your brow feels normal. You are a resilient woman to recover so quickly. Youth itself is a medicine." Mother Catherine smiled.

The nun who had earlier been seated beside Margarette entered the room carrying a tray. She pulled a small nightstand close to Margarette, set down the tray, and left.

Margarette looked longingly at the broth and milk.

"*Bitte,*" Mother Catherine encouraged.

The broth tasted like a succulent pot roast. The warm milk tasted like the richest cream that Margarette had ever tasted. Too soon, both were gone.

"Even the most humble meal becomes a margrave's feast after a fast," Mother Catherine commented with a smile.

Margarette nodded. *Had she eaten too quickly? Were her manners inappropriate?*

The two sat silently for a moment before Margarette asked, "George? Is George all right?"

"He is sleeping in another room of the travelers' house. He is the only one of you who came here in fairly good condition. You three have been through quite an ordeal and have traversed many miles."

"We have many more miles to go," Margarette said wearily.

"Just as I understand, dear. As soon as Brother Andrew is well, you three may finish your journey." Mother Catherine stood. "Now, do you feel well enough to join us in the dining hall for dinner? It will be served shortly."

"Actually, I can hardly wait."

The abbess extended her hand. "My name is Mother Catherine. You will be seeing me again. I will have Sister Esther bring you some appropriate clothing from our storage area. She will be your guide to the convent refectory, which is not far from here. She will also be your chaperone while you are in Corvey."

THURSDAY, OCTOBER 9, 1751—NEAR MIDNIGHT—NEAR FULDA

Wolfgang allowed *Donnerschlag* to have periodic drinks of water along the way to Fulda. The good treatment that his standardbred had received in Bamberg proved beneficial to both the horse and the rider.

Before midnight, Wolfgang arrived at his destination.

Chapter 23

George awakened with a start. Brother Anthony stood over him. "Get dressed and come with me. Brother Andrew has taken a turn for the worse."

George grabbed his clothing and in his haste put his trousers on backwards. "I will turn my trousers around later," he muttered to himself as he stuffed his feet into shoes and began following Brother Anthony while slipping his shirt over his head.

When the two entered the small infirmary, George halted. Father Francis and four monks stood around the bed on which the body of Brother Andrew twitched and jerked with tremors. Suddenly the body relaxed. One of the monks took the wrist of Brother Andrew and held it for some time. The monk looked at Father Francis and shook his head.

"He has left us for a better place."

Father Francis nodded in affirmation. "Prepare the body," he directed and turned to leave.

On his way out, Father Francis took the elbows of both George and Brother Anthony and said, "Come with me." He led them to his study.

After the three were seated, the cleric said, "I have been awake most of the night, weighing every consideration. I do not want to violate Father Benedict's instructions, so I think that I may have a solution."

"A solution to what?" Brother Anthony asked.

"To the plight of George Hempleman and Margarette Duffy." He leaned back in his chair and folded his hands over his rather ample mid-section. "Abraham Cohen is expected any day. He is a God-fearing man of the Jewish faith. I have known Abraham for years and I trust him. George, I am considering turning your journey to the coast over to *Herr* Cohen. He is a wine merchant from the Rhine and knows the territory well."

"So at the coast, Margarette and I will be on our own?" George asked.

"Probably not," Father Francis replied. "Both *Herr* Cohen and I have associates in Wesel. We will confer and come up with a solution. In the meantime, you and Margarette need to plan for colder temperatures. Of course, if the authorities come searching for you, I shall have to turn you over. That is my responsibility."

George said nothing in response.

FRIDAY, OCTOBER 10, 1751—EARLY MORNING—FULDA

Wolfgang awoke as sunlight fell upon his face. He turned over in the straw, lifted his weary body, and surveyed fellow travelers still sleeping on the floor of the Fulda Inn. Being careful not to step on any bodies, Wolfgang walked over to where the innkeeper was sitting behind the bar sipping from a mug.

"What's for breakfast?" he asked.

"Sausage, eggs, *das Brotchen*, and hot *der Kaffee*," the innkeeper said before taking another drink from his mug.

"Any chance that I might be able to order a hot *der Kaffee* right now?"

The innkeeper called quietly over his shoulder and in a short time, Wolfgang also nursed a morning awakener.

Sipping the steaming brew, Wolfgang asked, "So what news is there in Fulda?"

Eyeing the deputy with caution, the innkeeper said, "Who wants to know?"

"Lord Harry Sturzhelm in Cassel," Wolfgang replied.

"Ah! I have no details about a recent scandal, but I can lead you to a couple who does have details that will curl your hair."

"Who might they be?"

"Albert and Hilda Smythe. They live west of Fulda on a large farm. Nicest acreage around. You can't miss it."

Wolfgang laid a rix-dollar on the counter and turned to leave.

"Hey, where are you going?" the innkeeper asked. "I thought you wanted breakfast."

FRIDAY, OCTOBER 10, 1751—MIDMORNING—CORVEY

Sister Esther led Margarette into a storage room of the convent where Margarette did some shopping. After locating heavy winter cloaks for George and her, Margarette spotted two must-haves: tightly woven canvas for a tarpaulin and skeins of yarn.

"I could make gloves for both George and me." She looked hesitantly at Sister Esther. "If you do not mind and if you have plenty of yarn to spare, I might also make some sweaters."

Sister Esther removed several skeins from the shelf. "Will that be enough?"

"I am sure it will. Thank you ever so much. Of course, I also need needles."

Peering into a box off to the side, Sister Esther selected two knitting needles.

"Perfect! I will begin gloves for George today." Then Margarette pulled out her money pouch. "I have money to pay for these items."

"We do not charge here," Sister Esther said. "However, if you wish to make a contribution for future travelers, you may."

The tolls had dipped deeply into her dowry, but this did not prevent Margarette from donating her remaining few scant coins. She knew the money was well spent.

FRIDAY, OCTOBER 10, 1751—MIDMORNING—FULDA

The innkeeper was correct in saying that the home of the Smythes could be easily spotted. Wolfgang rode down the long lane to a cottage surrounded by fields, barns, cows, pigs, chickens, geese, and dogs. Albert Smythe heard the approaching hooves and stepped out of the barn leading a horse that was bridled and saddled.

"Albert Smythe?" Wolfgang called.

"You're speakin' to 'im," Smythe replied as Hilda Smythe stepped out of the cottage wiping her hands on a well-worn apron.

"The innkeeper said that you folks are the official gatherers of Fulda news."

"We have our sources," Smythe replied.

"I am in need of some information that is not carried in *die Zeitung*," Wolfgang said.

"For a price," Hilda Smythe said.

Wolfgang handed two rix-dollars to Smythe. "Lord Harry Sturzhelm in Cassel wants to know the whereabouts of George Hempleman who was in an abbey outside of Fulda last Saturday night."

"I know all about that," Smythe said. "*Ein bauer*, who is a solid source, told me about a couple of monks who were attacked in the abbey, probably by this Hempleman you're lookin' for. But Hempleman's gone. Brother Andrew's gone too. So is a nun. A deputy from Hessen-Cassel showed up lookin' for someone. Was that you?"

Wolfgang nodded.

"Anything else?" Wolfgang asked.

"Oh, *ja!* The boat behind the abbey is gone too. No one has seen it since. My guess is that all of the missing people took that boat and headed north. As you probably know, the Fulda flows north."

Hilda Smythe added, "Seems to me that all this nonsense began right after we were riding in a coach with a man with a Scottish accent. He had his daughter and son with him too."

Now this was new information. "When might that have been?" Wolfgang asked.

"About two and a half weeks ago," Hilda said. "Some people are nothing but trouble. The young girl looked very sad but was as closed-mouthed as you'll ever find. Not a peep from any of that family."

"There was a young lieutenant in the coach with us too," Albert interposed. "Is he mixed up in this too?"

Wolfgang raised a single eyebrow. "He stirred some of the toxic brew."

"Right under our eyes!" Hilda exclaimed. "Right under our eyes!"

"Anything else?" Wolfgang asked.

"Not that I've heard." Smythe said. "How about you, Hilda?"

Hilda shook her head.

Wolfgang gave the Smythes his last rix-dollar and headed for Cassel.

FRIDAY, OCTOBER 10, 1751—AFTERNOON—CORVEY

By midday, the body of Brother Andrew lay in the monastery chapel. George sat in the front pew and stared at the lifeless form. His former protector had become his friend, a man who had literally given his life for him and Margarette.

Dinner came and went. George declined Father Francis' invitation to join the brotherhood for the repast. He just sat and stared at the body, wondering about the journey Reverend Willis in Cassel had often spoken of, the journey from earth to a place filled with incredible peace, indescribable beauty, and complete answers for those who believed the Lord. Did Brother Andrew have access to all of that? If so, why did George himself fight so hard to stay on this side of eternity? Why did Margarette seem worth living for when the exchange was so unevenly balanced toward heaven?

Monks filed into the chapel for vespers. Just before the setting of the sun, George heard the entrance bell to the abbey ringing above the tenor, baritone, and bass harmony. A hurried step sounded across the stones of the monastery entrance enclave. Male voices resonated. The gate screeched open. Two sets of footsteps scudded over the courtyard pavement.

Abraham Cohen, his cart loaded with barrels of fine wine from the Rhineland, had arrived at Corvey Abbey immediately before the Jewish Sabbath had begun.

Chapter 24

SATURDAY, OCTOBER 11, 1751—SHORTLY BEFORE DAWN—CORVEY

Frederick Birkham banged his fists on the wooden gate of Corvey Abbey and yelled, "Open up in there. I am here on official business."

With his feet clad only in woolen stockings, Brother Anthony raced to end the disturbance while binding his woolen cloak snugly around him. With quiet aplomb, he ushered the haberdasher into the study of Father Francis, who stood sleepy-eyed behind his desk.

"Who might you be?" the cleric inquired.

"I am *Herr* Frederick Birkham from Hannoversch Munden, and I am seeking George Hempleman who evaded our customs officers on the Weser. The shallop he was sailing in is docked by the pier of your abbey. I insist that you turn him over to me so that I may take him to Hessen-Cassel."

"Your papers, *Herr* Birkham," Father Francis said as he extended his hand.

"I do not need any papers. I have been deputized," Birkham argued.

Father Francis continued standing. "I am sorry, *Herr* Birkham. If you have no official papers, I cannot do anything to assist you. Brother Anthony, lead this man out of the abbey compound."

As Brother Anthony firmly gripped Birkham's arm, Birkham sputtered, "You will live to regret this! That man is wanted by Lord Harry Sturzhelm himself! I will have this abbey shut down, I will."

SATURDAY, OCTOBER 11, 1751—EARLY MORNING—CORVEY

George did not abandon his vigilance when the brotherhood arrived for matins. A monk whom George had not seen before read in a rich baritone from what George understood was James 4:13–16. George recognized some of the Latin words, but not many. What he could piece together was that the officiating monk illustrated the passage with the story of Jonah. George remembered from Reverend Willis' sermons that Jonah had fully intended to go to Tarshish. Jonah had fully expected God to destroy the people of Ninevah. Jonah had anticipated eating the succulent gourd. However, each time God had surprised Jonah.

As the Latin words delivered their esoteric message to those who understood, George fell into introspection. He wondered if he were a Jonah. Was God about to surprise him? His mind kept returning to what the apostle James had written. Our lives are but a vapor. *A vapor! Here I am, nineteen years old. God calls Himself the Ancient of Days. How long shall I live? How long will Margarette live? Are we like Jonah, evading God's plan for our lives? Or are our lives together God's destiny for us? We have certainly been aided by well-meaning people. My parents have given us their blessing. Brother Andrew gave his life for us. Imagine! His life on this earth is called a vapor. Our lives are only a vapor! From now on I shall try to say "as the Lord wills." I know there is another scripture that tells us "to seek." So I will seek. I will push forward "as the Lord wills."* George planned to talk to Margarette about this. Perhaps they would agree on these principles. Perhaps their destinies lay elsewhere, beyond Hessen-Cassel.

The monks filed past the coffin on their way to the refectory. They seemed serene about the dying process. Father Francis was the last in the line of the brotherhood. He lingered at the casket, then turned to George. "Will you join me for breakfast?"

George shook his head. The archimandrite left.

Stillness prevailed until George heard a man clear his throat in the rear of the chapel. Then heavy footsteps approached the chancel. Glancing behind him, George saw a huge bearded stranger advancing. All thoughts of George's friendship with Brother Andrew left. He ran toward the door that Father Francis had left ajar. But George was not quick enough!

SATURDAY, OCTOBER 11, 1751—EARLY MORNING—CORVEY

After a hearty breakfast in the convent refectory, Margarette returned to her room in the travelers' house adjacent to the nunnery. She could barely keep from skipping and twirling about as she thought of the future that she and George would soon share. Grandmother would have white satin to make her a beautiful wedding gown. Her aunts, uncles, and cousins would celebrate the marriage with a lavish shower of gifts. Uncle Theodore would surely employ George and help him build a small stone cottage for the two of them on his acreage.

Margarette spiraled about before picking up the half-finished glove attached to a dwindling skein of yarn. She had studied the size of George's hands while he was rowing. Margarette pictured George putting on the gloves and exclaiming that they fit him perfectly.

"Now to work!" she said softly as her fingers, needle, and yarn flew in rapid circuits while the contour of fingers appeared one after the other on the grey glove. "This is my life," she sighed. "I am made to be a helpmate. The role fits me like this glove will fit George's strong hand."

SATURDAY, OCTOBER 11, 1751—EARLY
MORNING—CORVEY

A decisive grip closed over George's left forearm. Slashing his right arm toward the tightening fist, George felt his adversary catch his right arm in a similar hold and spin him around.

"Going someplace, George?" The rock-hard man with a full black beard grinned at him. George looked into the man's eyes. They were friendly. "How about you and me going to eat some of the breakfast that I smell in the air? It could do no harm to either of us." The man's eyes bore into George. "What do you say?"

"Do I have a choice?"

"What do you think?"

"I do not think I have one without a fight."

"You are right about that. So to the dining hall we go."

"To the dining hall we go," George agreed.

The man loosened his grip on George's right arm. The left arm he held even tighter.

Father Francis rose to greet the two as they entered the hall. "I see you have met *Herr* Abraham Cohen. He is quite a persuasive person, I see."

The two men positioned George between them as servers arrived with hot *der Kaffee*, eggs, sausage, warm *das Brotchen* filled with butter, and apple juice mixed with lime. The aroma was too enticing for George to refuse.

After the men had eaten their fill, Abraham Cohen invited George to take a walk outside the abbey grounds. The trees surrounding the abbey filled the morning with a startling array of orange, red, yellow, and scarlet. The leaves that had already surrendered offered a plush carpet of loose pile that tracked each step with a crunching, crackling, cavorting of color and sound.

Abraham sighed, "I have me a wife as lovely as Rachel in the Torah. She makes my heart sing. The first time I saw her I knew that she would be mine. Is that the way it was with you and Margarette?"

George did not answer.

"Oh, I am getting too familiar with you too quickly, I see. I think I understand. You have not been able to trust many people with this heart of yours, and you do not know if I am friend or foe. I could tell you that I will do you no harm, but words are sometimes hollow sounds when you prefer solid evidence. So I will tell you about myself, and perhaps you will believe me and perhaps you will not. If you do not, I suppose you will soon be caught and returned to Lord Sturzhelm. Of course, if you think that I am in Lord Sturzhelm's employ, then you might launch out on your own, use your own wit to evade the massive search that is intended to take you back to the arms of Lord Sturzhelm's daughter. So I will do my best to convince you that I am a friend.

"First, you have been told that Father Francis trusts me and has known me these many years. I am nearly thirty years old and have been delivering wine to Corvey Abbey since I was a newlywed at eighteen. So that makes Father Francis my friend for nearly twelve years. Twelve is a special number for Jews, being that our patriarch Jacob had twelve sons. So twelve is a good number.

"Now my wife Tamar and I are working toward the twelve mark. I myself thought the twelve must all be males, but Tamar says that the girls are to be counted in the twelve, so we are halfway to our goal if we go by Tamar's reckoning. Do you like children?"

George said that he did.

"Me too," confirmed Abraham. "When I look into the starry skies and consider what the Lord God said to the first Abraham, I lose my balance. Think of it. Abraham's seed being too numerous to count! We have a long way to go. Of course, you who are not Abraham's seed like to cut us down to size with inquisitions every few hundred years. But we Jews just keep sprouting back up, like the book of Ezekiel says.

"Well, enough of Tamar and me for now. What about you and Margarette? Is your love so strong that it will stand under intense pressure?"

Abraham paused and waited for George to reply.

Contemplating his response, George kicked mound after

mound of leaves away from his path. Eventually, George said, "Our love has been tested these last few weeks. We have nearly starved. Margarette survived a blow on the head at a customs stop. I rowed the shallop in complete darkness and intense cold without wavering, even though we both looked like wet rabbits and smelled like them too. Still when I look at Margarette, I see the one I cannot live without. I have never felt like this about any other woman. When I look toward my future, all I see is Margarette. Without her, any vision of the future goes dark."

"You are smitten, young man. You are smitten!" Abraham gave George a powerful clip on his shoulder. "I felt the same about my Tamar even though we do not always see eye-to-eye on all things." Abraham let out a mighty roar of laughter. "Are you ready for a squabble, George? You will have your share, I can assure you."

"I have already been severely scolded by Margarette when I left one night to check on my ailing father without telling her."

"So she taught you lesson number one, right? Never leave her in the dark! Women like to know what their men are doing. It drives them to distraction when they do not know where we are or what we are doing. I learned that lesson quickly too! Oh, that Tamar!" Abraham roared again.

The two strolled side by side, each thinking of the wonder of a woman. After several minutes, Abraham cleared his throat.

"Shall we get down to tactics, George? Father Francis has told me that he would like me to supervise you and Margarette until I can locate a replacement in Wesel, which is where I live, but you and Margarette must continue on toward Rotterdam. I think the idea of Margarette resuming her disguise as a young mute male is a good idea." Abraham poked George in the ribs. "That will work well for both of us, being that we men do not like too much input that we consider off course, right?"

George agreed.

"Okay, then. I just delivered five large barrels of wine to the abbey. We will use the cart and horse until we come to Lippe River. Being as today is the Sabbath for me, I dare not begin our journey until sundown. But travel at night can be slow and dangerous, so I am thinking that we could begin late Sunday morning after your church meeting," Abraham reasoned.

"I am not Roman Catholic, *Herr* Cohen. I am Calvinist," George corrected.

Abraham shook some more leaves off the trees with his burst of laughter. "We shall be an ecumenical trio. A Jew, a Protestant, and a Roman Catholic all in one wooden cart making our way peacefully through *Teutoburger Wald*. May God smile on our travels as we live the reconciliation."

SATURDAY, OCTOBER 11, 1751—MORNING—CORVEY

Frederick Birkham's patience was rewarded. He had waited outside Corvey Abbey after his ouster. Staying behind the cover of tree after tree, he crept within hearing distance as George Hempleman conversed with the large Jewish man. Birkham heard enough to plan his next move. He calculated that he had enough time to return to Munden to check with his wife, travel on to Cassel to get an official arrest warrant, and catch up with Hempleman and his companions on the Lippe River—with an official arrest warrant.

Chapter 25

SUNDAY, OCTOBER 12, 1751—EARLY MORNING—CORVEY

George did not hear much of what was said during the Sunday sermon. Seated near the front of the large sanctuary on the left side where all the brotherhood sat, he half turned in his pew to catch sight of Margarette, who sat toward the back on the right side where all the sisters of the nearby convent worshiped.

Margarette did not hear much of the sermon either, but she did know it was about the purity of Joseph's life. However, she delighted in knowing that her beloved sat in a rather awkward position for the express purpose of catching glimpses of her.

Abraham Cohen occupied a chair at the back of the sanctuary. He listened to every word of the text and sermon, knowing that Christianity was an outgrowth of his own religion. Realizing this nearly gave him an air of superiority, but he checked and subdued that attitude quickly. He and his people were not in a friendly land.

After the last hymn, the brotherhood returned to the monastery and the sisters to their nunnery. However, Mother Catherine held on to Margarette's arm while Father Benedict stood beside George and Abraham. The cart was loaded. Margarette, in her male disguise, positioned the broad-brimmed hat on her head. Just then, a gust of autumn wind swept the disc into the air, disheveling her blonde hair that caught rays of light red sunlight. George felt a tinge of resentment with everyone's presence except Margarette's. Margarette looked more than beautiful.

Mother Catherine caught the interchange, stooped to the ground, and picked up a handful of dirt. Smiling, she turned to Margarette, "You are too lovely, my dear. Allow me." She spat into the granules, dipped her forefinger into the mixture, and spread the mud onto Margarette's face. Then she ran her fingers through the girl's locks with her dirty hands, tied Margarette's hair back into a queue, and anchored the manly hat in such a way as to prevent wayward glimpses.

"Now I think you are ready to go." She took both of Margarette's shoulders, looked deeply into her blue eyes, and said, "Stay pure. You will never regret purity."

Father Francis took George's hand firmly into his own. "You, too, young man!"

"I will see to it," Abraham said.

The men seated themselves on the hard flat-board of the cart while *Marc* rode in the back with the food and luggage.

SUNDAY, OCTOBER 12, 1751—AFTERNOON—HESSEN-CASSEL

When Wolfgang saw the skyline of Cassel just miles away, he realized that he had arrived in time to enter the city before the gates were locked. Many horsemen, pedestrians, and carts passed him going toward the city. Others passed him leaving the capital, rushing toward home before nightfall. *Donnerschlag's* gait was so slow that Wolfgang could have outwalked him, but Wolfgang would not stoop to such condescension.

At the moat Gunther was recognized. An upstart in the military drew his pistol. "You there!"

Wolfgang commanded, "Sonny, put that thing away. You're going to hurt us both."

"I know what I'm doing, you deserter. I'm taking you to the barracks. Now get down from your horse!" He hollered toward the open gate, "Loren, I could use some help!"

Another young man came running across the series of culverts. "You have Wolfgang Gunther, Lawrence!" As Loren tried to bind Wolfgang's hands behind his back, Wolfgang hooked his leg behind the enlisted man and set him sprawling on the stone pavement. Lawrence shot his pistol and nicked Wolfgang's left arm. Wolfgang dove for Lawrence, wrestling the pistol from him. However, Loren was once again on his feet. With steady aim, he brought his pistol down on the back of Wolfgang's head, knocking him senseless.

Loren and Lawrence bound Wolfgang's hands behind his back. "You got a couple kerchiefs on you, Lawrence?" Loren asked.

"What for?"

"Gunther's head and arm are bleeding. I don't want him to die on us."

"He's not gonna die on us. You know his reputation. If there hadn't been two of us here, we could never have brought him down. And, no, I don't have kerchiefs on me. Now let's get goin'."

Lawrence and Loren threw Wolfgang over *Donnerschlag's* mid-section. The two sentries decided that Lawrence should stay on guard at the city gate while Loren led the horse to the army barracks. Colonel Giesler had left for the evening, so the officer in charge locked Wolfgang Gunther in a solitary cell without food, water, or bandages.

Donnerschlag was given a rub down and a hefty drink of fresh water followed by oats mixed with timothy hay.

SUNDAY, OCTOBER 12, 1751—AFTERNOON— TEUTOBURGER WALD

Abraham Cohen was full of stories. So, too, were George and Margarette as the cart progressed westward from Corvey to the Lippe River through the forested, rolling hills of *Teutoburger Wald.*

As Abraham guided *Treue*, the faithful Belgian horse, with expert rein commands, he asked, "Did you know that it was in this region that Arminius, alias Hermann, defeated three legions of well-equipped, well-trained Roman soldiers?"

"That was long ago. Was it not in the Year of our Lord 10 that Hermann defeated Varus?" George questioned.

"You are off a year. It was a.d. 9 according to your Gregorian calendar. Now with our Jewish calendar—"

George cut him short. "Please do not confuse me with two dates. I prefer to live in history, not remember it."

"The Roman general's full name was Publius Quintilius Varus," Margarette volunteered.

"George, are you willing to marry an educated woman?" Abraham laughed loudly before stifling his outburst.

"I would not want a wife any other way except educated," George looked back at Margarette, giving her a quick wink.

"Yes, it was Hermann who set the boundary of the Roman Empire west of the Rhine River. What shame Varus experienced with that defeat! He ended his own life!" Abraham spoke with such passion that it seemed that the battle had just been lost that day.

"But the Romans needed a good bruising!" George insisted. "I am not in agreement with any man taking his own life. That is pagan! But I am in favor of a man defending his own land. I think it would be fitting that a tribute to Hermann be erected. He was a great Cheruscan."

"Well said!" Abraham conceded.

The sturdy Belgian trudged steadily up the gradual incline, which never seemed to end.

"Are we going to reach the summit of Heaven on this trail?" Margarette asked.

"I thought the same when I first made this overland journey twelve years ago," Abraham said. "By dusk we should reach our highest elevation. We will make camp and touch the stars. How does that sound?"

"Very romantic," George said.

"I will rephrase that," Abraham countered. "We will set up camp and hope that the wild animals do not encroach too closely."

"I am sleeping in the cart," Margarette said.

"George and I will be sleeping right beneath the cart on that tarpaulin you have brought with you," Abraham added.

As the wind tore down the colorful leaves and allowed the sun to penetrate the diminishing deep growth of the *Wald*, Margarette looked for a blanket to ward off the chill. Picking up the woolen wrap, she spotted George's saddlebag, and she thought of the sacrifice George had made in giving up his horse.

"George," she began, "when we get to Scotland, I will ask my family to give us a wedding present of a thoroughbred. I know it was hard for you to give up *Beleuchtung*."

"I will work for a horse, Margarette. I will not accept charity."

Abraham observed, "Now there's a proud man, Margarette. Can you live with a proud man?"

"Is that pride or is that integrity?" Margarette said. "Had you said *stubborn* in your observation, *Herr* Cohen, I could not agree with you more."

George whipped his head around only to see Margarette twitching her nose with a twinkle in her eyes.

"Woman, you are a challenge! We could head north and see if you might be a witch."

"My father told me about the witch hunts in Lemgo during the last century. I think I prefer to stay on our current course."

"Thank the good Lord for our Age of Enlightenment!" Abraham bellowed. "But Lemgo also has a noble history. Bernhard II von Lippe founded the town in the late twelfth century. Having membership in the Hanseatic League helped this entire area economically."

"Until the Thirty Years War brought devastation to the entire European continent!" George observed. "Why can we not live together in peace?"

"Jews have been wondering about that for a long while," Abraham sighed.

"Well, we cannot do anything about wars and feuding. My father brought us to Hessen to avoid conflict, and see what that proved," Margarette joined Abraham in his melancholy.

"I know. We have rumblings to the north and to the east of us. Prussia has been flexing its muscle since Frederick II became ruler. But enough of this," George concluded. "It is time to tell some fairy tales!"

Thus, until they reached their campsite at dusk, each of the travelers took a turn at telling a story about frogs, soldiers, princesses, giants, tailors, witches, charcoal-burners, magic spells, and living happily ever after.

SUNDAY, OCTOBER 12, 1751—MUNDEN

Frederick Birkham reached Munden late Sunday night. Naturally his shop was locked, as was his second-storey home above the shop. Instead of trying to unlock his entrance door in the dark of night, he stood beneath the bedroom window, lobbing stone after stone against the shutters.

Soon he heard his wife scrambling across the wooden floor. "Who is out there? Is it you, Frederick?"

"I am home and with good news, Sophia. Now let me in."

Chapter 26

MONDAY, OCTOBER 13, 1751—BEFORE DAWN—TEUTOBURGER WALD

Margarette awoke when she felt the first drops of rain on her face. It was still very dark, but she did not know if the darkness was from an overcast sky or the dead of night. She whispered, "It is beginning to rain. Are you two awake?"

She heard rustling as the men abandoned their slumber.

"I am awake," George yawned expansively.

"We will not have a camp fire this morning," Abraham announced as he stamped his feet into his shoes and stretched. "George, get the gear in the cart while I bridle and harness *Treue*. We will eat breakfast on the way."

Margarette folded the bedding that George handed to her. Then George fashioned a very loose canopy over the cart with the tarpaulin. "Do you think you can stay well during this storm, Margarette?"

"This is entirely different," Margarette argued. "I am going to be fine."

Sprinkles gave way to cold rain as the Belgian labored west and the three munched on bread and dried apples. Margarette was well covered by the tarpaulin, but the lashing wind did not spare the men. Abraham pulled out a pair of leather gloves.

"Do you have any gloves, George? I never knew a nobleman who did not have a pair of fine leather gloves."

"Margarette, could you hand me my saddlebag please?" Margarette gave the bag to George.

As George riffled through the bag, he pulled out a leather pouch. "What is this doing in here? I thought I had found a glove." Reaching into the pouch, he pulled out several rix-dollars and a note. But there was something else in the pocket that was cold, flexible, and heavy. "My mother's necklace!" he exclaimed. Grabbing the note George read:

> *My dearest son,*
>
> *I have enclosed some of your inheritance. I pray that it will aid you and Margarette as you begin your lives together. The Bible is for your spiritual growth. Without God's Word, your journey in life is in vain. As a favor—*

Here the rain rushed to wash away the life-giving message of his mother.

> *—your loving mother, please read and study this daily.*

> *The money will help you on your journey, but the neck—*

Again the words dissolved into an obliteration of black puddles.

> *—establish yourself in a home of your own.*
> *I love you forever, my dear son. I trust God—*
> *Mothe—*

George handed the letter to Margarette. "Try to keep this dry. It is a note from my mother. Some of her words have already been smeared by the rain and lost forever."

"May I read your note?" Margarette asked.

George was having trouble keeping back the tears. "*Ja, bitte*," he said.

Margarette did not attempt to hold back her tears. However, she allowed none to fall upon the precious script. She wondered if the necklace George was given was the same one she had been accused of stealing. If so, how had the necklace been recovered? She thought through endless possibilities which only complicated the matter. She concluded, *Some events we must put on the shelf. Some are mysteries we can never solve without duress.*

Margarette came out of her reverie when Abraham asked George, "Are you all right? Where are your gloves, man?"

"I am fine," George answered. "I am better than fine. My mother put a note and some help into my saddlebag. I will be able to pay you for your kindness."

"I am not going out of my way. You are wonderful company. This trip is my gift to you. When we get on the Lippe, however, the owner of the boat as well as the customs officials will be wanting payment. Can you take care of your part of those fees?"

"My mother has seen to both!"

MONDAY, OCTOBER 13, 1751—MORNING—CASSEL

A guard shook Wolfgang Gunther awake. "You have visitors," he announced as he loosened the ropes from Gunther's wrists.

Another guard handed Gunther a basin of water and a towel. "You had better spruce yourself up. Your visitors are Colonel Giesler and Maxwell Braun, the newly appointed constable.

Wolfgang forced himself to stand, doused his head with the water from the basin, and hurriedly rubbed the dirt and blood away. His head throbbed and his body ached, especially the wound on his left arm, but his mind began to clear.

He turned to the two guards. "Good enough?"

"You would not pass inspection, but you look good enough.

Follow me," the first guard said. The second guard followed behind with a musket.

A puzzled Wolfgang entered Colonel Giesler's office.

"I am sorry for all this confusion," Braun said as he led Wolfgang to a seat across from Colonel Giesler who stood until Gunther was seated.

"What happened? I was fulfilling my mission in tracking down Hempleman, came back to Cassel, and the first thing I know I am attacked. The next thing I know is that I am in the barracks in solitary confinement."

"Terrible case of mistaken identity," Giesler lied. "The men thought you were Garvey."

Wolfgang detected Giesler's falsehood. One of the men at the bridge had identified him by both his first and last name. Argument or correction would not work to his advantage, so he opted not to challenge his superior.

Instead, Wolfgang tipped his head back in acknowledgment. "So what is on the agenda now? Do you want my report?"

"Yes, we do. Have you spotted Hempleman?"

"He was within my grasp. Garvey interfered and the gander got away. I tracked him to near Nuremberg before realizing that Garvey had misled me. Heading back to Fulda, I located a couple named Smythe."

"I know that couple," Giesler said. "They have been a wellspring of information in the past."

"They were again. It appears that Hempleman, the girl, and a monk left from an abbey outside of Fulda. They used a shallop to head north."

"That confirms his appearance in Cassel a week ago when Schroeder and Schuster let Hempleman drug both of them," Giesler said.

"So he is on the run to the north, just as I thought," Wolfgang said as he ran his fingers through his hair. "If you could give me a fresh mount and money for expenses, I will have him in your hands in a week."

"Your horse is doing fine. He just needed a bit of pampering. If you would treat that horse of yours right, he would be more than adequate for your job," Braun cautioned. "So what is your plan?"

MONDAY, OCTOBER 13, 1751—MORNING— NEAR LIPPE RIVER MOUTH

The rain did not let up. Abraham Cohen guided a drenched *Treue* onto a path leading up to a farmhouse. A farmer came running out of his cottage to check the condition of his valued Belgian.

"Is he all right, *Herr Bauer*?" Abraham called.

"He seems to be. He doesn't look any worse than the likes of you," Bauer replied cheerily.

"Want to check the cart, too?" Abraham asked.

Bauer walked around the wooden vehicle, kicked the wheels, and shook the cart with his hand. "Good as new!" he pronounced.

"So, will you give us a lift to the river?" Abraham asked.

"I always do. Give me a minute to tell my wife. You sure picked a nasty day to travel."

Abraham laughed, "I did not pick this day. It picked us."

MONDAY, OCTOBER 13, 1751—MORNING—CASSEL

Maxwell Braun secured permission from Lord Sturzhelm to join the search. Braun would carry the purse and be the strategist interacting with the higher stratum in society. Gunther would provide the muscle and move among the disenfranchised. Knowing that he would get three full meals a day, Gunther was satisfied with the arrangement. Realizing that he would not get any blood on his hands, Braun felt his confidence building.

The two men hoisted the last of their provisions on their horses when a servant of Lord Sturzhelm called for the lord's chamberlain.

"I will be right back," Braun told Gunther before adding, "I hope!"

As Braun stepped inside Lord Sturzhelm's office, he saw a tall, slender man with a stylish hat.

"Meet my chamberlain and constable Maxwell Braun, *Herr* Birkham," Lord Sturzhelm said. "Maxwell, this is Frederick Birkham, a hatter from Hannoversch Munden. He is simplifying our task."

Braun studied the *burgher* as Lord Sturzhelm explained Birkham's first contact, his hunch, and his successful search.

"So Hempleman is on the Lippe River by now," Braun said.

"So it would seem," Lord Sturzhelm agreed.

"Are you a traveling man, Birkham?" Braun asked as he took the hatter's hand in a firm handshake.

"I am at your service, *Herr* Braun."

Lord Sturzhelm sat down at his desk, wrote up a warrant for George Hempleman's arrest, and handed the document to Braun who added his signature.

"*Herr* Braun, you, Gunther, and Birkham will be living lavish lifestyles if you bring back the booty."

MONDAY, OCTOBER 13, 1751—MORNING—LIPPE

In the drenching rain at the Lippe dock, Abraham Cohen conferred privately with George and Margarette. Margarette was to resume her role as Marc Lubeck. But this time she was to be a mute *cousin* of George; the physical similarity between them was non-existent. George was to become Franz Lubeck. The two cousins' pretense for being on the river would be their trying to locate a third cousin by the fictitious name of Arnold Hagen. Since Abraham was a regular on the river, his presence remained unquestioned.

Franz and Abraham agreed to talk about nothing except the weather, the history of the region, their pursuit of Arnold—or remain quiet. No personal information would escape their lips.

With the strategy agreed upon, Abraham hailed down a boatman sailing a dinghy. The two negotiated a price, and Franz insisted on paying two-thirds. With their scanty gear stowed, the four began their voyage down the Lippe toward the Rhine.

Boatman Wilbur Kern was well protected with a canvas hood and cloak that shed the driving rain. Abraham and the "Lubeck cousins" formed a tight circle under the tarpaulin to protect themselves. Fortunately, by midmorning the rain stopped, although the wind still beat against the sails, the tarpaulin, and the shivering passengers. Very few protective trees grew along the banks since *Teutoburger Wald* had been left behind.

Kern's curiosity regarding the deafness of Marc egged him to test the validity of the frail cousin's condition. When the sun sneaked out from behind vanishing clouds, Kern let out a series of obscenities that caused both Abraham and Franz to look toward the boatman with apprehension.

"What seems to be the trouble?" Abraham asked.

Marc, never showing any indication of hearing the vulgarities, continued to look forward at the bow or starboard at the scenery on the riverbank.

"Nothin', mate," the boatman replied. "I was just amazed at the sight of the sun. It's been many a day since I saw her light." Then he turned his piercing eyes on Franz. "So where did you and Abraham meet?"

"In the travelers' house at Corvey, *Herr* Kern," George responded.

"Come up from the south?" Kern asked.

"Actually from the northeast where Charlemagne and Widukind fought the battle over Saxony," George replied.

"Charlemagne should have kept his nose out of religious affairs," Kern said rather belligerently.

"Why so?" Abraham asked.

"A man and his nation should be able to choose his way of worshiping without any interference from the sword," Kern said.

"I could not agree more," George said. "Yet Charlemagne did enlighten us to the truth."

"That was supposed to be our job," Abraham remarked with tongue-in-cheek.

Kern remained quiet for a while as Marc, Franz, and Abraham pointed out landmarks, beautiful manors, and an occasional hart along the bank. Marc never responded to a verbal comment, only using gestures and eye contact.

"We will be staying at Lippstadt for the night and not at the Schwarzenraben unless you have royal blood running through your veins," Kern said. "Get your purses ready. The custom officials here have a special fondness for taxing."

MONDAY, OCTOBER 13, 1751—MORNING— OUTSIDE CASSEL

"I have mapped out our course," Braun explained to Gunther and Birkham. "We will go overland directly to Lippstadt, which would be the first stop for anyone going west on the Lippe River. You have already seen their disguises, Birkham. Wolfgang, you know Hempleman from working with his father. This should be an easy arrest. I do not care about the girl. She is expendable. We might even use her as a hostage; it might be easier to capture her to get to Hempleman." Then he added, "Tonight we will stop in Liechtenaw. Tomorrow we will scout for leads in Lippstadt."

MONDAY, OCTOBER 13, 1751—EARLY EVENING—LIPPSTADT

Abraham, Franz, and Marc carried their gear to the Lippstadt Inn. Abraham knew the proprietor who kindly placed their belongings in storage for the night. After a warm dinner of *Karpfen,*

Kartoffelklosse, fresh vegetables, and apple cider, the three selected a corner section of the room to bed down on fresh straw.

All the while the proprietor mulled over in his mind the inconsistency of Abraham having companions on this trek from Corvey. He cornered Kern when he was sure that Abraham and his friends were soundly asleep.

"What do you know of Abraham's companions?"

"Not too much. They are very closed-mouthed. The little cousin, they say, is mute. I am still testing that."

Chapter 27

TUESDAY, OCTOBER 14, 1751—LIPPSTADT

Kern awakened his clients before daybreak. "Looks like a fairly decent day, even though it is a mite chilly," he said. "We need to be boarding and on our way. I would like to take advantage of the fine wind that is blowing out there."

The companions quickly and quietly ate warm slices of *das Brotchen* dipped in hot mugs of *der Kaffee*, gathered their gear, and walked two blocks to the Lippe as the sun peered out of the east.

Franz and Abraham made small talk while Marc took to whittling. Margarette's mother had told her long ago of how the Welsh families gave their daughters a narrow chip of wood when courting to keep their hands occupied. Marc, not wanting to give up her identity, did not carve a spoon as Welsh girls did, but rather a small bookmarker.

All day long Wilbur Kern devised ways to test Marc's inability to hear.

TUESDAY, OCTOBER 14, 1751—LIECHTENAW

Maxwell Braun, another early riser, had Gunther and Birkham fed and on their horses before dawn. With methodic calculation, Braun kept the company on his time schedule as the earth rotated like a sunbather seeking the golden rays before the inevitable dimming of light cooled the air and caused creatures everywhere to look for refuge.

TUESDAY, OCTOBER 14, 1751—HAMM

A beautiful sunset splashed the western horizon as Kern anchored his boat at a pier in Hamm. Abraham, Franz, and Marc again lugged their gear to the nearest riverside inn, ate a warm dinner, and bedded down on the floor of the inn.

WEDNESDAY, OCTOBER 15, 1751—BEFORE DAWN—HAMM

Because of the stress of maintaining a false identity and the constant movement from one unfamiliar place to another, Margarette neared exhaustion. However, this worked to her advantage when Wilbur Kern stood over her before daybreak with metal pan and spoon and beat a clamorous racket beside her head.

George jumped up immediately as if to ward off any danger.

Abraham bellowed, "What do you think you are doing, Kern? Waking the dead?"

Gathering his wits, George nudged Margarette who opened her eyes, then closed them again. He then grabbed her by her arms and pulled her into a seated position. Pointing toward Kern, he hoped she would realize the test taking place.

She did. Nodding, she began brushing the straw away before standing and motioning for a mug of steaming *der Kaffee*. George hoped her feminine movements would be overlooked.

WEDNESDAY, OCTOBER 15, 1751—DAWN—LIPPSTADT

Braun felt the blood pulsating through his body when he awoke from a dream. The dream was too real, yet surreal. He had caught a wild stag and smeared the blood of the kill on his face. Questioning if his motives in tracking George Hempleman bordered on paganism, Braun quickly reassured himself that he was obeying the law, that sometimes doing the right thing required extreme measures. *But am I doing the right thing?* He touched his face. He had a bit of a beard but no blood that he could detect. Staring at his hands, he reassured himself. *Of course I am doing what is right! Many are in agreement with my course of action.* Having convinced himself, having rationalized his actions, he shook Birkham and Gunther awake. The men grabbed a light breakfast and saddled their horses at the dawn of a new day.

By midday they reached Hamm and learned that their quarry was within reach.

WEDNESDAY, OCTOBER 15, 1751—NIGHT—HALTERN

In pitch darkness Kern guided the small dinghy toward the lights of Haltern. If all went well, he could deposit his strange passengers in Wesel tomorrow. On his trip back to the source of the Lippe, he hoped to get people who were company and not just cargo.

Yet their very reticence led him to suspect that they might be very valuable cargo indeed—if only he could prove that suspicion.

After sailing up to the pier, Kern had the help of Abraham and Franz in tying up his boat. Marc slung the backpack on her shoulders and handed the saddlebag, blankets, and tarpaulin to George. It was obvious to Kern that the two cousins trusted no one with their belongings. Abraham grabbed his satchel, and the four walked to the town gate. After Kern gave the gatekeeper a brief explanation, the gate swung open. The inn came into sight.

Although it was too late to have a warm dinner, the travelers munched on cold leftovers of *Weisswurst*, beer pretzels, and cider.

Afterward, all but Kern bedded down on the floor of the inn for the night.

Kern waited until he heard Abraham and Franz snoring. Marc, he had observed, was not a snoring man. But even if Marc were awake, *he* was stone deaf and not a problem.

Kern approached the proprietor of the inn to ask for directions to the office of the constable. "No need for directions!" the innkeeper said. "The constable is sitting right over near the door. His name is Otto Olsberg."

Olsberg was filled with information. He told Kern of a young nobleman in Cassel who had a big reward on his head. Kern looked over at the sleeping, snoring duo that stopped snoring momentarily, shifted positions, and returned to their slumber.

"Let's step outside," Kern said. "I think I have some information for you."

At that moment riders could be heard outside of Haltern's gate. As Kern and Olsberg left the inn, Margarette shook George.

"Yeah?" he said as he lifted himself on one elbow.

"We need to leave. Now. Do not awaken Abraham. We must not involve him."

"What is going on?"

"Shh. The innkeeper is looking this way. He introduced Kern to the town constable. Kern is outside right now giving him details about us," Margarette explained.

"Okay," George agreed. "I will distract the innkeeper. Take the backpack and crawl out that side window. I will follow you and bring the tarpaulin and saddlebag. But do not move until the innkeeper has his back turned. Got it?"

Margarette nodded.

George yawned, got up, and walked to the door where the proprietor was trying to keep track of what was happening in his inn and what was going on by the town gate.

"It is hard to sleep around here," George complained as he blocked the proprietor's view of Margarette as she moved toward the window.

"There is a lot of confusion by the gate. Horsemen yelling about a nobleman being on the loose. What's so new about that? Noblemen are always on the loose, trampling through people's fields, knocking down their fences, causing chaos."

"Well, let me know what you learn. I am going to try to get some sleep."

"Good idea," the innkeeper said. "I will stay here and check on what is happening. I will let you know what I learn in the morning."

Margarette was already outside the window when George picked up the tarpaulin and saddlebag. He too slipped through the window opening just as the gatekeeper allowed Braun, Gunther, and Birkham into the city proper.

"We must get out of town," George whispered. "I recognized Gunther's voice."

"The killer?" Margarette asked.

"The same," George said.

Taking Margarette's hand, George guided her through the shadows toward the opposite side of Haltern. Dogs announced their presence. Owners yelled for the canines to be still. But nothing was still. Soon horses prowled up and down the streets in organized fashion.

George yanked two dresses off a clothesline as well as two linen caps. He left four rix dollars attached to a nail on a nearby post. "Here, put this on, Margarette. It looks as if it would fit a youth."

"A youth, am I?" Margarette said as she easily fit into the linen dress.

George slipped the larger gown over his tall frame. It was loose around the waist but so short that it only covered to the middle of his calves. "Oh, well, it is dark." He turned his eyes to inspect Margarette as he covered his hair with a linen cap. " No one knows the sound of your voice except Abraham, so pretend that I am your mother who is dragging you away from your lover. I will not say a word, but you must continually protest that you do not want to go home to milk the cow, feed the pigs, hoe the garden, spin the yarn. You know what is expected of a country girl, right?"

"Exactly!"

"We need to put our gear in the saddlebag and dump the tarpaulin and backpack. They have served their purpose. Now adjust your linen cap and off we go."

"Where are we going?"

"Outside of the gate, of course."

"You are presumptuous, George Hempleman."

"When you cannot hide in the dark, you hide in the light."

WEDNESDAY, OCTOBER 15, 1751—NIGHT—HALTERN

Otto Olsberg led the search through the dark narrow streets. Maxwell Braun and his two deputies followed, almost tasting the catch. They scoured the streets, looking behind and inside of water barrels, carts, stables. They knocked on doors alerting citizens of money to be had if they informed on any strangers matching the description of George Hempleman and a woman disguised as a man. Some residents joined the search. Babies began crying. *Burghers* yelled out their windows for peace and quiet.

The loud disturbance roused Abraham Cohen from a deep sleep. Seeing that his companions were gone, he decided to leave also. He did not want to be caught in the middle of an inquisition.

George and Margarette kept breathlessly close to the shadows while weaving down one street and up another. Abraham wove a different pattern through a mirrored section of Haltern. When all was clear, Abraham latched his belt onto the top of the spiked fencing, pulling himself up and over the impediment. For now he was a free man.

As George and Margarette neared the town gate, George got a clear view. What he saw caused him to step back into an alleyway while yanking Margarette behind him. A courtyard away the city gatekeeper was talking to a man on a thoroughbred.

"It is Maxwell Braun!" George whispered. "We need a miracle, Margarette."

Chapter 28

THURSDAY, OCTOBER 16, 1751—MINUTES PAST MIDNIGHT—HALTERN

George cautioned, "Stay here! I will be right back!"

Margarette froze. "Are you leaving me again?"

"Not on your life!"

George removed the female disguise and crept through the alley toward the center of Haltern. He heard a man shouting orders. Horses' hooves echoed from the outskirts of the town's limits.

With a deep guttural tone, George yelled toward the city gate, "*Herr* Braun, I think I have found them!"

Within minutes Maxwell Braun rode toward George, who had concealed himself in the shadows. "In that stable!" He indicated with his outstretched arm.

Braun slid off his horse, drew his pistol, and ran toward the cheerless stable where horses whinnied, sows squealed, and chickens fluttered. George followed Braun inside the barn. He brought both fists down heavily on the chamberlain's neck. Braun collapsed on the floor.

George removed Braun's cloak and decorative hat, bound his mouth with a gag that he fashioned by ripping a strip of fabric from Braun's shirt and tied Braun's arms behind him with rope that he found on a nearby hook. With Braun's pistol snugly inside his back belt, George ran outside the barn, mounted Braun's horse, and raced toward Margarette. Pulling her up behind him, George spurred the steed.

The gatekeeper smiled snidely as he opened the gate. "I see you have the girl, *Herr* Braun."

"My deputies have the man. They will be coming shortly. Tell them that I will meet them in Dortman."

THURSDAY, OCTOBER 16, 1751—HOURS BEFORE DAWN—HALTERN

The gatekeeper waited for a good long time, all the while listening to the commotion in the town. When he realized that the man on the horse was probably not *Herr* Braun, his stomach began to churn. "I will lose my job, I will."

He ran the short distance to his home, awakened his wife, gathered some twine, and picked up an iron skillet. "You have been wanting to do this many a time, my lady," he said to his wife. "Now come with me. This is a matter of bread on our table."

The good wife followed her husband to the town gate. He instructed her as she secured his hands and feet. "Now hit me in the back of my head with the skillet, just enough to knock me out."

"How will I know what 'just enough' is?" she asked. "Dear, I really don't want to do this."

"It's the only way. Now be quick about it before Olsberg gets back."

The good wife lifted the heavy utensil above her husband's head, bringing it full force upon his skull. Her husband fell whispering, "That's enough." He blacked out.

All the while the innkeeper peered through the front window wondering what on earth had happened to this once tranquil town.

THURSDAY, OCTOBER 16, 1751—HOURS
BEFORE DAWN—ROAD TOWARD DORSTEN

George and Margarette rode the sturdy thoroughbred southwest toward Dorsten. George's body protected Margarette from much of the brutal wind that slashed through the dark night.

"Are you with me, Margarette?" George asked.

"Who else would be behind you, George?"

"Getting sarcastic, are we?"

"I am just so tired, George. Where do you get all your energy?"

"Did I ever tell you about my great grandfather from one thousand years back?"

"You can trace your ancestry that far?"

"Well, I do not know how much is fiction and how much is truth, but it makes a great story. Do you want to hear it?"

"I have left all my books behind. So tell on, George."

"Do you remember the famous Charles Martel who defeated the army of Islam at the Battle of Tours?" George asked.

"Of course. My father told me about him. That was Europe's historic battle of a.d. 732."

"Getting back to Martel, do you know who his famous grandson was?"

"Charlemagne?" Margarette asked.

"Correct."

"You are not going to tell me that your lineage goes back to Charlemagne!"

"Not by blood but by association," George said. "My great grandfather Hermann fought under Charlemagne during the invasion of northern Spain."

"I am impressed, George," Margarette said as she gave him a hug. "But my father said that Charles the Great was stopped at Saragossa."

"Otherwise known as Zaragoza," George interrupted.

"Okay, smarty," Margarette laughed as the two rode forward into the night. Suddenly she was not feeling nearly so tired.

THURSDAY, OCTOBER 16, 1751—HOURS
BEFORE DAWN—HALTERN

When Wolfgang Gunther rode back to the town entrance to check with Braun, he spied the gatekeeper bound and unconscious. Loosening the man's wrists and ankles, he called for the innkeeper. "Krendle, get out here with some water!"

Krendle obeyed.

Gunther poured an entire basin of water over the unconscious man.

As the keeper of the gate opened his eyes, he tried to focus but everything was spinning so rapidly that he dozed off again, laying his head back on the gravel.

Gunther ordered, "Get some more water! Do you know this man's family?"

Krendle nodded.

"Well, get them, man! And bring me some more water!"

The innkeeper in Haltern was not particularly fond of the gate-keeper. Yet he began to feel a greater affinity toward Jacob Weller when Gunther snarled and made demands.

Martin Krendle ran to his inn and yelled for his wife. Refilling the basin with water from a large jug, he told Mary what had happened and asked her to fetch Jacob's wife

Krendle and Gunther were standing over Jacob as the gatekeeper's wife came running toward the men holding her skirts above her ankles so as not to trip in her haste.

"What have you done to my husband?" she sputtered to the men hovering over him. She knelt and cradled her husband's head in her arms. "Jacob, wake up." Krendle placed the basin of water beside her. She dipped her hand into the water and sprinkled droplets onto Jacob's face. "Jacob, you have to be all right! Jacob!"

The man responded with one eyelid opening slightly. Soon the other eye cooperated, and Jacob's wife eased him into a reclining position as Birkham rode up and slid off his horse.

"What's going on?" he asked.

Jacob began to remember his ruse. "Oh, my head!" he groaned. "What hit me?"

"You were attacked?" Gunther asked.

"Well, obviously!" Birkham sneered. "Where's Braun?"

"I haven't seen him," Gunther answered. "Oh, no! Has Hempleman given us the slip again?" He turned toward the innkeeper. "When is the next watch?"

"Clyde will be here shortly. I will help Jacob back to his home."

"No," Gunther ordered. "You stay with the gate until the next watch. The wife can see to her husband."

Martin Krendle was not a man of noble birth, nor a man of high esteem in the community, but he had enough wealth to command respect, and he felt the heat of bile rising. Immediately he resolved to keep Jacob's secret.

With arms clasped over his chest, he sat at the gate with a protruded lip and an angry scowl.

THURSDAY, OCTOBER 16, 1751—HOURS BEFORE DAWN—ROAD TOWARD DORSTEN

"To get back to Grandfather Hermann," George said, "my family says that he escaped the massacre of Roland's forces in the Pyrenees."

"I heard that the entire rear guard was cut off due to some kind of betrayal."

"The betrayal was from Roland's stepfather, who alerted the Saracens to attack at a mountain pass," George confirmed.

"Beware of stepfathers!" Margarette observed. "But Spain was not lost. I remember that."

"Correct. Charlemagne invaded in another campaign and claimed the Spanish March."

"What a warrior!" Margarette marveled. "But tell me about your grandfather."

THURSDAY, OCTOBER 16, 1751—HOURS
BEFORE DAWN—HALTERN

Olsberg, Gunther, and Birkham combed the town for Braun. As they neared the stable where the chamberlain lay tied and gagged, they heard boots kicking against the barn siding.

Braun was a furnace of anger. Had he touched his wrath to the hemp that bound his wrists and ankles, the rope would have disintegrated. Once Gunther removed the gag, Braun set off a fireworks of oaths. He stomped out of the stable.

"Where is my horse? I know Hempleman is headed toward the coast. We need to leave immediately."

A quick search revealed that Braun's thoroughbred had been used in the getaway.

"Gunther, you and Birkham go on ahead to Wesel. Seize him and the girl any way you can. I will follow with the warrant as soon as I can get me a mount, a pistol, a cloak, and a hat. Now go. Go! *Go!*"

THURSDAY, OCTOBER 16, 1751—HOURS
BEFORE DAWN—ROAD TOWARD DORSTEN

"My grandfather Hermann was not actually part of the rear guard," George explained to Margarette, "but a section of Charlemagne's troops who returned to rescue that remnant. When the commander of Grandfather Hermann's cavalry saw the massacre, he would not permit any of his men to enter the fray."

"Thus Grandfather Hermann returned to Cassel to continue the family line," Margarette concluded.

"Actually, the Hemplemans did not arrive in Hessen-Cassel until generations later," George said as Braun's thoroughbred brought the couple ever closer to Dorsten.

The night air enfolded the couple as stories of chivalry and heroism flooded their thoughts.

Margarette almost jumped when George broke through her reverie. "Just think—Charles the Great was an illegitimate son who later became the king of the Franks and the Holy Roman emperor of the Germans!"

"And an entire ballad was composed over one reference in history to Charlemagne's nephew, an officer in the rear guard!"

"If I had an instrument and a singing voice, I think that I would begin the *Chanson of Roland* right now," George said.

"I have never heard you sing, George."

"You do not want to hear me sing, Margarette."

The two laughed until they heard hooves approaching from behind.

THURSDAY, OCTOBER 16, 1751—HOURS BEFORE DAWN—OUTSKIRTS OF HALTERN

Otto Olsberg took Braun to a *bauer* outside of Haltern.

"He has the best stock around. He won't mind waking up in the middle of the night if you can pay him well."

"I will pay him what his horse is worth!" Braun fumed. "Not a rix more!"

THURSDAY, OCTOBER 16, 1751—HOURS BEFORE DAWN—ROAD TOWARD DORSTEN

George looked frantically for an escape route. He reined in Braun's horse abruptly and guided the steed away from the main road toward a field of corn. "Now dismount, my lovely," he said as he helped Margarette to the cold ground. They walked deep inside the rows of stalks, yet they kept close enough to the border of the field to see the road.

Within seconds two horses sped by at a full gallop.

"We will have to enter the city gates separately," George said. "I will take you as close to Wesel as I can without arousing suspicion. Since you are dressed as a town peasant, no one will question you. I will meet you at the first inn inside the gates. There you are going to be treated like nobility, Margarette."

"You are leaving me again?" Margarette asked. "If this continues, I may turn around and go home."

"Go home to what, Margarette? Your father will put you back in a convent, if he owns you at all. We have come this far. We are nearly on the Rhine River."

"I just want to go to sleep."

"You shall sleep to your heart's content in a proper inn in a proper room as soon as we both get inside of Wesel."

"George, we are not going to be together as husband and wife until we are in Scotland."

"I promise you that. Now trust me. Here are some rix dollars to get you through customs. I will be watching for you at the first inn."

"If I had a pistol, George Hempleman, you would be fearing for your life about now."

George reached below his cloak and pulled out Braun's pistol. "Here you go, Margarette. Aim accurately."

"You are impossible!" Margarette said. "All right. You win. I will walk into town with my peasant garb. You had better be in that first inn!"

"I will be, Margarette. May I?" He leaned his face toward hers. She turned her head.

"In Scotland, George. In Scotland after the wedding ceremony."

Chapter 29

THURSDAY, OCTOBER 16, 1751—MIDMORNING—WESEL

George had no trouble gaining entrance to Wesel. However, he knew that he had to dispense of Braun's horse, cloak, and hat quickly. Going into the inn, he sat close to a window. Before long he sighted a *bauer* heading toward the city gates with an empty cart. George caught up with him.

"Good morning, *Herr Bauer*," George said as he approached the middle-aged man. "I hope you had good success while in Wesel."

"Couldn't have been better," answered the *bauer*.

"Could I interest you in a fine thoroughbred, a handsome cloak, and a fashionable hat—all at a bargain price, I assure you?" George asked.

The *bauer* stopped and looked at the warm cloak and fashionable hat on George. "Where's the nag?" he asked.

"*He* is not a nag. He is a thoroughbred, tied up at the hitching post near the inn."

The *bauer* looked amazed. It was the finest horse he had ever seen. The *bauer* imagined himself riding proudly down the streets of Hattingen mounted on the horse and wearing the cloak and hat.

After haggling over price, the smartly dressed *bauer* rode away on Braun's thoroughbred while leading his aged horse by tethers.

George secured a room in the inn and went shopping, purchasing a most extravagant gown and hat for Margarette and a fashionable cloak and hat for himself. He returned to the inn and waited by the window in his room for sights of Margarette.

THURSDAY, OCTOBER 16, 1751—MIDMORNING—ROAD TO WESEL

Braun had been on the road all night. He had to admit that the horse he had purchased was a good steed. Denying his appetites, Braun had whisked through Dorsten. As the black of night had bowed way for dawn, a fog clung close to the Lippe River road and became thicker as the Lippe and Rhein converged. Like a wolf's shadow falling upon a lamb, soon fog crept over the outlying Wesel area.

Braun passed coaches, carts, horses, and pedestrians going and coming from the large city. He was particularly curious about one lone bucolic girl whom he had just ridden past. He shifted his balance back in the saddle, then pulled the right rein tightly while leaning toward the right. The horse obeyed. For several seconds Braun studied the girl walking toward him. She never flinched, never missed a step, just kept getting closer and closer.

It cannot be her. She would stop. Run. He reined the horse around toward Wesel.

During this interlude the happy *bauer* wearing Braun's hat and cloak and riding on Braun's horse passed by.

THURSDAY, OCTOBER 16, 1751—MIDMORNING—ROAD TO WESEL

Abraham swung his feet back and forth as he sat on the edge of a wagon laden with fruits, vegetables, eggs, and chickens. A friend on his way to the Wesel market had recognized him outside of Haltern.

Abraham would repay his good friend with a bottle of vintage wine once he reached home.

Despite the fog and the irregularities of his trip, his heart was light. He would soon be home with his Tamar and their children. He began singing a psalm of David.

Just as he sang, "The Lord delivered me from my enemies: yea, He lifted me up above those who rise against me: He has delivered me from the violent man," Maxwell Braun sped by on his newly purchased horse.

Abraham did not know Maxwell Braun, had never met or heard of the man, yet he felt the cold breeze of approaching winter when the rider skirted around the wagon.

THURSDAY, OCTOBER 16,
1751—MIDMORNING—WESEL

Margarette flowed into Wesel with the flood of humanity that crowded through the gate. When she explained that she would be visiting a friend in the city, the customs officer took the toll and let her pass.

Inside the city gate, visibility was better. She spotted the inn. Before she had taken a dozen steps, she saw George bounding out the door of the inn and rushing toward her.

"Thank God, you have arrived!" he said as he led her to the lodge, through the dining area, and up to their room. Waiting for her was a large bowl of clear water with clean towels and a bar of perfumed soap.

"Thank you, George," she smiled weakly. Then she poured out the anxieties of her close encounter with the man on the horse.

"I am so sorry, Margarette." He fought the urge to enfold her in his arms.

"A horseman alone must be Braun. Remember. We saw only two go past us. So all three of them are probably in the city by now. I will think of something. You clean up. I will have a breakfast tray sent up for you. Sleep as long as you wish. I will stay close to the dining hall." George turned to leave before remembering the gifts. "Look on the bed. You have a new gown and hat to wear. This is my betrothal gift to you."

"No strings attached?"

"Only to the hat," he said.

THURSDAY, OCTOBER 16, 1751—MIDMORNING—WESEL

Because they were in yet another Germanic city-state, Gunther and Birkham alerted the local Prussian officials of their search and asked for cooperation in the apprehension. They took a room near the constable's office in the center of town before leaving on foot to comb the area for clues.

THURSDAY, OCTOBER 16, 1751—LATE MORNING—WESEL

Tamar listened intently as Abraham described his trip.

"You must find your friends. I insist. Bring them here. To stay for any length of time in a public inn is too dangerous." Tamar whisked Abraham out the door.

I must begin at the main city gate near the Lippe, Abraham thought as he left the house. *They will undoubtedly go to the first establishment they see.* Locating the inn, Abraham entered the bustling dining area. All the straw had been cleared away hours ago. Now servers laden with heavy trays of soups, breads, and steins met the demands of customers. Abraham roamed through the masses looking, circling, twirling about. Just as he was about to leave, he saw George Hempleman humped over at the bar finishing a bowl of *Pichelsteiner*.

"Mind if I join you?" Abraham asked.

George reached for Braun's pistol as he slowly turned toward the man who addressed him.

"You do not need protection from me, young man," Abraham said. "My wife insists that you stay with us until we can get you on the road or river again. Remember, I am to locate another chaperon for you two."

George did not know if staying with Abraham in Wesel was such a good idea. He turned around to leave and saw Wolfgang Gunther standing at the entrance.

Slowly turning back to face the wall, he said to Abraham. "I will meet you in the alley behind the inn. One of the sleuths just walked in."

"Agreed." Abraham said. "I will order a stein of cider, then meet you in five minutes."

THURSDAY, OCTOBER 16, 1751—LATE MORNING—WESEL

The Prussian officials were of no help to Gunther or Birkham, so Gunther stood watch beside the city gate through which he had entered. Birkham continued interrogating innkeepers and shop owners, making them financial promises he knew that he could not keep. But his promises produced many watchful eyes stealthily examining strangers.

Gunther's vigilance was rewarded when *Herr* Braun passed customs before noon. Wolfgang's stomach was growling and Braun held the purse.

THURSDAY, OCTOBER 16, 1751—LATE MORNING—WESEL

The bath, breakfast, new garment, and fashionable hat revitalized Margarette. But to be walking through alleys needed explanation.

Abraham reasoned, "My home is a short distance. The Good Book says 'A prudent man foresees evil and hides himself: but the simple pass on, and are punished.'"

"George told me it was wise to hide in the open," Margarette argued.

"Forgive him, *Fraulein*. His reason is obscured by love."

George defended, "We are here in Wesel in one piece!"

Margarette countered, "With the help of many kind friends."

George threw up his hands. "I know when I am outnumbered."

Tamar stood in an open doorway with children hanging onto her apron and strings. Once the children saw their father, they ran into his open arms. With the exuberant welcome over, the children found fortress behind their father's legs and their mother's skirts, looking curiously at the pretty lady and handsome gentleman in their fine attire.

"Come in. Come in," Tamar said. George removed his hat while stepping through the doorway.

The table was set for a luncheon feast. Tamar had placed her best china out for the adults. "Sit down. Sit down. All is ready."

Abraham quietly closed the door and slid the hinge to secure a lock. He looked between the front window curtains, scouting for the unfamiliar.

Tamar piled the plates with *Karpfen*, potato dumplings, and string beans.

"Abraham, please," she said.

Abraham spoke the blessing over the meal.

Tamar concluded his prayer with a loud, "Humph!"

Abraham laughed as George and Margarette looked askance.

Abraham explained, "I did not pray in *Yeshua*'s name."

"*Yeshua?*"

"You call Him *Jesus*. We Jews called Him by His Hebrew name. Tamar believes as you do even though she does not use the name *Christian*. I have yet to be convinced," Abraham said.

"Stubborn is what he is!" Tamar said. "God sends His only Son to Earth, mind you, sent Him to us Jews first, and my husband refuses to accept God's gift!"

George and Margarette exchanged a glance of incredulity before George said, "I realize you are an agreeable man, *Herr* Cohen, but I am amazed that you would marry a Christian. No offense intended to you, *Frau* Cohen."

A slight smile erupted on the lips of Abraham. "Oh, my Tamar did not become a Christian until after we stood under the canopy. Tell our guests of your subterfuge, Tamar."

Tamar became entirely serious. "It was after the birth of our first child. I was shopping one day and walked into a bookstore, one that I visit regularly. Abraham was away for a few days delivering wine to his customers, and I was seeking some reading material to occupy my time while Jacob napped. Out of curiosity, I picked up a New Testament. I had often wondered why Christians were so hostile toward us. Perhaps I would find the answer in this book. Well, I did not find a complete answer except in passages relating to the trial of *Yeshua* and in others where Paul alludes to Jewish interference during the spread of Christianity. But those passages were internal disagreements among Jews. Never mind those. My point is that while I read the Testament, I realized the books were written by Jews who were doing what God Almighty wanted us to do from time immemorial, to share His love with the world. I was convinced that no hindrance kept me from becoming a follower of *Yeshua*, Himself Jewish, just like Paul, Peter, and all the apostles."

To avoid conflict and to renew the friendly atmosphere in her home, Tamar refilled each person's mug and served large slices of a fruit-filled torte to the delight of everyone.

"What a torturer my wife is!" Abraham exclaimed as he slid a large bite of *der Kuchen* into his watering mouth. Tamar snapped him with the edge of her skirt, and everyone broke into a merry laugh.

"I have not been this light-hearted for months," George said. "Margarette, we must always remember to fill our future home with laughter and good times even when we disagree—momentarily."

"You make me happy, and I will keep you happy," Margarette responded with a sly smile.

Abraham roared so loudly that the window glass nearly shattered. "She learns quickly, George," Abraham gasped, then roared again.

Late into the day, the Cohens listened to the life histories of their fugitive guests. During the telling of the stories, Abraham devised ways to get the couple safely on the Rhine and to the coast. The problem was solved when Margarette mentioned her brother Hank who was a coxswain on the River Rhine.

Abraham edged up in his chair. "So your last name would not be Duffy, would it?"

"Well, yes," Margarette affirmed.

"I have known your brother for a few years. He has transported many a barrel of wine for me to take inland. Fine fellow. And the final piece of our puzzle," Abraham said.

"You know Hank?" Margarette marveled. "He became a boatman only three years ago."

"Yes," Abraham beamed. "He will be your final chaperon to the coast. He can locate a ship going to Scotland. You will be free." Abraham stood and reached for his hat and cloak.

"Where do you think you are going?" Tamar asked.

"I am going to find Hank. I may not be back for a few days."

THURSDAY, OCTOBER 16, 1751—LATE MORNING—CASSEL

Maurice Hempleman looked out of his upstairs bedroom window toward the center of Cassel at the spacious mansion near the margrave's palace. Inside those walls Rhonda Sturzhelm became more beautiful and more elusive every day.

Since the evening of George's homecoming banquet, Maurice had been able to think of nothing else other than capturing the beauty's hand in marriage and securing his own future. What

George had run from, Maurice would embrace. He was strong and intelligent enough to operate a large cotton plantation in Togo. Next July he would reach the age of eighteen. To be able to prove his mettle and gain the hand of Lord Sturzhelm's second daughter was a gauntlet he wanted to grab.

Prodigious obstacles haunted him. The Hemplemans had become social pariahs of Cassel since George's disappearance. This was unacceptable to Maurice. He had been reared as nobility and had been treated as nobility. He would settle for no other lifestyle. An unyielding determination prodded him to rise above his brother's betrayal of the family and salvage the Hempleman reputation.

Maurice knew that Lord Sturzhelm was a proud and greedy man. Lord Sturzhelm had been eager to marry his eldest, homely daughter to the dashing George Hempleman. That was why the betrothal had occurred so early. But if he, Maurice, could persuade the powerful lord that Charlotte could find fulfillment as a companion of her younger sister in Togo, he and Rhonda would have a most faithful liaison between them and Lord Sturzhelm.

The last thing that Maurice wanted to do was to move south to the Hempleman manor with his family. He wanted his father's title and was sure to get that. But he wanted more, and he knew that he needed to conclude a contract quickly.

Chapter 30

WEDNESDAY, OCTOBER 22, 1751—LATE MORNING—WESEL

Six days had passed since Abraham had left. Tamar not only managed her household well but was also a gifted and protective hostess. She would not allow George or Margarette to step outside, and if a knock came at the door, she ushered Margarette into the girls' room and George into her sons' room. Thus, the interval during which Abraham searched for Hank Duffy was more like a secluded vacation for George and Margarette than a period of anxiety.

Each morning after breakfast Tamar called her six children around her and asked, "What are you about to do?"

In unison, the six children, even two-year-old Enoch, would say, "We are studying to show ourselves approved unto God. We are correctly dividing God's Word."

With great care, Tamar opened the Book, reading first from the Pentateuch, then from the wisdom literature followed by a passage from the prophets. Then Tamar picked up a New Testament and read.

The first day she read from the Gospel of John about being born again. The second, third, fourth, and fifth day she read from the same passage. On the sixth day Margarette asked Tamar why she continued to read that passage repeatedly.

Tamar explained, "Because being born again is the most important decision one can make."

"I am not sure I understand what you mean," Margarette said.

"This is how I see it, Margarette. Have you ever done any gardening?"

"Of course," Margarette said. "Our family has always had a small plot of ground we work."

"Then you have taken refuse, like rotten potatoes or bad corn, and turned them under for fertilizer, correct?"

"Yes, sometimes what we threw away actually sprouted and produced delicious vegetables."

"Exactly," Tamar agreed. "But sometimes the plant just rotted and became soil."

"So you are saying that as willful as we are, we can either become the soil or become the productive plant."

"You understand well," Tamar said.

"Reverend Willis used the passage about the seed and the soil nearly once each year," George said. "He must have thought that its message was very important."

Tamar continued, "If you were a gardener, would you not want your plot of ground to produce an abundant harvest?"

"So into the soil we go, stinking and rotten," George caught the idea. "Then the rain comes."

"And the sun shines on us," Margarette said.

"And the Gardener breaks up the soil, removes the stones and weeds, and drives off the predators," George added.

"All the while there is a tiny seed within each plant yearning to see light, to stretch, to grow, to live. That is what I call our seed of life, or spark of life, that God puts in every one of us," Tamar said.

"Everyone?" Margarette thought of the many evil people she had met during her short life.

"Everyone, Margarette. Some people keep ignoring the seed of life and develop a hard heart. Other people think that they are good enough and that they do not need the True Light. But both are wrong. I am a much better mother and wife because I died to myself and allowed *Yeshua* to live in me. Abraham is so naturally good that it may take him a long time to realize that his 'good enough' is not good enough for God."

"So what do we do?" George asked while thinking of his own trail of sin.

"We do what the Hebrews did long ago. We put blood over our sins," Tamar explained.

"You mean the blood of Jesus," Margarette said.

"Exactly. Only His blood is good enough to cover all of our sins. *Yeshua* is the perfect Sacrificial Lamb of God."

"You tie the whole Bible together beautifully," Margarette said. "How can I be born again?"

"Admit your sinfulness, Margarette. Admit that you cannot go through life without the One who put that spark of life in you. Depend upon Him always. *Yeshua*, your Jesus, said He would forever live in us as He lives in the Father. Now that is close fellowship."

"Jesus sent us the Holy Spirit to stand along beside us," George added. "In fact, He lives in us, too, if I understood Reverend Willis correctly."

"You understood correctly," Tamar agreed. "But you must guard your new heart all the days of your life. The world, your flesh, and our adversary want to crowd out what God plants and nurtures."

A man cleared his throat at the foyer. "Thus, you must daily do what you are doing now. Study. Fellowship. Love." Immediately Abraham was swinging children in his arms and making his way to Tamar, whom he hugged until she begged for breath.

"I have missed you, my love," he said. "But enough about us. We have another visitor."

WEDNESDAY, OCTOBER 22, 1751—LATE MORNING—CASSEL

The marriage had been hurried yet extravagant. All parties were still reeling from the flurry of the wedding and the departure preparations. Yet a refreshing calm settled over the newlyweds and both of the families.

Maurice, Rhonda, and Charlotte settled themselves into a private stagecoach. Maurice waved a last good-bye to his parents, sisters, and baby Siegfried while Rhonda and Charlotte threw kisses to their parents and young Gertrude. In the last week Lady Sturzhelm had repeatedly explained to Charlotte that her eldest could escape much of the social stigma she now felt by joining Maurice and Rhonda in Toga, and Lord Sturzhelm had volunteered to grant her a generous yearly income. Charlotte began to see the advantages. The spurned lady would not be without social interaction. Both Lord Wolff and Lord Hamler had unmarried sons, none quite so desirable as George Hempleman, but possible marital partners. *Would they not be making frequent journeys to Togo to supervise their fathers' land holdings? I know I am not pretty like Rhonda, but I have known women who are not attractive physically but are beautiful in spirit and have successful marriages. I will try to gain control of my tongue, emotions, and, yes, my self-centeredness. I, too, want to be whisked away by a husband who loves me.*

Maurice had accomplished the impossible. Having convinced Lord Sturzhelm of his abilities, Maurice had arranged a reconciliation between Lord Sturzhelm and Maurice's father, Lord Hempleman. Even though Johann was not able to resume his role as constable, he and his family were no longer outcasts. This acceptance helped the ailing Johann to regain much of his stamina, although he still needed a cane to walk.

Lord Sturzhelm heaved a sigh of relief as he watched three of his coaches roll out of Cassel. He was sending the servants he had recently employed in Amsterdam to attend to the needs of Charlotte, Rhonda, and Maurice in Togo.

Perhaps Charlotte will find solace, Lord Harry thought. *At least I will not be listening to her occasional wails lamenting her betrayal. No wonder George Hempleman chose the little strawberry blonde.*

WEDNESDAY, OCTOBER 22,
1751—LATE MORNING—WESEL

"Margie, what have you gotten yourself into?" Hank asked as he walked toward his younger sister and held her by her shoulders at arms' length. "You were always the homebody, the one with her nose stuck in a book. Now you are the subject of conversation up and down the Rhine and in all of Hesse."

Margarette did not know how to respond.

Hank looked around. "So this is the notorious George Hempleman," he said as he took stock of George's appearance. "Forgive my manners, *Herr* Hempleman, but I do have the best interests of my sister at heart. You have not taken advantage of her, have you?"

"Not at all," George responded. "I respect the value you place on Margarette. I hold her in high esteem, so high that I have forsaken all but her."

"That is noble of you, but what are your plans?" Hank asked sarcastically.

"We plan to settle in northern Scotland near your kin."

Hank swung his head toward Margarette. "Father took us out of there in '42. Why would you be going back, Margie?"

"It is not safe for us here, Hank. I could help Grandmother. George could tend sheep."

"Is that what you want, George?" Hank asked incredulously.

"I just want a home of our own. I want to marry your sister. Life without her would be no life at all."

Hank pulled out a paper from beneath his cloak and handed it to George.

George unrolled the flyer, which gave a brief description of him and Margarette before listing the reasons for his apprehension: theft, multiple aggravated assaults, drug dealing, false identity, manslaughter. The paper was signed by Constable Maxwell Braun, acting on behalf of Lord Harry Sturzhelm of Hessen-Cassel.

George limply handed the sheet to Abraham. "What have I done? What seemed so right to me has an entirely different script here. I could be condemned on each and every one of those counts in a court of law." George sank into a chair and ran his fingers through his hair. "Margarette, I am so sorry. I never intended this."

For the next hour George explained to Hank the events that had led up to each of the accusations. Hank interrupted with question after question, asking for clarification, explanation, and more information. At times Hank directed his questions toward Margarette.

Growing tired of Hank's investigation of the obviously biased allegations, Abraham and Tamar quietly tended to the business of their hearth and home, what they knew were the important issues in life.

At long last, Hank stood and rubbed his lower back. He studied his sister with a long and serious gaze. "Okay, Margie, let me hear from you. Do you want to spend the rest of your life with *Herr* George Hempleman?"

"I believe that you know the answer to that question is *yes*, Hank. I do."

"Well, I am satisfied if you are. While I have been listening, I have also been planning."

When Abraham heard these words, he pulled up a chair to enter into the confabulation.

Hank thought that the quickest way out of the sundry German states was the use of the Rhine River road. "Then inside the border of the Dutch Republic, we could travel northwest on the Lek River into Rotterdam."

Abraham cautioned, "I believe disguises need to be maintained. The economy in The Netherlands is at an all time low, which means that men will trade information for money."

"Good point, Abraham. However, emigrants are flowing out of the German states to other lands on a regular basis. We will be three among many. I can help with expenses. Being a normal Scot, I save much of my wages."

Margarette was relieved to hear her brother brighten the conversation. "You are sounding more like the Hank I remember," she gave his shoulder a loving squeeze.

Just then a solid knock on the front door of the Cohen home silenced all the adults.

Abraham motioned to Tamar that she should take the guests to the back of the house. A second series of louder staccato thuds echoed throughout the room.

As Tamar directed Hank and George toward her sons' room and Margarette into the room of Deborah and Rebekah, George whispered to Tamar, "With or without Hank, Margarette and I are leaving now. I will not implicate you in any scandal."

Hank overheard and said, "I plan on being your chaperone until you two are married in Scotland. I may even settle there myself." He continued. "Grab only what you absolutely need. We travel light."

Margarette argued with Hank over leaving her new gown and fashionable hat behind. Firmly, Hank took the garment and hat from Margie's grip and handed both to Tamar, who was weeping. The three left by the back door just as Wolfgang and Braun stormed from the front toward the back of the house.

Outside in the alleyway Hank led his sister and her betrothed through seldom-used trails toward the Rhine. By sunset they were on the waterfront where the wide river reflected the lights of the city. Hank pulled his charges into a darkened alleyway. "Stay here. I am going to call in a favor." He sauntered toward a group of men sitting on benches, holding steins, and conversing. Pulling one man aside, Hank spoke briefly, reached for his money pouch, paid a sum, and shook the man's hand.

Waving good-bye to the group of men, Hank headed for a small boat, pushed away from the pier, and began rowing. George and Margarette observed her brother's skill as he propelled the vessel northwest around a bend where he could no longer be seen.

"Where has he gone?" George whispered.

"He will be back for us," Margarette affirmed.

The couple waited until twilight listening to the slow, measured *clip-clop* of horses' hooves on Wesel streets and the rise and fall of male and female voices. By dusk the peaceful monotony was interrupted by a burst of flurry caused by three horsemen.

Braun and Wolfgang slid off their horses and ran toward the startled men with whom Hank had spoken earlier. Birkham, still mounted, held the reins of his cohorts' horses steady. George and Margarette could not hear the conversations, but they saw one man point in the direction where Hank had rowed.

Just then George felt a tap on his shoulder and swung around with ready fists. Hank whispered, "Easy, George. We need to get out of here."

Hank led the way through the darkened alleyways toward the outskirts of the city while Braun, Wolfgang, and Birkham took the river road northwest.

"My friend's boat is just around the bend. He knows where it is anchored. I doubt if he gave your 'friends' any helpful information. If we stay on this route leading toward The Netherlands, we will be behind your pursuers, which is always a safe place."

"You are a fox, Hank," Margarette said.

"Father did not rear any dummies, Margie," Hank reminded his sister.

"So we are going to walk to the coast?" George asked.

"I hope not," Hank said. "If the three of them come back this way, we will watch them pass, then go to a boating dock. For now, we are on foot."

"At least it is not raining, and we all have warm cloaks," Margarette observed.

"Speaking of clothing, Margie, I think that you had better disguise yourself again as a male," George suggested.

"You want me to change into my male clothes here?" Margarette asked.

"Unless you want to go back to Hesse," George teased.

"All right. You men, turn your backs. I know it is dark, but no peeking."

So by the light dodging through the cirrus clouds, Margarette became Marc once more, and the three left Wesel, hugging the edge of the river road. As midnight approached, they passed Xanten, the fabled birthplace of Siegfried. George entertained Marc and Hank with the retelling of the *Nibelungenlied*, making sure to mention that his youngest brother had also been christened Siegfried.

Chapter 31

THURSDAY, OCTOBER 23, 1751—EARLY MORNING HOURS—KLEVE

Braun and his men stayed the night in Kleve. Before bedding down, they developed a scheme to catch their prey. Birkham would retrace the route back to Wesel, talking with locals. Braun would proceed to Amsterdam and employ enough dockworkers to flush out the elusive Hempleman. Gunther would do the same in Rotterdam. If Birkham gathered enough information to indicate that Hempleman was headed toward the coast, he would join Wolfgang in Rotterdam. Pleased with their plan, they all slept soundly as the object of their search passed by Kleve in the cold dark of night.

THURSDAY, OCTOBER 23, 1751—EARLY MORNING HOURS—ROAD TOWARD THE NETHERLANDS

The moon hid behind the windswept clouds. Hank kept his arm under his sister's elbow so she would not stumble. Despite the cold breeze, the three were perspiring. If they lingered only moments, their sweat turned icy cold. Knowing that food could keep them going, Hank reached into a pouch that hung beneath his cloak, pulled out a handful of oats, and told George to cup his hands together.

"What is this?" George asked as the grains fell into his hands.

"Sustenance," Hank replied. He handed Margarette her ration. "Now, scoop as much dew off the grass as you can and rub the dew into the oats. This will be your breakfast, lunch, and dinner until we reach the coast."

"Impossible!" George said.

"Not at all," Margarette corrected. "Hank, tell him about our Scottish warriors."

"The basic food for us Scots is oats. By mixing the oats with dew, an oat ball is formed. It lies on the stomach for three weeks and sustains you. Warriors carried oats as a last resort."

"No honey?" George asked in jest.

"You nobility!" Hank responded in kind.

THURSDAY, OCTOBER 23, 1751—DAWN—KLEVE

At dawn, Birkheim left his two companions and began spreading his net east. Braun and Gunther headed toward the Dutch border.

In The Netherlands at the fork in the Rhine, Braun would head northwest while Gunther would take the Waal River road toward Rotterdam.

THURSDAY, OCTOBER 23, 1751—NEAR DUTCH BORDER

By early morning Hank, George, and Marc moved off the main road and into a forest to secretly enter The Netherlands as Braun and Gunther rode their horses adjacently on the main road. Soon the Rhine split into two channels.

"We veer to the right here and keep by the Lek River," Hank said. "Hopefully we will board a passenger boat at Arnhem." Hank increased his gait.

Margarette tried to keep pace. She would not tell her brother or

George, but blisters erupted on her feet. She longed for rest, a place to lie down.

The sun battled the clouds for supremacy, but the mass of small water droplets suspended in the sky refused to give way to the daystar.

Energetic farmers and tradesmen passed by on the road leading into Arnhem. Thinking Margarette was just another young man on the road, the strangers indiscriminately jostled her in the same manner that they bumped against Hank and George; Margarette's two protectors immediately took defensive positions by walking on each side of her.

Once inside the city borders, Hank pointed to an inn he frequented. Before Hank reached the entrance, Braun rode up to the establishment and tethered his horse.

George casually turned away, taking Marc by the elbow.

Hank looked up toward the sky the way coxswains study weather currents.

Once Braun was inside the inn, Hank whispered, "There is another place a few blocks away."

Hank guided George and Margarette through the narrow streets of Arnhem where intricate lace window coverings individualized each dwelling. Stopping at one particularly lovely, spotlessly-clean threshold, Hank walked up the single step and tapped on the door. The upper section of the door opened, revealing a stout blonde male of about twenty years of age.

"Hank! I have been concerned about you. No one has seen you for days. Come in. Come in." The young man loosed the lower door section to allow the three entrance. A woman, apparently this young man's mother, bustled about the kitchen giving orders to a seemingly endless number of children, all younger than Hank's friend.

"Mother," the young man said, "I have guests. Could you bring some hot tea into the parlor and perhaps some *schoonbroodt?*"

Hank declined the food. "Thank you, Allan, but we must be leaving. The reason my companions and I have stopped is because we need your help."

Hank gave a short explanation of the predicament that he, George, and Marc were in, and of the close encounter they had with Braun a few minutes ago.

"I will send my brother Lem to the inn to see what he can learn," Allan said. "He is a smart lad and keeps his mouth tight."

THURSDAY, OCTOBER 23, 1751—AFTERNOON—ARNHEM

The Arnhem innkeeper read the flyer that Braun had given him.

"No, I have not seen the likes of any of them. I have heard of the search though. I will tell you what. I will be glad to take this flyer to the town authorities for a small fee."

Braun placed a guilder in the innkeeper's hand. "I would prefer going myself."

The man supplied the directions.

Lem followed Braun and stood leisurely outside the office of the civil authorities. When Braun left on his horse, Lem rushed home.

"So the hunter has apparently left Arnhem for Amsterdam, and the local constable is now aware of two companions with Hempleman," Allan said as he distributed well-worn Dutch caps with visors to Hank, Margarette, and George. "We must move hastily. I have a boat that can take you to Rotterdam. Then you are on your own."

THURSDAY, OCTOBER 23, 1751—AFTERNOON—WESEL

Birkham tried repeatedly to enlist help from sojourners. He had no success. He was one angry haberdasher when he reached Wesel. There the officials listened and took the information, yet could report no such sightings. Furious for his loss of time, Birkham spurred his mount toward the coast, wondering if he would be left empty-handed when the reward for Hempleman was distributed.

THURSDAY, OCTOBER 23, 1751—AFTERNOON—WEST OF ARNHEM

A capable boatman, Allan took the first shift of rowing. An hour later Hank paddled without a slowdown. Then George manned the oars for the third shift. All the while Margarette nursed her feet with cool water from the Lek, reaching into the water with a sock and applying the liquid balm to her blisters.

"I can see that I will need to build us a wagon as soon as we reach Scotland," George commented.

"Make that a three-seater," Hank joked.

Margarette smiled, reached into a large pocket under her cloak, and pulled out a skein of yarn.

"What are you doing now?" Hank asked.

"Knitting all of us some warm gloves. My hands are freezing, and I suspect yours are too." She handed a pair to George. "Yours and mine are already finished." George pulled the woolen gloves over his cold, calloused hands.

"These fit perfectly, Margarette." George was astonished.

Margarette set her fingers to knitting.

Hank laughed. "If you are not a paradox, sister! There you sit looking like a mariner yet knitting."

"You had better keep quiet, Hank Duffy, or you will be last on my list."

"Yes, ma'am," he grinned.

THURSDAY, OCTOBER 23, 1751—LATE AFTERNOON—ROTTERDAM

Gunther reached Rotterdam in time for a fine dinner before resuming the search. Most people with whom he spoke had heard bits and pieces of the Hempleman story and were eager to learn more. Arguments erupted as friends took opposite views of the young nobleman's plight. Few remained distant from the scandal. Gunther realized that the interest worked to his advantage as many volunteered to help for the sake of adventure. One was an independent boatman named Gilbert whom Gunther especially befriended and enriched, thus tightening the net.

THURSDAY, OCTOBER 23, 1751—EVENING—ROTTERDAM

The lights of Rotterdam sparkled in the west. Allan slowed his rowing and searched for an embankment in the scant light the city jealously hoarded.

"I must leave you on your own and wish you the best," he said to Hank as the boat touched land and jerked to a halt. "I vowed to my mother when my father was lost at sea that I would not go near the ocean or any of the harbors. She and my brothers and sisters depend upon my keeping that vow."

"I understand, friend," Hank said. "Thank you for all your help. I did not know where else to go."

The two shook gloved hands as George stepped ashore and helped steady Margarette as she planted her sore feet on solid ground.

Allan pushed off. Hank, George, and Margarette headed westward.

Chapter 32

FRIDAY, OCTOBER 24, 1751—MINUTES PAST MIDNIGHT—ROTTERDAM

The darkened buildings shielded the harsh wind. The cold night temperatures played havoc on all who dared to remain out of doors. Hank suggested that George and Margarette stay near the waterfront under a pier while he checked on tickets to Aberdeen, Scotland.

Margarette did not resist when George put his arm around her shoulder as they sat in the sand with their backs against the lashing wind. They dared not talk or move. They simply shared their body heat and watched the course of the moon through a filmy web of clouds.

After an hour Hank stole under their shelter and crouched beside them.

"The news is not good. Your story is well known even here. A German from Hessen-Cassel has been asking for assistance in your capture, so to think that we are going to sail out of here on a passenger ship is next to fantasy. Do you have any suggestions?"

George fingered his leather pouch. "I have my mother's emerald necklace. Would that buy us a vessel?"

"We cannot purchase a vessel strong enough to carry us across the German Ocean. But if we had a sailboat, we could sail down the coast to Calais, spend the winter in France, get jobs, and save our money."

"Maybe find a priest or minister who would perform a marriage?" George asked.

"George, I insist that we wait until we get to Scotland. I want a few of my family to be a part of our wedding," Margarette asserted.

"You are one headstrong woman, Margarette," George said.

"You have not seen the half of it," Hank chuckled quietly. "So we stay the winter in Calais. Hand me that necklace. I will locate us a vessel."

George pulled the ornate jewelry from the leather pouch. Hank examined the treasure in the starlight and whistled quietly. "This should purchase us a sea-worthy vessel."

He pocketed the necklace and skipped off to find a seaman down on his luck.

With a cord of hemp washed onto the beach, George reverently secured around his chest the leather pouch that contained his mother's Bible and her parting note. With tears in his eyes, George winked at Margarette who realized that the man she loved had given up nearly everything and everyone for her love.

FRIDAY, OCTOBER 24, 1751—2:00 A.M.—NEAR ROTTERDAM

Dozing off in the saddle, Birkham forced himself to stay awake by smacking his face, adjusting his hat, and flexing his tired muscles. The nightglow of Rotterdam drew the greedy man into its clutches. He stopped at the first inn he encountered and made arrangements for the night's stay, asking the proprietor to awaken him in three hours. Then he inquired about the search for a George Hempleman and grew encouragement when the innkeeper said that a German was already in Rotterdam searching for the same subject. Birkham placed a guilder into the man's hand and asked, "Could you give me directions to the law enforcement office?"

The owner of the inn was quick to supply the information.

"Three hours and I am up!" Birkham reminded his informant.

"Three hours it is!"

FRIDAY, OCTOBER 24, 1751—3:00 A.M.—ROTTERDAM HARBOR

Hank knew a few of the sailors who drifted in and out of Rotterdam. Going from tavern to tavern, Hank asked those he could trust for leads on the purchase of a sailboat "for a friend." To represent himself as the purchaser would make him more of a suspect than he already was. Time after time Hank received a shake of the head or a churlish grin. Losing track of the number of public houses where he had been, he decided to return to Margarette and George to devise a different plan.

However, before reaching the pier, he located a fellow leaning against a lamp pole who spent weeknights observing incoming and outgoing traffic. On a whim, Hank asked the man if he knew of a sailboat for sale.

"That I do," the man replied. "At a premium price."

"Is she a sturdy vessel?" Hank asked.

"Indeed. You can look her over come dawn. She belongs to me."

"Actually, I am in a bit of a hurry. I have two companions with me. Could I see your boat now?"

The stranger stepped back. "Are you with that young nobleman causing a ruckus in Hessen-Cassel?"

"What would you say if I told you I was?" Hank replied.

"I would say if you have the right price, I have the merchandise, and god-speed to you."

Hank pulled out the necklace and held it up in the fleeting glimmer of moonlight. The man gasped at the dazzling beauty of the encased gems.

"My one condition is that I would like to buy the necklace back from you at a later date," Hank said.

"Sonny, the price increases each day that I hold those gems in my possession."

Hank hesitated, then said, "Let me take a look at your sailboat."

FRIDAY, OCTOBER 24, 1751—3:45 A.M.— ROTTERDAM HARBOR INN

Wolfgang Gunther slept in a chair beside the window of his rented room overlooking the harbor. When he heard the crack of lightning, he awaked. In the street below Wolfgang saw three figures in dark cloaks and sailors' caps running through the rain and down a small pier where they boarded a sailboat.

Gunther pulled on his boots, stomped down the narrow staircase, and burst out the door onto the boardwalk.

Hank and George expertly trimmed the lone sail to tack to windward while Margarette found herself a spot in the bow. Then Hank sat at the rudder while George adjusted the sail to the shifts of the westerly wind.

Gunther ran toward the boat as it left the pier shouting into the wind, "Turn back, Hempleman, or I will shoot!"

"Margarette," George ordered, "lie flat on the bottom of the boat *now* and do not raise your head." Margarette dropped onto the hull where icy rainwater drenched her clothing.

George kept one eye on Margarette and the other focused on tacking. He knew that speed and distance were their common allies.

Gunther ran back to the boardwalk keeping his sights on the sailboat, which zigzagged in and out of his vision. He drew his flintlock from his back buckle and took aim. A burst of sparks identified Gunther's position followed by a tear in the lower part of the sail.

He fired his gun a second time and heard a man's cry from the boat.

Margarette crawled on her elbows over to her brother.

"Stay down, Margarette," Hank ordered. "I just have a scratch on my right arm. I will be all right."

A third shot rang out. George reached beneath his cloak and pulled out Braun's pistol.

"No, George!" Margarette shouted.

George replaced the handgun just as a gust of wind caught the sail, surging the boat forward.

"We are nearly out of his range," Hank said. "Steady now."

A fourth shot penetrated the dark of night. In a few moments George felt the sensation of warm blood flowing down his frigid right leg.

In a stage of light slumber, Birkham heard the shots being fired in the harbor. *It's Gunther!* After tossing payment for his spot on the straw to the innkeeper, Birkham ran into the night storm toward the echoing blasts.

Gunther fired the rest of his ammunition in an angry rage. As the sailboat continued its course, he remembered Gilbert's boat tied up along the bank. Locating the vessel, Wolfgang kicked at the veteran seaman as he slept under canvas in the shallow hull of his boat.

"What's going on?" Gilbert yelled.

"I need your boat! Now! The man I am after is getting away! If you want a share in the reward, you will get this vessel rigged and sailing!"

Accustomed to crises, Gilbert immediately loosened the holding rope and readied the sail just as Gunther spied a man, with arms flailing, running toward the boat.

Gunther ordered, "Cast off!"

Gilbert guided the boat away from the shore as Birkham shouted, "Gunther! Stop! It's me! Birkham!"

Gunther yelled for Gilbert to ease back to shore.

"Do you have any ammunition, Birkham?"

"Enough for what we need to do," Birkham yelled and jumped aboard.

George tore a strip from his cloak to wrap his bleeding leg. Then he ripped off another and told Margarette, "See to Hank's wound."

As torrents of rain lashed around her, Margarette wrapped the cloth snugly around Hank's right bicep.

"Thanks, Sis," Hank said before ordering. "Now lie flat. I imagine Gunther will be sailing up behind us before too long."

A skilled seaman, Gilbert closed the gap between the two vessels as both boats raced through the shrouded harbor toward the North Sea.

Dawn demanded supremacy over the eastern horizon in a tangled struggle with the dark threads of night.

Cargo and passenger ships, with their lanterns swinging devilishly in the cruel wind, awakened in the harbor. Crewmembers hoisted anchors, pulled the lines, raised the sails. Soon ship after ship left the safety of Rotterdam harbor to plow through the white-capped waves.

Seeing what was about to converge on them, Hank yelled, "I only have a scratch, George. You take the rudder. I will get us out to the open sea before these monstrous ships push us aside. Margie, hold the rudder steady until George takes over."

Margarette strained against the rudder, which wanted to follow the waves. Hank took the lines from George, who dragged his body toward the stern leaving a trail of blood behind. Margarette tried not to focus on George's blood loss as he took the tiller from her hands.

Behind them, cries of "Stop, Hempleman!" followed curses as Gilbert drew on a reservoir of nautical knowledge that swept his vessel over the dark waters. But the more powerful sea-worthy ships gained prominence in the harbor and edged up behind the tiny sailboats.

"My vessel cannot outrun the fleet behind us!" Gilbert roared over the wind, which now and again grabbed the sails and tipped the vessel dangerously close to the waiting waters.

"It can, and you will catch the boat ahead of us!" Gunther growled and pointed his flintlock straight at Gilbert's head.

Nearing the mouth of the estuary, the winds increased intensity as Hank struggled to control the sails. George's vision began to blur. A huge pool of blood pushed aside the puddles of rainwater below George's leg. Gunther's oaths resounded in the morning fracas as Gilbert guided his rig to within shooting range. Wolfgang fired another shot. The blast reverberated in the tempestuous squall, but a huge wave created by a square-rigger swallowed the bullet. The massive ship parted the waters.

A spew of vicious vulgarities lasted only moments before the garbled wrath sank into the depths of the estuary. The fierceness of the wind fought and roared against the intrusion of a second square-rigger heading toward the German Ocean. Hank trimmed the mainsail to avoid a collision. Then he adjusted the sails to tack into the wind as the sailboat skimmed out of the estuary.

Margarette shouted, "Go back, Hank! Go back! The wind is getting worse! George is bleeding to death! We are all nearly frozen! Turn back!"

George shouted, "Stay the course, Hank! We can make it. Just follow the coastline south!"

With a final crescendo, a gust of wind and rain grabbed the boom and knocked Hank into the ocean. Margarette screamed as George jumped into the sea trying to locate Margarette's brother. With the boat drifting at the whim of the wind, Margarette grabbed the tiller and tried steadying the wayward vessel.

Denying his pain, George dove again and again into the violent churning sea looking for signs of Hank. The dark skies and darker waters prevented any visibility. All the while George's strength ebbed from his body. Then the westerly wind had its way and tipped the sailboat onto its side as a third square-rigger sailed up from behind, soared past the small sailboat, and created a wave that threw Margarette out and away from the boat.

George heard her scream and abandoned his search for Hank. He reached her just as she began sinking toward the ocean's depths. He unclasped her cloak and let it float away.

"Kick your shoes off?" he ordered. "You will be able to tread water more easily."

"I am not going to lose my shoes, George!" Margarette yelled.

"Stubborn is what you are!" George grabbed for a loose board floating in the foaming waters. "Well, hang on to this while I locate Hank."

"Do not leave me, George!" Margarette screamed and clutched his shoulders.

The two drifted farther out toward sea when they both heard a faint call in the distance. "Protect Margie, George! Preserve her honor!" Then only the roar of the storm beat against them as the sun required a view of the scene below.

Another ship headed their way. Using one arm to hold onto the splintered board keeping both him and Margarette afloat and his second to wrap around Margarette, George coached, "Hold onto the board, Margarette, and use your feet like flippers on a fish. We need to get clear of this ship. Together we can do this. Kick and hold on!"

The ship cut through the water dangerously close to the terrified couple who clutched the board, fought their way through the debris of two sailboats, and used their waning strength to survive a third impasse between the propulsion of the storm's waves and the violent wake left by the ship's passage.

"George, we are going to die!" Margarette screamed.

"Keep kicking, Margarette! Hold on tight!"

On board the ship, a midshipman heard a woman's cry. At first he thought it was the wind, but another scream resounded. He rushed to starboard and saw the sun's rays catch hold of a mass of reddish-blonde hair being whipped in the wind.

"Man overboard. Man overboard!" he yelled and ran for the life preserver. Securing the end rope onto the ship's railing, the sailor took aim and thrust the white ring toward the bobbing reddish-blonde ball. Sailors gathered round the midshipman, straining for a view.

"Who is it?"

"I don't think we've lost anyone."

"Probably part of the crew on that sailboat."

Meanwhile, Margarette and George saw the airborne object coming toward them. The precious circular gift fell into the waters tethered by a rope held aboard the swiftly moving ship. The aim was good. But Margarette and George had to grab hold quickly or they would be left behind. The ship was on the run. The couple used the last of their remaining strength to reach for the preserver. George would not let go of Margarette, so he ordered, "You take the preserver, Margarette. I will follow later."

"I am not leaving you, George!" she yelled and grabbed the rope that held the preserver.

The couple pulled the lifesaver within their reach. A semi-conscious George resisted her efforts to throw the ring over his head. "You first, Margarette! You first!"

"I have all my blood and can wait until after they pull you aboard!"

Still George argued. "It would not be right. You first, Margarette."

"If I give you a kiss, will you let me put this preserver over you, George?"

George's eyes immediately gained clarity. "I could probably float on the wind if you kissed me about now."

Margarette gave him a quick peck on his cheek, threw the pre-server over his head, and helped George pull his long arms through the opening. At that moment, a second life preserver splashed into the tumultuous waters.

"He is going to recover, young lady," the ship's surgeon said. "I removed a bullet from his right leg. He lost a lot of blood, but the rain and seawater kept the wound cleansed. What he needs now is a lot of encouragement and a good diet. This ship does not provide either. Yet he is young and strong."

"When may I speak to him?" Margarette asked.

"As soon as he awakens."

The surgeon left the small room.

Margarette walked toward the narrow bunk where George lay and took his large hand in her small grasp. George lay perfectly still.

"Is that you, Margarette?"

"I am right beside you, George."

"We are on a ship?"

"We are."

"So where is the ship taking us?" George asked.

"To America, George. To America. A ship carrying indentured servants picked us out of the sea and is carrying us to a new land."

"Margarette, I am so sorry that our dreams have turned into nightmares."

Margarette patted George's hand.

The somber couple quietly reviewed their weeks of narrow escapes.

In a whisper George observed, "I remember my mother tell-ing me that I was entering into an honorable deception by leaving home and pursuing you." Slowly George heaved a sigh filled with anguish. "My mother is a wonderful woman, but she was wrong. There is no honorable deception. I have left behind a wake of destruction. Deaths. Heartaches. Uncertainties. I should have faced my father and Lord Sturzhelm, asked your father for your hand in marriage, and lived with the results." George paused, opened his eyes, and searched for forgiveness in the depths of those beloved blue starlets which assured him of her love. "We will be servants, Margarette. Servants!"

"For only four years, George. Only four years."

George ran his hand across his chest as if searching for a lost object. Peace replaced anxiety as he felt the familiar Book still strapped close to his heart. Then he remembered.

"Hank. Is Hank on this ship?"

"No. Hank was swept away." Tears gathered in Margarette's eyes.

"He could still be alive," George said as he opened his mother's small Bible soaked with salt water.

Margarette broke into sobs. "The Book will guide us, George, just as Tamar said."

George drew Margarette toward him as she convulsed into tears on his strong, broad chest.

"I am so glad that you have not left me, George. To be alone without you—"

"We are never alone, Margarette. Somewhere in this Book I am holding, God tells us that He will never leave us or forsake us. God does not lie. God does not deceive."

"No," Margarette agreed. "Our God is an honorable God."

A preview of the exciting sequel to Honorable Deception . . .

Honorable Passage

Margarette Duffy awakened in a paroxysm of coughs. Where am I? Darkness enveloped her. Unfamiliar voices pierced the air like stagecoach wheels skidding over gravel. A rolling movement tossed her to one side. I am being taken back to Hessen-Cassel. We have been captured. She heard cries of children and babies somewhere in the close abyss. Her thoughts coalesced. Sensations of a frigid sea, images of full-riggers, emotions of terror hurled through her mind. From the bunk that held her, she pushed her shivering body to lean upon one arm, straining to create order from chaos. I am on a ship. George and I were pulled from the German Ocean. Hank! My brother! Hopefully he survived, but will I ever know?

A thin quilt covered her. Damp clothing and tangled tresses informed that her rescue was recent. She pulled the wrap tightly around her quaking body and coughed again. As she adjusted to the deep realm of shadows, a strange odoriferous emission surrounded Margarette. She felt nauseous. The young Scot heard rustling movements before seeing a ringlet of slatterns hovering over her.

"She's wakin' up," a feminine voice announced.

"Welcome to life in the hold," a second woman rasped. A chorus of titters and laughs erupted only to be silenced as a door opened off to the side. A middle-aged woman entered carrying a lantern that revealed the bearer's sharp facial features and heavy age lines. As the woman moved forward, Margarette clarified the macabre host staring at her. I remember now. Life preservers saved George and me after the wreckage of our sailboat. A ship physician removed a bullet from George's leg. I must have blacked out after that.

Coughing again, she managed to ask, "Who are you?"

"We, sweetie," said the woman holding the lamp, "are bound servants seeking a better life in a new land, and I am your overseer on this voyage. Who might you be?"

"I, I am Margarette Duffy."

"That tells me nothing," the lantern lady glowered. "What's your story?"

"Where is George?" Margarette evaded the questioning. "I want to see George,"

"She wants to see George. George will make everything right, like most noblemen," the taunter sang mockingly to the delight of her audience. "Looks like the gentleman got you into one sorry mess, dearie"

Perhaps the woman had more information than Margarette wished, although she knew not how the woman could come to know so much. "You do not know him," Margarette defended while swinging her feet onto the ship's flooring. The abrupt movement sent a piercing pain through Margarette's head. Swirling images reflected and refracted in a whirlpool of confusion. For stability, she clutched the edge of the bunk on which she sat, slowing the dervish dance. Gradually the lantern glow undulated over every flaw, line, wrinkle, and frown of the assembled hags, accentuating Margarette's horror.

A short tap preceded the door opening again. Heads swung toward a buxom woman in a grey garment. Beside her stood a young lady as streamlined as the lady was ample. Margarette's gawkers, except for the woman with the lantern and a quiet lass sitting on the bunk opposite Margarette, filed out of the compact cabin.

"I am *Frau* Leininger and this is my daughter, Beth," the newcomer said. She flourished her arm toward the woman with the lantern who remained immobile. "*Frau* Finster is the ship's overseer for unmarried women without family. You will be seeing her quite often."

Frau Leininger sat her rather plentiful body beside Margarette. "You must be terrified, child," she said while brushing one of Margarette's damp strawberry blonde locks away from her forehead. "Rescued from the sea. Your companion injured. Boat splintered into pieces." The sympathy dislodged Margarette's senses, shifting her focus to her chilled feet, compacted into frigid soggy shoes, and her shivering body, leeched of heat by cold, damp clothing.

Margarette wanted to trust the kind lady, yet she had trusted others who had proved false. Her uneasiness heightened as she puzzled over the information about George and her that people spewed like common knowledge.

"I want to see George."

"He is resting. When your companion awakens, you may see him. He is under our care."

"Your care? The physician has released him?"

"Yes. *Herr* Van Doren summoned my husband hours ago. You see, my husband is a minister. We care for the sick."

Margarette sighed, wanting desperately to cry on this woman's shoulder. She could not afford the luxury of consolation. Questions plagued her. Without hesitation, she asked, "How did I get here? The last I remember is being in a type of infirmary after a physician operated on George."

"There you lost consciousness. *Frau* Finster carried you here. The women you saw earlier and—" *Frau* Leininger gestured toward the young woman sitting opposite. Her eyes spoke an unnamed question.

"Claudia," the petite girl announced. "My name is Claudia Schmied."

"—and Claudia are your roommates. This cabin holds eight."

Just then a quiet knock sounded on the thin wooden door. A deep, resonant voice urged, "Eliza, you and Beth bring the girl. The young man may be dying."

For more information on Karen Bowden-Cox
and her books, visit karenbowdencox.com.